# inVision

CHRONICLES
*of* NICK

# invision

## SHERRILYN KENYON

WEDNESDAY BOOKS
NEW YORK

INVISION. Copyright © 2016 by Sherrilyn Kenyon. All rights reserved. Printed in the United States of America. For information, address St. Martin's Press, 175 Fifth Avenue, New York, N.Y. 10010.

www.stmartins.com

The Library of Congress has cataloged the hardcover edition as follows:

Names: Kenyon, Sherrilyn, 1965– author.
Title: Invision / Sherrilyn Kenyon.
Description: First edition. | New York : St. Martin's Griffin, 2016. | Series: Chronicles of Nick ; 7 | Summary: Now that Nick and his team of ancient gods and demons have claimed the Eye of Ananke and see the missteps of the future, he must battle demons more treacherous than ever before.
Identifiers: LCCN 2016006376 | ISBN 9781250063885 (hardcover) | ISBN 9781466868878 (ebook)
Subjects: | CYAC: Supernatural—Fiction. | High schools—Fiction. | Schools—Fiction. | New Orleans (La.)—Fiction.
Classification: LCC PZ7.K432 Iqm 2016 | DDC [Fic]—dc23
LC record available at https://lccn.loc.gov/2016006376

ISBN 978-1-250-06390-8 (trade paperback)

Our books may be purchased in bulk for promotional, educational, or business use. Please contact your local bookseller or the Macmillan Corporate and Premium Sales Department at 1-800-221-7945, extension 5442, or by email at MacmillanSpecialMarkets@macmillan.com.

First Wednesday Books Edition: September 2017

D 10 9 8 7 6

As always to my family and friends who keep me semi-sane, and who tolerate my weirdness and flighty state while I work. Especially my gorgeous sons and husband who are my daily sources of hugs and inspiration.

For my friends/family who are spiritual warriors and who fight the good fight for all of us every day against the evil that seeks to do us harm (and Mama Lisa a most special hug to you for all you do). To my ever patient and incredibly wonderful editor Monique, and the entire SMP team who put so much into every title (and Alex, Angie, and John who are ever at the ready)—you guys really are the best ever! For my agents Robert and Mark Gottlieb, who are my champions whenever I need their strength and guidance.

And last, but never, ever least, to you, the reader, for taking another journey with me into a realm beyond the normal. Love you all!

# inVision

# PROLOGUE

S o this is your great solution? Really? When the
going gets tough, the tough drown themselves
in chocolate milk and beignets?"

Irritated at being disturbed, Nick Gautier arched a
brow at the sarcastic tone that normally he'd appreciate. But right now, he didn't want to hear it, especially
not from some cocky demon overlord who was supposed to be his subordinate bodyguard.

Besides, it was easy for Caleb to judge. Lord Malphas was tall, ripped, and had those perfect dark good
looks that got him anything he wanted. *Any* time he
wanted it, without even having to use his powers of
persuasion.

Provided it didn't come from one surly, unreasonable Cajun half-demon teen who was currently trying

to drown his misbegotten woes in a mountain of beignets and chocolate milk.

So yeah . . . Caleb had it right. This was what Nick wanted to do with the rest of his life.

Growling low in his throat, Nick reached for another powdered sugar–covered pastry. "Don't you have a baby to eat or village to terrorize or something?"

With a deadly grimace, Caleb dared to pull the sugary confection from Nick's hand before Nick could stuff it in his mouth.

He was lucky Nick didn't take a plug out of his flesh.

"Or are you trying for a diabetic coma?" Caleb dropped his gaze to the six plates on the small round table that were stacked in front of Nick. All of which attested to just how upset Nick was that he'd gobbled them down like a Charonte demon on a three-day bender after an all-week fast. "Please tell me you didn't eat all of those on your own."

He would tell Caleb that, but it would be a lie.

Nick passed a grudging grimace to his friend. "What do you care?"

"We care, boyo."

He winced at the sound of Aeron's deep, lilting

accent as the ancient Celtic god came up behind him through the small crowd that was seated at the Café Du Monde around him and Caleb. Tall and muscled, the blond war deity moved to stand beside the demon so that the two of them could stare down at him with the same disappointed smirk.

Beautiful. Just what Nick had put on his Christmas list. The mutual disdain of two ancient beings who wanted to collectively kick his half-demonic ass for being a churlish baby.

And why not?

He was long past due for a good old-fashioned pity party. All that was missing was the balloon animals. And Häagen-Dazs.

Along with zombie clowns from hell, trying to eat the tourists and kill Nick for his powers. 'Cause face it, here lately that was how every party Nick attended ended.

"So that's it, then? You're just going to quit?"

*Oh yeah, that helps. Bring in the girlfriend. 'Cause I just don't feel worthless enough.*

Nick sighed as Nekoda Kennedy piled on with the other two. Lithe and ever graceful, she was still the most beautiful girl he'd ever seen offscreen. With brown hair and vivid green eyes that usually lit up whenever she looked at him, Kody had won his heart the first day they met and had held it in her hands ever since.

But right now . . . .

He just didn't want to hear it from anyone. Not even his angelic girl.

Hanging his head, he pushed his chair back to face her. "What do you want me to say, Kode? You saw what I did. It's hopeless. I'm going to end this world. Whether it's tomorrow or a thousand years from now. I'm going to lose it all. Break bad and tear humanity apart. . . . Doesn't matter what we do. Whatever we try. We just delay the inevitable outcome. So I'm going to sit here with my eats. And just . . ." He let his voice trail off as the full horror of his future played through his mind for the five millionth time.

He was the end of everything.

Everyone.

All he loved.

The entire world would one day fall to Nick's army of demons.

Yeah, there was something to put on his college applications. That ought to have schools lining up to accept him. Who wouldn't want *that* as their alumnus? *We have graduated senators, presidents, movers-and-shakers, and the Malachai demon who ate the world whole . . .*

It was the one reality Nick wanted to deny and couldn't. Everything eventually came back to that one inescapable fact he wanted to run away from and couldn't.

*I'm only sixteen. Too young to deal with this crap.*

He was supposed to be worried about his grades. About keeping his girl happy. Staying out of trouble. His mom finding his friend's porn magazines stashed in his room. Getting to work on time. Making curfew.

Not hell-gates and demons coming for the throats of his family and friends.

Definitely not about the fact that his birthright was to bring on the destruction of the entire human race.

Suddenly, Nick stood up as a severe panic attack hit him so hard that it left him reeling. Unable to cope with it, he stumbled toward the rear exit of the café that led toward the French Market that ran parallel to the Mississippi River.

This time of day, it was completely empty. Thankfully.

His heart pounding wildly and with no real destination in mind, he rushed down the back alley where bronze statues were poised beside benches as he tried to catch his breath and find some semblance of sanity in this madness that had become his extremely complicated life.

Yet as he ran, those statues seemed to be watching him today with their beady, blank eyes.

Yeah, it was a stupid thought, but what the heck?

Nothing made sense anymore.

After all, the River Walk was actually a front that opened to a back-world prison ward that held off demons. So why couldn't these statues be as alive as the ones there? For all he knew, Caleb could pass his hand over them and they could be just as mocking and demeaning. Made as much sense as the fact that Nick's girlfriend was a ghost, his best friend an immortal demon, and his newest crew addition was a Celtic god of war who'd been cursed into the body of a púca that Nick had rescued from a hell realm where he'd been sent as a test to save his mother's life.

And that *he* was the Malachai . . .

Yeah! His life was *that* screwed up.

"Nick!"

Caleb tackled him to the hard concrete sidewalk. Ah, jeez! He seriously needed those additional bruises to explain to his mother, who already thought he was getting mugged on a regular basis.

"Get off me!" he roared in his demonic tone as he shoved at his friend.

But Caleb didn't flinch. He kept him pinned on the ground. "What's going on in that head of yours, Gautier?"

Nick pulled the Eye of Ananke out of his pocket. "I saw it!" he snarled. "Everything. All outcomes lead to the same final conclusion. Don't you understand? It's hopeless! I'm a monster and you're all dead!"

Kody staggered back.

The color drained from Caleb's face an instant before he let go. "You're wrong." But the conviction was missing from his words this time.

Nick shoved the medallion at him. "See for yourself. I'm going to kill you, too, Cay. And Aeron. All of you!"

Caleb took the ancient amulet that looked like some freaky green dragon eye set in the middle of a beveled, rust-colored disc, and held it to the center of his forehead so that he could see the future that had haunted Nick since he'd made the mistake of looking at it.

Nick scowled as he realized that by doing it, Caleb had just admitted to something he'd been concealing from all of them.

He had the blood of a fate god in his veins. Otherwise, that amulet would have destroyed him. Not even Kody dared to touch it.

But Caleb hadn't thought twice about taking it in his hand.

Very interesting.

Kody sat down on a bench a few feet away as unshed tears glistened in her green eyes. "I refuse to believe it. There has to be a way to stop the future. The Arelim wouldn't have sent me back unless there was hope."

Aeron swallowed hard. "You know the cosmic laws. A pith point is a set piece. If it's to be . . ."

"It's not." Caleb pulled the Eye away, then rubbed at his forehead. "There are other outcomes." He glanced at Kody. "But you're not going to like any of them."

Nick glared at Caleb. "That's not what I saw when I looked into that thing."

Caleb snorted at Nick's churlish tone. "You're fatalistic. You know . . . Caleb," he mocked Nick's Cajun drawl in a falsetto, "I don't have a headache, it's a giant brain tumor eating the flesh off my head. I know it. I didn't stub my toe, Cay. I amputated it! Look! That's not a hangnail. It's a bleeding stump."

Nick shoved at him. "Shut up."

"It's true and you know it."

"So what's the solution?" Kody asked.

"The simplest?" Caleb sighed. "What Ambrose said. We erase everything. Reset his meager little brain to zero and let his life play out to the first pith point."

"No!" Nick growled. "My mother is *not* some arbitrary pith point we lose! I've seen a different solution. I will not sacrifice her life in this. *I'd* rather die. Just kill me and be done with it."

Aeron laughed out loud as if the mere suggestion was preposterous. "You've got your full Malachai powers, boyo, and Adarian's dead. There's no dying for you now. Only slavery. With torture being optional."

"Until you have a child . . ." Yeah, Caleb just had to toss that reminder into the mix.

"I have a brother. Can't I give this to him and let him be the Malachai instead of me?"

Caleb shook his head. "That ship left the harbor

when you took the Malachai sword and picked your šarras for your army. You are the full Malachai now, Nick. There's no undoing it. Not until you have a son who kills you for your powers, and he designates his own generals."

Pressing the heels of his hands to his eyes, Nick cursed them all. "Why didn't you stop me from taking that stupid sword from Livia?"

Caleb stood up. "Like you would have listened."

"I might."

Kody shook her head. "No, you wouldn't have. You never do."

They were right. He just didn't want to hear it. "If we erase everything, where does that leave me?"

"With a migraine," Aeron said under his breath.

Before Caleb could answer, the statue beside Kody opened its eyes and turned its head to stare at Nick.

"I knew it!"

They all ignored his Tourette's as Kody jumped away from the statue to eye it warily.

"Malachai." It smiled eerily before it stood and headed for Nick.

Both Aeron and Caleb cut its path off.

The statue tsked at them. "Still hiding behind your

friends? Shame you don't have the same loyalty to them."

Rising to his feet, Nick scowled. "Excuse me? I emphatically disagree. I protect my friends. Always."

"You can disagree all you want. But I know the truth and so do they." The statue held its hand out toward Nick and opened its palm. A ball of light hovered there, showing him images of another ally they'd thought had died in their last battle against the demons that had been trying to kill Caleb in his own home. "Zavid isn't dead, Malachai. He's only abandoned by you. Have you the nerve to come get him? Or will you stay and protect the princess?" It glanced meaningfully at Kody before it turned back to sneer at Nick. "After all, he who leaves Rome, loses Rome."

And with those words spoken, the ball vanished and the statue returned to being immobile again.

Nick's jaw went slack. "Zavid's not dead?"

"It's a trap." Caleb turned to face Nick. "Don't listen."

"You knew?"

Caleb shook his head. "It's not as simple as you think. Noir used his body to attack you. No one survives that kind of possession. Not even an Aamon.

While his soul might be with Noir now, his body isn't."

In that moment, Nick's Malachai powers kicked in and fed him the information he needed. The aether around him began to whisper with information and facts. He saw Zavid in the Nether Realm, being tormented in a pit where Noir threw his enemies.

Wincing, he couldn't believe that no one had told him about this. "I have the powers to bring him back and restore him?"

"Again, not that simple."

Nick stared aghast at Caleb. "How is it not that simple?"

"You haven't learned those powers. Yes, you sort of . . . kind of . . ." Did Caleb always have to use that mocking tone? "Learned *some* necromancy—"

"A little bit," Kody added for emphasis.

"But you're not at the level where you can actually command those powers with any degree of skill."

"Yeah, boyo, you could bring him back as a goat."

"Already did that to Madaug," Nick mumbled, then louder, "but I got him better and made him human again."

"Sort of."

Nick rolled his eyes at Caleb's sarcastic tone. Was it too much to ask for his friends to have Alzheimer's? They were old enough to be senile and then some.

But no . . .

Leave it to him to be surrounded by demons with perfect recall.

"You're not being helpful." Nick growled under his breath. "I can't leave Zavid in Azmodea." That was a hell realm of unimaginable horrors. He'd only been to it once, and briefly, but it'd been long enough to leave a crappy impression.

Cocking his brow, Caleb crossed his arms over his chest. "Thought you were out of the fight? What happened to drowning your woes with beignets?"

Nick glanced at Kody then Aeron before he met Caleb's gaze. "That was before I found out one of our own was being held by He-Who-Wants-Me-Chained-to-his-Bony-Throne. I don't leave my friends behind to suffer in my stead. Especially not Zavid. Not after he saved my life and not after everything he's been through. I made him a promise and I intend to keep it."

With those words spoken, he headed toward home to make plans.

Kody watched as Nick lowered his head and went

into that sexy predator's lope that he always fell into whenever he had a mission to protect someone he loved, or was heading to fight for someone else. He had no idea that he even did it, nor did he know just how incredibly adorable he was when he did so. That stubborn Cajun blood and his ever-faithful heart were why she couldn't bring herself to complete her mission to assassinate him. Why she loved him even though he would one day kill every member of her family.

*Kill her.*

It was so hard to reconcile this decent young man with the beast she knew she'd one day face in battle. How could anyone change so much?

She cut her gaze to Caleb. "What did you see in the Eye? What changes him?"

"The ruthless bitch who ultimately betrays us all. Death."

A single tear slid past her tight control. Caleb was right. Death changed everyone. Each time she'd buried a member of her family, it had left a savage hole in her heart. One that never fully healed.

Nick had so little family to begin with, and as a Malachai, his natural state was that of hatred and cruelty. His mother and her unwavering love were the only things that kept him from becoming the same monster his father had been.

The monster he was destined to become.

"So Cherise is definitely a pith?" she asked Caleb. Pith points were those events that were chiseled solid in everyone's life. Predestined intersections, such as birth and death, that were unstoppable moments nothing could alter. What happened in between to bring them into being were transitory and subject to free will. Humans and other creatures could move things around the pith points and make a thousand changes—those arbitrary events were never predetermined.

But a pith . . .

It was set in firmly in the *Divine Book of Fate.* Nothing and no one could change that.

Caleb shook his head. "No. She's not a pith. Her death isn't necessarily what sends him over."

"So we can save her?"

He nodded. "At the cost of *your* future. Everything's a trade-off."

Aeron flinched. "All magick comes with a price."

"And the balance must be maintained." Caleb sighed before he returned to speaking to Kody. "You and his mom were both born of the primal source to balance the Malachai. Cherise in the past and you in the future—both of you his possible anchors. The two of you should have never met."

But the Arelim had cheated and altered the rules. Now the law of the universe was attempting to right itself and correct their audacity for daring to tamper with fate and natural order.

Of all beings, as the Keepers of Cosmic Order they should have known better. Unfortunately, desperate people moved in desperate ways and did desperate things.

"And what of the prophecy? Can we save him?"

Caleb rubbed nervously at his neck. "Maybe. But it's not so simple. It requires a supreme sacrifice. One of utter love to reach him at his darkest hour . . . even then, there aren't any guarantees."

Kody despised those last four words.

Every bit as frustrated as she was, Caleb raked his hand through his hair. "We wanted Nick motivated . . . but not *this* motivated." He dropped his hand. "He goes into Azmodea and we're screwed."

She couldn't agree more. However, they had one not so small problem. "We can't stop him. His powers are too strong now."

"Believe me, I know. I'm lucky I got him tackled just then. Worse? I can't go in there with him. Neither can Xev. Our father would chain us down beside your uncle and hand-feed us to Noir's demons if he saw us protecting the Malachai." He looked at Aeron.

"Don't be cutting them eyes at me, Malphas. Not sure if I can or not. Might be able to swing an invite from Thorn. But that'll only get me so far into that realm. Same for Dagon. You know how it goes when you're born of other pantheons. They tend not to let us come a'playing in their backyards."

Caleb let out a fierce groan. "Have I said today how much I hate your boyfriend, Kody?"

"Only a few dozen times since lunch."

"Good. Don't want you to forget it." Growling, he headed toward the street.

"Where are you going?"

"To get my butt kicked again. You should come watch. You might actually enjoy it. I know I won't."

How she wished that was a joke. Unfortunately, before this was through, they were all likely to get their butts handed to them.

And their heads, too.

# CHAPTER 1

Nick stood in the center of his bedroom, staring at the symbols on his wall. They were ancient protection sigils that Caleb and his aunt Menyara had placed there to keep out anything that could harm either him or his mother. The first time he'd noticed them as a small child, Menyara had told him they were special Monster Away sprays that she'd made for him. It'd made him feel extra-loved and protected.

Little had he known then that they weren't just for protection. Those scrolled emblems had also been there to restrict his powers and bind them so that he couldn't accidentally uncover his birthright.

As a result, he really didn't understand a lot about who and what he was.

Even now.

But it was time he learned. He was through guessing and flying by the seat of his pants. If he was to save Zavid and not get enslaved by the oldest, most primal evil, he needed to really comprehend what he was capable of pulling off.

And there was one person he knew who could answer this.

"Xevikan?"

Mr. Fuzzy Boots rose up from the sofa to arch his back and yawn.

Nick snorted at Xev's alternate feline form. "I need you as a human, dude. Shed the cat skin for a while."

He flashed himself into his extremely tall human body. Although Nick couldn't blame him for wanting to spend most of his time in the lazy house cat incarnation. He wouldn't mind spending his days snoozing, either.

Not to mention, the old powers had done a number on Xev when they'd cursed him to this state. Instead of being the boy-band member he'd been born, his perfect good looks were now off-putting, and there was nothing they could do to change them. Heaven knew they'd tried enough L'Oréal products to convert the

entire North American *and* European Goth commu-
nities to normal hair colors.

Instead of his natural black, Xev's hair was an
unnatural shade of red on one side and a vibrant, fake
yellow on the other. If that wasn't bad enough, his eyebrows were a light, electric blue that clashed with his
rusty-greenish-blue hazel eyes.

At least he could fake being emo in this time period, but still . . .

It had to suck to have your own family be so cruel
as to condemn you to such a fate.

Crossing his arms over his chest, Xev scowled at
Nick. "What's trying to eat you now?"

Nick rolled his eyes and ignored the question. "Did
you know Zavid was still alive?"

He made a peculiar noise. "*Alive* is an interesting
term when one attempts to apply it to a soul-eating
hellhound who was possessed by the source of all evil.
But to be honest, I hadn't thought about it, one way or
another."

"Would you mind applying your skills to it and
telling me what you think?"

Xev nodded slowly. "Yes. Given that he most likely

couldn't be killed per se, he probably does exist in a noncorporeal state in Azmodea."

"Can I have the English translation of that?"

Xev rubbed at the corner of his eye with his middle finger in a deliberate manner before he answered. "Remember when you were divided? Your soul not in your body?"

Like that wasn't seared into his brain? Especially given the number of things that had tried to eat him and it was how the two of them had bonded. "Not something one forgets easily."

"Well, there you go."

"Um, you lost me, Sparky." Nick scowled at something that confused him. If the soul was divided from the body . . . "Then he's dead."

"Define *dead*."

He glared at Xev as he continued to play vague in a way that would make the ancient Atlantean god Acheron proud. "Would you stop with the head games and please answer the question?"

"I'm trying. It's not that simple."

"You and Caleb . . . what is it with the two of you? Did you take asshole pills this morning? Gah, you *are* brothers. I don't know why you can't get along. You're just alike."

Xev snorted. "You think we're bad? You should meet our father sometime. Your great-great-grandfather is a total piece of work. But to answer your question, Nick. Zavid would need to be reborn here. Yes, you *could* do that. The Malachai theoretically has power. But that kind of thing will cost you. It's not free, and the universal powers frown upon it. It's like altering time. Just because you can, doesn't mean you should. The hardest part of life is knowing when to walk away and let fate run its course. Even though it's a kick in the stones to let it do it."

"And if that was you trapped there? Would you still be advocating a retreat?"

"It was me trapped there, for countless centuries. And yes, it sucked." He reached over his shoulder to rub at his back. "You want to know why I choose to stay in my cat form most of the time?"

"You hate people."

He shook his head. "When I'm a cat, I'm not reminded of the fact that my own father ripped my wings off my back in a fit of anger over something I didn't do. You've no idea how many times I instinctively try to move them, only to remember they're gone. And why."

Yeah, that had to burn. Soul deep. Having wings himself, he knew they were the same as an appendage. It would be the same as someone ripping off an arm or leg. "I'm sorry."

Xev shrugged. "The point is we all have our own version of misery we deal with. And I do feel badly about Zavid. But you go down there, and there's no easy way back. It's a trap for you. Trust me. Noir will own you for eternity."

"My father escaped."

"By betraying a friend. You ready to do that?"

Nick snorted. "Depends on the friend."

Xev gave him a flat, droll stare.

"Lighten up. It was a joke. . . . Sort of." Letting out a tired sigh, Nick checked his watch. "Anyway, I've got to get to work. Keep an eye on my mom?"

"Always."

"All right. See you later." He left Xev, knowing the ancient being would die before he allowed anything bad to happen to Cherise Gautier.

That was the only good thing that had come of the deception that had been played with their lives. Xev wasn't just an immortal houseguest Nick had taken in, the ancient cursed god was also his great-grandfather.

Yeah, it really messed with his head whenever he stopped to think about it. While they physically appeared to be only a couple of years apart in age, their births were separated by thousands of years. He'd had no idea they were related when he'd saved Xev and allowed him to move in here.

Neither of them had known.

It was something they were slowly coming to terms with, especially since Xev had been forced to give up his son and had never thought to see him again. The last thing Xev had ever expected to find when Nick had rescued him was that he had a living granddaughter, never mind the addition of her smart-mouthed son.

Life as a Malachai was ever a strange, strange thing. But Nick was slowly acclimating to it.

Leaving Xev behind, he exited his condo and dug his car keys out of his pocket. His mom was still at work and would be there for another hour. Until Xev had moved in with them, Nick would have been worried about her walking home from the bar and grill where she worked by herself. But Xev would head over and see her home for him.

And he'd die before he allowed any harm to come to her.

That was the only thing that allowed Nick to function these days, especially given the number of creatures out to claim a piece of his hide. And who were willing to use his mom as a bargaining chip to get to him.

*Thanks, Dad, for* that *birthright.*

'Course, he couldn't blame it all on his father. A large chunk of it had to do with his own surly attitude of pissing off everyone around him and in particular the Grim Reaper, War, and the essence of all evil himself. Nick had done all that on his own.

No help whatsoever.

In retrospect, he should have thought it through a little better before he lipped off at them. But at the time, he'd been a little put out. It'd seemed like a good idea.

Now . . .

Well, he wasn't gutted yet. They hadn't captured or killed his mother or Kody. So, he was almost winning.

Some days.

Yeah, that was the lie he was going to go with for now. It allowed him to sleep a few hours at night so long as nothing scratched at the windows or walls.

Pushing it out of his mind, he headed for Kyrian's and tried to focus on the next forthcoming near-death experience—facing his immortal boss with bad news.

"Nick?"

Nick blinked at the deep, thick, indefinable accent that belonged exclusively to Acheron Parthenopaeus. An accent that came and went on Ash's whims, much like his bizarre hair color that often rivaled Xev's for garish hideousness. But in Ash's case, it was a personal choice. As were the facial piercings and extreme Goth wardrobe. Something Acheron did in order to be off-putting and intimidating.

Not that he really needed it given his mammoth six foot eight inches of height. And that was without the additional three inches he gained by wearing his red Doc Martens combat boots. Or the terrifying aura that said he'd rather rip your spine out than converse with you.

A normal person with any kind of survival instinct would run for cover.

Luckily, normality had waved good-bye to Nick a long time ago and taken his sanity with it.

Turning to look at Ash, he raked a teasing grin over the ancient immortal's intimidating lope and let it linger on his waist-length hair. "Nice shade of green you got going on there, buddy. Should I call Commissioner Gordon and let him know the Joker's back in town?"

Ash didn't comment on his snide tone as he used his inhuman powers to close the door behind him, as he drew closer to Nick's location. 'Cause that wasn't unnerving at all.

Good thing Nick was used to Ash's idiosyncrasies, otherwise Kyrian would be looking for new help. After having to clean up a massive urine stain from his expensive carpets.

Ash paused beside Nick to frown down at him. "So, if I'm the Joker, that would make you—"

"The Boy Wonder."

"Ah, so what are you doing in here . . . *Dick*?"

"Ouch! Somebody call me a burn unit!" Shaking his hand, Nick laughed and tried to deflect Ash's attention from the fact that he'd been caught in Kyrian's solarium where his boss kept the ancient Greek statue of his three sisters. It was one of the few things Kyrian had in the house from his days as a Greek prince. While he was proud of his heritage, Kyrian didn't keep a lot of his past around. It was as if it was too painful for him to bear.

His sisters, however, were another matter. At least once a night, he'd come in here and "visit" with them. Sometimes he'd even leave flowers at the base of their feet.

Nick screwed his face up, unwilling to admit that he'd come in here trying to use the Eye to see if he could detect scenes from Kyrian's past. "Nothing."

Ash arched a brow that said he knew Nick was lying, but didn't feel like calling him out on it. "Where's Rosa?"

"She wasn't feeling well. I beat her down and made her go home early."

"What act of Congress did that take?"

Ash wasn't joking about that. Kyrian's ornery housekeeper never neglected her duty or Kyrian, whom she saw as another child and treated with utmost care and regard. There was only one other male who had any kind of power over her . . .

"An act of Miguel. I've learned to play dirty. One call to the son and the mothership caves."

Ash sucked his breath in sharply. "That's harsh, Gautier."

"Yeah, I fight to win."

"I'll remember that in the future." Ash started to withdraw.

"Hey, Ash?" Nick hesitated as Ash paused to look back at him. "Can I ask you something?"

"Sure, kid."

"How do you live when you know the future?"

Ash snorted. "Wow, you just dove right in there with no preamble."

"Yeah, I tend to do that sort of thing. You taught me to drive. You know how I am. Full throttle. All the time. Trash cans and pedestrians be danged."

"And I'm still in therapy over it, too. Eleven thousand years without any serious trauma, and five months of driving with you and I have more PTSD than five tours as a war vet."

"Ha-ha."

"You laugh," Ash scoffed. "I'm serious."

"So am I." Nick sobered as he touched the Eye he still held in his pocket. "How do you cope with knowing what's going to happen to everyone around you? Doesn't it ever freak you out?"

Ash let out an elongated breath before he answered. "I try not to look."

Nick rolled his eyes. "I'm serious," he repeated.

"Me, too. It's all you can do. Because when you look in and see what's coming for those around you, that's when you really screw things up."

"How do you mean?"

"Simple. You try to avoid this and cause that, and the minute you do . . . you get blindsided by an unexpected twist caused by the actions you took. Case in point, the worst events in my life were a direct result of someone trying to help me. I'd have been better off had the ones who loved me just let fate play out, instead of trying to circumvent it. It's why I try really hard not to involve myself in the free will of others."

"Does it work?"

Ash shrugged. "Yes and no. It's painful at times. Like watching a child you love on the playground when you know they're about to tumble. You have that split second where you think, do I catch them or let them skin their knee and learn about gravity? It's an innate craving to want to keep them from harm, but if you don't let them learn now, the later repercussions can be a lot more catastrophic. Unfortunately, you don't know how bad until it's too late."

"Like marrying my wife."

Nick turned at the sound of Kyrian's unexpected Greek accent behind them. There was no missing the pain in his tone. He rarely spoke of Theone. Not that he blamed him. His ex had done a number on him when she'd handed Kyrian over to his bitterest enemies to be tortured and then crucified as a traitor of the Roman Empire.

It was one thing to read about history in school. Another thing to interact with the people who'd actually lived it and been affected by it.

Glancing at Acheron, Kyrian moved to stand next to Nick. "You remind me so much of myself at your age, boy. Hotheaded and stubborn. No one could ever tell me anything. I had to learn it for myself. My father did everything he could to talk sense into me and I wouldn't hear it for anything. I thought he was prejudiced and old-fashioned. Set in his ways. How stupid he was to judge a woman he didn't even know, based on her occupation that I thought she'd been forced into."

Perhaps, but it didn't change one basic thing that Nick would always come back to. "She shouldn't have betrayed you."

"I shouldn't have been blind."

Ash clapped Kyrian on his shoulder. "We make our own realities, brother. See what we want to in others and ourselves. Always."

Kyrian nodded. "And I saw a heart where there was only greed. Truth where none was spoken. It's easy to get suckered when you're young." He laughed bitterly. "My father used to always say, 'Kyrian, my son, you're not a pot of gold to anyone but me and your mother. And we will always love and worship the ground you tread upon. Sadly, the rest of the world won't cherish you for your worth. All they see is a smart-mouthed brat. For everyone loves a self-made man and despises his spoiled, entitled issue.'"

Nick grimaced. "Man, that's harsh."

"But true. And I never turned my ear. Rather, I chased the shiny apple only to find the swallowed fruit bitter on my tongue." He reached up to touch the marbled hand of his youngest sister as if he could still feel the flesh of her skin. "You would have thought with my sisters forever nagging me and pointing out my endless list of flaws that they'd have broken my spirit when I was young, and I'd have known not everyone would seek or enjoy my company."

Nick snorted at his self-deprecating humor, especially given that he normally said his sisters didn't criticize him at all. "Your wife was stupid."

"No, Nick. Theone was quite clever and calculating. She knew exactly what she wanted and wasn't afraid to go after it. I was the idiot who closed my eyes to things I should have seen." He narrowed his gaze. "She was nothing like your Kody. But to answer your earlier question, it's not as hard to live with the future you know as it is to live with the future you don't. Uncertainty is the hardest cross to bear. You will spend most of your life letting that shred your time. Does she love me? Should I do this or that instead?"

Ash nodded. "Kyrian's right. Nothing tears at the soul more than making a decision when you don't know how it's going to ultimately play out. And what you're going to be left with when it's all over."

"Except living with the burden of making a bad one," Nick mumbled.

Kyrian snorted. "Wow, Acheron, he does listen to us, after all. I think I'm scared now. Surely, this is a sign of the Apocalypse."

Nick blew him a raspberry. "Well, boss, as long as it doesn't involve any more zombies, I can handle it."

They both groaned at his reminder.

"Madaug hasn't been programming again, has he?"

Nick shook his head at Kyrian's question. "We've all banned him from computers. Threatened to break all his fingers, toes, and glasses."

"Good. He's brilliant, but terrifying."

"I know, right? And poor Bubba. He and Mark have nothing left to chase. They're stuck with survival classes. Maybe we ought to throw them a bone?"

Kyrian scoffed. "I think I could use some boredom for a while. What do you think, Acheron?"

"Boredom . . . what is this foreign word you speak of, General? I fear I know nothing of it."

Nick laughed. It always amused him when Ash and Kyrian acted like kids.

At least until Ash's phone went off. Excusing himself, he went to answer it in private.

Kyrian crossed his arms over his chest. "So why are you in here?"

"I was curious," he admitted. "I know you've told me about your sisters. And since I don't have any siblings, I was just trying to imagine what you must have been like as a kid with them. It screws with my head."

Sadness haunted Kyrian's eyes as he looked up at

the huge statue. "It's sad we don't appreciate our child-hoods until it's too late. At least those of us who had good ones."

"What do you mean?"

Kyrian sighed. "Just that I took mine for granted. Didn't realize how lucky I was until the day I left home and saw the homes other children grew up in."

"Your friend Julian?"

He nodded. "Yeah. He opened my eyes to a lot I'd never seen before."

Nick would have liked to have met Kyrian's mentor. The more he heard about the ancient Greek general Julian of Macedon, the more he respected him.

"Speaking of . . . you ready to train tonight?"

"Sure. I can always use another butt-whipping. Stone didn't stuff me in a locker today or slam my head into a fountain. I was beginning to feel neglected."

Kyrian laughed. "Boy, you are all kinds of wrong."

"I know. I blame it all on my mom. She hugged me so tight when I was little, it deprived me of oxygen. Gave me brain damage."

When Ash returned, he had the same grimace on his face that Bubba wore whenever someone told him zombies weren't real.

Or that *Oprah* was being preempted for another program.

Yeah, those were bad days for everyone.

"What's going on?" Kyrian asked.

"Squire's Council. There were a couple of deaths last night."

"Couple?"

He nodded slowly.

Nick didn't like the sound of that any more than Kyrian did. "By the look on your face, I'm assuming they didn't choke on a bad plate of red beans and rice."

"Of course not."

Nick wrinkled his nose. "Do I want to know?"

"Given your reaction the last time one was killed, probably not. But at least we're not in my car now so I don't have to worry about you clawing up my upholstery again."

"You're never going to let me live that down, are you?"

"You all but stained my seat." He passed a dry stare to Kyrian. "Wonder if we neuter him if it would calm him down any?"

Kyrian laughed. "Might, however his mother would neuter us afterward. Don't know about you, but I would miss those body parts."

"I could definitely live without them," Ash mumbled in a barely audible tone. "Unfortunately, the beast I have to endure couldn't, and she'd make me miserable." He growled in the back of his throat. "Anyway, it was bad." He spoke those last four words much louder and in staccato. "They're thinking Daimons got to them."

Nick went bug-eyed at the thought. "Okay . . . I don't care for this thought of Daimons eating Squires." Even if he was a Malachai. It just seemed like bad form.

"Don't worry. We won't let them eat you. Alive anyway."

Nick snorted at Kyrian's dry tone. "Thanks, boss," he said sarcastically. "Now I'm glad I didn't save you any of Rosa's cookies. You're not worthy!"

Kyrian clapped him on the back. "That's okay. You'll have earned them before the night's over."

"How you figure?"

"It was payday today. Artemis dropped my money in the pool. You get to dive for it."

Nick bristled indignantly. He hated that the ancient Greek goddess Artemis couldn't get with the times and pay her Dark-Hunters in cash or electronically. No, she still thought it was the Dark Ages, and once a month plopped a buttload of gold bars and gems on them. Saddest part was that, for a goddess renowned for her unerring archery skills, she had no aim. She always dumped it somewhere extremely inconvenient—then again, she might be doing it on purpose. That made the most sense.

He glared at Kyrian. "Are you . . ." He paused as he realized what that look on Kyrian's face meant. "No, not *there* again. Anywhere, but there."

"Oh yeah . . . it landed at the bottom of my pool in the backyard. Have fun digging it all out. Make sure you don't miss any diamonds this time." And with that Kyrian walked off with an evil laugh echoing behind him.

"I hate you!" Nick called after his departing back. "And I quit!"

"You can't quit. I own your sorry ass, and your mom won't let you quit until you pay off the hospital debt you owe me."

Nick mocked his words while Acheron laughed at him. He grimaced at the ancient being. "Don't you need a cute, tacky-shirt-wearing, indentured servant?"

"Like a hole in my head. . . . No."

"You both suck."

"Yeah. It's what the fangs are for." Acheron ran his tongue down one of them to emphasize his point.

Sighing irritably, Nick shook his head. "Fine. Just don't let me get eaten like those other Squires. Remember, you can't kill me 'til I'm twenty-four. That's our bargain."

Acheron shoved at him. "You're so weird."

"And yet you like me. What's that say about you?"

"That I don't get out much."

As Nick headed for the door, Ash stopped him. "You want me to lend a hand with the pool?"

"Nah, I got it. Go save the world. But if you want to zap me some swim trunks, I'm sure Kyrian's neighbors would be eternally grateful. Otherwise I'm going commando."

No sooner had he spoken than a pair appeared on his head.

Groaning in agony, Nick pulled them off. "I see now where Artemis gets her aim. You two train together much?"

Acheron muttered something in Atlantean as he walked away. That wasn't unusual.

What made Nick pause was the fact that this time,

he understood the words as well as if they'd been spoken in English or Cajun.

*Kid, don't even say Artie right now. Last thing I want to do is deal with her tonight. Don't stir that redheaded dragon. She might hear you and come calling.*

At least one of his Malachai powers was working the way it was supposed to. But that actually scared him. He wasn't used to it. They normally backfired. Misfired. Went sideways or flat-out did nothing.

And as he looked back at the statue, for the first time he saw Kyrian's sisters not in their pale marble forms, but as they'd looked in his lifetime. Phaedra, who was younger by only a single year. She'd sang with the voice of an angel. Althea, the baby of the family, who had been Kyrian's favorite sister. The one he'd doted on incessantly and coddled to the point that his parents had complained that he'd spoiled her rotten. While his whole family had been devastated by his death, she had taken it the hardest of his sisters. So much so, that she'd shaved her blond hair that had been a match for Kyrian's and had refused to speak.

And Diana. The sister he'd been the most like and as a result, they'd fought constantly. About everything under the heavens. Both stubborn and unyielding.

Ironically, she'd ended up married to one of his best friends, who was very similar in temperament and form to Kyrian—as if she'd missed her brother so much that she'd gone looking for someone who reminded her of him.

Not only could Nick see them, he felt Kyrian's love for them. Their love for Kyrian. It was so incredibly strong that it traversed the aether and spanned the centuries to form a protective cloak for his boss even two thousand years later.

No wonder Kyrian had taken so much care to protect and carry this one memento of them with him throughout time.

Kyrian was right, he'd been blessed by the gods. His family had done their best to protect their son and keep him safe. Even when he insisted that he fight as a soldier, his father had surrounded him with a personal guard of the best soldiers he could find, and sent him to train under Julian of Macedon—the most skilled and respected commander of the Greek city-states of that time. Alkis of Thrace had spared no expense to protect his only son. He would have done anything for Kyrian.

And when Kyrian had married a prostitute against

his wishes, Alkis had tried his best to make his unreasonable son see the truth of her.

Kyrian had refused. In love with the façade she presented to him, and deluded by her lies, he'd listened to no one about his Theone. Nothing could make him let her go, not even when his father had disinherited him as a last resort.

Theone had been his life and he'd abandoned his troops when he'd heard she was in danger. Riding day and night, he'd gone to her side to rescue her, only to have her drug him and turn him over to his enemies for torture and execution.

His family had done everything they could to try and save him. Alkis had offered to surrender all of Thrace to Roman control. Kyrian's sister Althea had offered herself up as a slave to his mortal enemy, Valerius Magnus the Elder.

That was true love. Unconditional love. After all the bitter words Kyrian had spoken to his father, King Alkis had still done his best to save him and spare him from Theone's treachery.

Unfortunately, the Romans had no intention of letting him go. He'd been too good a commander for that. They knew if he were to ever go free again, he'd defeat them and destroy their empire. As the ancient historians had written, when Kyrian of Thrace led his army to war, Rome fell like leaves during a bitter frost.

And on the day his father had received word of Kyrian's execution, the proud King Alkis of Thrace had killed himself over it.

Nick blinked back tears as he choked on grief. He could feel the anguish and guilt that Kyrian lived with every day for what he'd done. By seeking his own happiness and believing the lies of one treacherous woman, he'd ruined his entire family and destroyed his nation.

One moment of blind selfishness . . .

No wonder he didn't talk about it. No wonder Kyrian didn't trust anyone. How could he?

But that was the trick in life. Deciphering who had your best interests at heart. Who was in it for you and who was in it for themselves. More often than not, you didn't find out until you were like Kyrian and left hanging to die.

Nick reached up and touched Althea's hand. For the merest instant, he could have sworn that she gripped his fingers.

Yeah, that was freaky.

"Don't worry," he whispered to them. "I won't let anything happen to your brother. I've got his back for you."

*But who has yours?*

Nick jumped at the disembodied voice that whispered in his ear.

What the heck?

Using his powers, he scanned the room with his demonic eyes.

There was nothing here. No sound in the aether. No scent . . .

Yet that had definitely been a feminine voice speaking English.

"Crap." The one thing Nick had learned these last couple of years . . .

A disembodied voice whispering in his ear was a harbinger of bad things a'coming. And it definitely didn't help that both War and Death had declared open warfare on him already. The Grim Reaper had told him to buckle up.

Obviously, it was on.

# CHAPTER 2

Whoa, Gautier! You're jumpier than normal, which given the fact that you could double as a hyperactive squirrel most days, says a lot."

Nick grimaced as Brynna Addams and LaShonda Thibideaux stopped beside him at his locker. "Thought you were Caleb sneaking up on me to do something foul . . . like wedgie me before class," he lied, hoping Brynna would accept his excuse. Not that Caleb needed to sneak up on him to give him a wedgie.

Evil demonkyn snot could do that with his Jedi mind tricks from across the room. And had been known to do so in his crankier moods.

One day, Nick was going to fully master his and return that favor.

Then run like heck into another dimension where hopefully Caleb would never find him.

"Ah. That explains it." Adorably cute as she stepped up to reach for her lock, Brynna was an average girl-next-door who dressed in understated khaki pants and conservative button-downs, while LaShonda was her flamboyant best friend with a flair for stylish J-pop trends. Today, Shon had gone in for that whole sexy Japanese *Lolita* schoolgirl uniform that reminded Nick of something out of a fantasy manga—right down to the frilly white cuffs and bright frou-frou red bow tie, and a blazer that was two sizes too small, which seriously emphasized a part of her ample anatomy he wasn't looking at because he didn't want to get Jack-slapped for sexual harassment.

Not that it was the only reason. . . . Also, because he wasn't a lech.

However, he would be a most happy and well-behaved boy if *his* woman would borrow some of LaShonda's outfits from time to time.

Yeah, Kody would look incredible in that.

And as usual, Shon had gone all-out with the theme. She even had her sisterlocks pulled back with a matching navy headband, and white knee-high socks and stacked Mary Jane shoes.

Nick cringed the second *that* thought went through his head and was highly mortified that he knew what those black shiny shoes were called. But then Kody was slowly "civilizing" him on such things. Any day now, he'd be eating off plates and drinking out of glasses like a real person.

Though to be honest, he was coming to his education under duress. He still didn't really understand why women needed more than two pairs of shoes—those you wore and the pair your mom forced on your feet for church and special occasions because your regular shoes were holey and not *holy*.

Blushing, he stepped out of the way so that Brynna could open her locker door to grab her books. "Did you get all of the English reading done last night?"

"No!" Brynna let out a sound of supreme annoyance. "It was too much. Did you? And if you say yes, I *will* hurt you."

"I cheated and just had Kyrian tell me about it. Great thing about working for an ancient Greek boss. He knows *The Iliad* like the back of his hand, and

actually enjoys lecturing me on it. I think he personally knew Achilles."

She snorted. "He's not *that* old."

"No, but Ash is."

She laughed.

"Actually . . ." Tightening her grip on her books,
Shon looked around before she leaned in to whisper, "I
heard a rumor from my mom that Kyrian slept with
the granddaughter of an Amazon queen who fought at
Troy."

Nick snorted in denial. "No way!"

Shon held her right hand up to testify to its truth.
"That's what they claim."

"Who's *they*?" Brynna asked.

"Other Greek Dark-Hunters." Shon flipped her
hair over her shoulder. "Zoe being one of them. And
she's old enough to know . . . and *was* an Amazon princess."

Nick considered that. Shon would know. Like
Brynna, she came from one of the older Squire families
that had been protecting the identities and existence
of Dark-Hunters for generations, and providing ser-
vices and cover for them. Even better, Shon's father was
the New Orleans' Council lead historian and archive

keeper, and had been for years. So when it came to the history of the Dark-Hunters—what they'd done and who they knew, he was the authority for the region.

"I'd ask Kyrian about it, but he gets cranky when I get too personal with inquiries. . . . Wonder if Ash knows."

"Probably." Brynna pulled her books out of her locker and shoved them in her tote. "He knows everything."

Not quite. He had no idea Nick was a Malachai. Or that Kody was his niece. For all the powers Acheron commanded, there were a surprising number of things that could be kept hidden from the ancient Atlantean.

But Nick didn't correct her. He was quickly learning that most everyone and everything had a weakness of some sort. Nature tended to build in an off-switch.

Every *Titanic* met its iceberg.

That's what Kyrian had told him the point of *The Iliad* was. Balance and moderation. Regression to the mean.

Every Hector met his Achilles. Every Achilles met his Paris. Every Priam had an Agamemnon and every Agamemnon had a Clytemnestra.

Sooner or later, everyone paid for the wrongs they

did to others. And when karma came home to roost, she brought nasty, irritable friends with spears.

It was making the hardest choices at the hardest times, and learning to stand by them and bear out the consequences.

Speaking of . . .

He turned as he felt the powerful presence of a preter who never failed to put a dopey grin on his face. The minute he saw Kody's bright green eyes and tight red tee, he realized he should have worn looser pants. Thankfully, he had on a really baggie Hawaiian shirt.

*"Ca viens, ma bebelle cher."*

Her gorgeous smile only made his condition worse. "One day, I have got to learn Cajun." She scowled at him. "For all I know, you could be insulting me with that deep smooth drawl of yours."

Nick dropped his backpack as casually as he could from his shoulders and pulled it around to the front as an added layer of protection—just in case. *"Non, cher.* I would never do that to *ma belle."*

Brynna laughed. "I don't know, girl, long as I've been here, I still haven't gotten the hang of it."

Shon tsked at her. "Y'all break my native heart!"

Nick broke out into his thickest Cajun drawl. "They

just don't know, *cher . . .* they just don't know. What we gonna do with the likes of them?"

"I vote we feed 'em to some gators later." Shon winked at him.

Brynna scowled at Kody. "You ever feel like you need subtitles when he does that?"

"No. Unless he's actually speaking Cajun, I can understand it, even when it's thick and fast. But Bubba and Mark . . . I definitely need subtitles when they get excited and start babbling. I've no idea what language they're speaking."

"That be middle Tennessee good ole boy," Nick teased. "Their accents aren't *that* thick."

"For *you*," Kody teased. "But you have to remember that English isn't my native tongue, anyway."

Brynna's eyes widened. "It's not?"

Kody went pale as she realized that she'd slipped up in front of Brynna and Shon. "Um, no. I was born in Greece, and my mother's Egyptian."

"Really?" Brynna gaped as she passed a glance to Nick. "We were just talking about Greece. So did you learn Greek or Arabic first?"

Nick arched a brow as he waited to hear this. . . . While the language of modern Egypt was Arabic,

Kody's mother was an ancient goddess. So she'd grown up speaking hieratic and demotic Egyptian—languages long dead and forgotten. Even her Greek predated Kyrian's native Koine Greek dialect that was very different from the modern-day spoken language of Greece.

"Greek," she said quickly.

*Nice save.*

Kody slid an irritated frown toward him. *Don't take that tone with me. I'll have you know, I'm fluent in Arabic, too. My dad spent a number of years living in North Africa and traveling among the nomadic tribes there.*

That was something he hadn't known before. Weird.

"I'm impressed," Shon said. "You have no trace of an accent. How did you manage to be so lucky?"

Kody shrugged. "Good genes. While my parents pick up languages fast, they never could quite shake their accents. But my brothers did."

Brynna gaped even wider. "I didn't know you had brothers, too. Why don't they go to school here?"

*You are letting out all kinds of secrets today. What? Someone cast a truth spell on you?* Nick shot his thought to her.

*I know! Help me!*

Nick cleared his throat. "Her brothers are a lot older. Neither of them live in the state."

"Ah." Brynna nodded. "Believe me, I get it. My family's huge, and spread all over. It's such a pain."

The bell rang.

Nick groaned out loud as students scrambled for their classes. "Where's my hemorrhoid? Not like him to not have attached himself to my hip by now."

"Maybe he's sick," Brynna offered innocently, not knowing that Caleb, as a demon demigod, couldn't get sick.

Well, he had gotten sick *once*, but there were extenuating circumstances and it shouldn't have happened again.

God, he prayed *that* hadn't happened again.

As they broke away to head for class, Caleb came rushing down the hall toward them.

Nick arched a brow. "Something wrong?"

"My alarm didn't go off."

"That's odd."

"Yeah," Caleb said sarcastically. "You've no idea. Aeron overslept, too."

That was strange. Lucky Charms Legolas would give Nick's mom a run for her money on his ability to keep accurate time and never be late. Not to mention, he kept a rigid military schedule that was terrifying. Instead of a god of war, he should have been one of obsessive-compulsive disorder.

Nick screwed his face up. "Zeitjägers again?"

"Not funny."

"Really not trying to be." 'Cause time guardians carrying adamantine sickles they used to behead those who abused the time sequence weren't something to joke about. Especially not when they looked like jacked-up plague doctors that had escaped from some voodoo horror movie on an acid trip.

And they dripped blood all over your only pair of shoes while they followed you around like gruesome shadows you couldn't shake.

Yeah, Nick would *never* joke about that.

Maybe there was a good reason for having more than one pair of shoes, after all. Girls might be on to something with that.

He was still having nightmares and flashbacks from his last encounter with those creepy things.

"You know," Nick said slowly. "I'm thinking we could all benefit from some therapy. But then given the stuff we deal with . . . if we ever began to talk about it to an outsider, they'd lock us up and throw away the key."

"Yes, they would." Caleb led them into class. "And having lived in a cage, I don't recommend it."

"Yeah, but in your case, you had demons eating your entrails on a daily basis."

"True. And your father trying to tear my wings off." Caleb visibly shivered at the memory. "Have I told you today how much I really hated your father?"

"Nah, but I feel you, brother. He was not on my party list, either."

Kody shook her head. "You two are so bad."

Nick choked indignantly. "Oh, like you had any more love for him than we do. As I recall you tried to kill him yourself."

"Your father was a sadistic beast."

"Yes, *our* point exactly. No one cried when he died." Nick let Kody enter the classroom first before he headed to his usual seat.

"Well, you don't have to *say* it."

He made demon noises under his breath as he cast a disgruntled look at Caleb. "There she goes trying to civilize me again. What is it with women? Gah! Next thing you know, she's going to tell me not to pick belly lint."

"Nick! That's so gross!"

"See!"

Covering her eyes with her hand, she shook her head. "You're so awful. Thank you, Caleb, for being a gentleman and minding your manners."

"No, problem. Lil housebroke me for you. But if it makes you feel better, Nick, I was much worse than you when she met me."

Laughing, Nick took his seat. And as he dug through his bag, a strange image went through his head.

It was of Caleb and Lilliana. The image was so raw and vivid, and potent, that it froze him to the spot.

Agonizing grief and physical pain laced through him.

Malphas had been wounded in battle. He'd taken a spear straight through his side, and been forced into retreat by the Sephirii forces that had fought against the first Malachai's army.

After a long pursuit, Malphas had finally lost his enemies and had found a place with fresh water. Because of the agony of his injuries and the effort it was taking to remain conscious, he didn't have the strength left to waste his powers on concealing his true demonic form. So he lay beside the stream on his stomach with his black wings spread wide and his red skin scuffed and smeared with his black blood.

His breathing labored, he'd been trying to stave off the bleeding when he heard the sharp gasp to his left. Furious, he'd angled his sword at the interloper, intending to murder whoever had dared disturb him.

But the moment his gaze locked onto those two celestial blue eyes that had been filled with fright, he'd hesitated. Those large eyes had dominated the face of an angel—and not the kind he fought against.

Her nose was a bit large for her pixie-like face, but it hadn't detracted from her beauty at all. That small flaw had somehow made her even more beautiful. She'd worn her white-blond hair pulled back into a long, thick braid, yet defiant strands had come free to curl and tease her skin.

Even though she was obviously terrified of him, she'd bitten her lip and approached him very slowly.

Cautiously.

"Are you injured?"

Stunned that she wasn't screaming or running away, Malphas scowled at her.

"Can you understand me?"

He bared his fangs as she came closer, then hissed, hoping to send her fleeing.

Instead, she froze instantly. "I mean you no harm, demon. I'm a healer. I can help you, if you let me."

Those words baffled him. She was human . . . why would *she* help him? They were enemies in this war. She had to know that. His kind had slaughtered hers by the hundreds, everywhere they found them.

Without fail. Without prejudice.

*Without hesitation.*

Still she stood there with her arms held out at her sides. No guile. No deception that he could sense. She seemed as sincere as any creature he'd ever known. Not that he'd known all that many who were sincere, or any, for that matter. The majority of his acquaintances were backbiting snakes who would betray faster than a heart could beat.

"Please . . . let me help. If anyone else finds you here, they'll call the others to slay you."

"Why aren't you calling them?"

"You've personally done me no harm. I don't believe in holding someone accountable for the deeds of others. Only what he, himself, has done." She moved forward again until she reached the tip of his outstretched sword that was still coated in the red blood of his vanquished enemies.

Only then did she hesitate as she saw it.

Malphas lowered the tip to the ground, and let the sword fall from his hand. He tucked his black wings down by his sides, then hissed as that action caused more pain to slice through his abdomen.

With the most tender expression anyone had ever given him, she knelt by his side and laid a gentle hand on his cheek. It was the first time in his life anyone had given him such a touch. For a full minute, he couldn't breathe as unknown feelings went through him. More than that, her skin smelled of rosewater and honey. A delectable scent that awoke a fierce hunger in his soul.

Yet it wasn't for her blood or bones.

He wasn't sure what he wanted from her.

"You're burning with fever."

He couldn't believe that she didn't recoil from his unnatural bloodred skin. Or long orange hair. Rather, she cupped his cheek and stared into his yellow demon eyes without flinching as she wiped away the black demon's blood on his cheek and lips.

"Can you stand?"

He nodded.

To his even greater shock, she helped him to his feet. And when her gentle hand brushed against his black wings to help support him, he was lost to her kindness. "There's a cave where I played as a girl, just over that hill." She jerked her chin to show him the direction. "No one ever goes there. They believe it's haunted. You should be safe to rest within its shelter, and I can tend your wound and bring you food."

"I still don't understand why you would help me."

"Because you need it."

He shook his head. "Aren't you afraid of me?"

"Petrified."

And she should be. He towered over her frail, fragile human body. It would take nothing to break her into pieces and use her blood and bone marrow to restore his strength and heal his injuries. He'd torn apart men twice the size of her, and those were trained warriors who'd been armed war heroes.

Yet here she stood . . . unarmed. Defenseless. Her only armor a thin, light yellow flaxen dress that was so thin, he could see the outline of her body whenever the sun passed through it. She didn't even have on a single piece of jewelry she could stab him with.

Nothing.

Even her nails were trimmed to the quick so that she couldn't scratch him. She was as harmless as a little mouse.

A part of him wanted to taste her blood to see if it was as sweet as she smelled. That same part of his soul hated her for daring to stand before him like this—for that innocent trust that said she knew he wouldn't hurt her.

It was as if she dared him to prove he was ruthless and uncaring. Things he'd vowed to himself he would always be. That he would feel nothing for anyone, ever again.

Numb to the world and all its pain.

She was his enemy. The very thing his father sought to protect. Malphas had sworn his sword and army to the utter destruction of every member of her pathetic race. To see them put down like the infectious disease they were.

Humanity . . .

The very word was bitter on his tongue.

Yet as he looked down at her and felt the heat of her hand on his skin . . .

This wasn't hatred inside him. He wanted to comfort her and chase away the frightened light in her eyes.

Even more peculiar, he wanted to know what a smile would look like on that innocent face.

"I won't hurt you, little one." He wasn't sure who was more stunned when those words came out of his mouth.

She or he.

For the first time, the terror faded from her eyes and her gaze softened to warmth. Placing her arm about his waist, she gently helped him toward her cave. "Are all demons as gigantic as you?"

He snorted at her question. "Depends on the species." He sucked his breath in sharply as he stumbled on a hidden bramble, and pain hit him anew. She didn't flinch as he put more weight on her than he'd meant to.

Amazed by her, he gentled his grip on her shoulder, not wanting to hurt her in any way. "Are all women as brave as you?"

Finally, a smile curved her lips, and it was as breathtaking a sight as he'd thought. "Depends on the species."

He'd arched a brow at her flippant, teasing tone. "Well, aren't you a cheeky one?"

"So says my father. It's ever a fault of mine that I don't know my place. But who better to know my place than I, says I? And who so better to determine it? For I will not be hemmed in by anyone else's expectations. This is my life, such as it is. And it will be lived under my rules so long as I have it." She led him into the dark cave where his sight quickly adjusted.

To him, this was home.

Even more surprised by her spirit that was unafraid of the dark he called home, he sat down on the floor while she went to a corner and uncovered a small tinder box. If he didn't know better, he'd think her part demon the way she moved about in the darkness as if she could plainly see.

But it was merely the fact that she was familiar with the place, and knew where everything in it was located. She struck a match and lit a small tallow candle to burn. Holding it aloft, she returned to his side and placed it in a small makeshift sconce she'd created.

Once she could see, she returned to his side and knelt down. When she reached for his armored cuirass, he caught her soft hand with his claws. "What are you doing?"

She gave him a blank stare. "I was going to inspect your injury. Surely, you don't think I could do you harm?"

No, but trust didn't come easy for him. He'd never had anyone who hadn't sought in the past to give him all manner of pain.

That list included his own parents.

Reluctantly, he loosened his grip and surrendered to her care. As promised, she didn't hurt him. Rather she carefully examined his wound then tore away a section of her underdress to bandage it.

That selfless act hit him twofold. One, that she destroyed her own dress for his care. And two that her touch was feather-light and seared him to the core of his rotten soul.

When she was done, she sat back to smile down at him. "You lie still and rest. I shall get you something to eat and drink."

"Thank you."

"You're welcome . . ."

By the way she said that, he knew she wanted something from him, but he had no idea what.

After a second, she laughed. "What's your name?"

"Malphas."

"Malphas?" she repeated in distaste. "That name doesn't suit you at all."

"How do you figure?"

"You're far too handsome to be a *Malphas*."

Was she insane? He was completely demon in her presence. The one thing he'd learned early in his life was that humans hated them whenever they wore their demon skins. Everything about his kind was repugnant to the human species.

Yet it didn't seem to faze her at all.

Not even the darkness of his blood or the length of his claws that had been designed to shred human flesh seemed to bother her. She acted as if he were as normal to her as daylight.

And it softened his hardened warrior's heart in a way nothing ever had before. "What name would you have for me, then, little one?"

She pursed her lips into an adorable frown as she considered it. Then, to his complete consternation, she reached up and gently brushed his orange hair back from his face so that she could cup his cheek and study his features. "Caleb."

It left him speechless that she'd instinctively picked a name so close to his summoning name . . . as if she could sense it somehow. But more than that . . .

"Caleb?" He shuddered. "Why such an awful thing?"

She dropped her hand to the center of his chest.

"Because I sense in you a true heart. A *faithful* heart. And by your wounds and scars, I can tell that you are fearless. So I shall call you Caleb, the faithful, fearless warrior who defends what he believes with everything he has. That is what I see when I look upon you. Not a demon. An ever-courageous, noble warrior. One day, I suspect, you shall look into a mirror and see the same noble man I do."

And with those handful of words, Lilliana shattered the icy barrier that had caged his heart since the moment he'd been forsaken to this harsh bitter world without friend or family. "I can assure you that I will never look into a mirror and see a man there. At least not that I don't scream. Then kill it."

She laughed. "You know what I mean. Now let me see about collecting your sword before it's found and they begin looking for you. Then I'll make sure you have supplies until you're well enough to rejoin your army."

Malphas's breath had left him in a rush as he realized that he'd completely forgotten his weapon.

What the hell?

He'd *never* in his life set his sword aside. Never been disarmed by anyone.

Until now.

Malphas had set it aside without a second thought. What magick did this human wield so effortlessly that she could ensnare the most lethal demon commander in the entire Mavromino army? For weeks now, he'd been pursued by their deadliest forces. Even wounded he'd put down their best soldiers with minimal effort.

And she had done nothing more than smile and he'd laid aside his sword.

*I'm an idiot.*

One who expected her to return with enemies to use his sword to kill him. After all, they would need such a weapon, forged by the gods, to damage his flesh, as mortal weapons were harmless against him.

But she didn't. Instead, she returned, just as she'd promised, his weapon in hand and a basket of food for him in the other. Without a single reservation, she'd handed his sword to him. Then given him food and drink, and redressed his wound.

When she finally left the cave later that day, she'd carried his heart with her. A heart he hadn't even known he possessed. With nothing more than a handful of spirited words and a kindness he'd never known, she'd taken the most lethal demon ever spawned by the most vicious, callous creatures the Source had spat out, and captivated him.

Centuries later, Caleb still loved her. He still grieved for her and kept her memory sacred. And he continued to use the name she'd given him to remind himself that his wife, alone, had seen something inside him besides a monster.

Lilliana had taught him to fight, not simply against his father because he hated him, but *for* his convictions because that was what a man of honor did.

It was the right thing to do.

*I pray that you never again reach for this sword, Lord Husband. But should the day ever come when you must return to war, then it should be to protect what you love. Never again for hatred or fear. And never should you battle for vengeance.*

Nick felt the same emotions Caleb had felt on the day he'd plastered his demonic sword into the wall of his cottage bedroom. Wrapped in enchanted cloth and bound with a protection spell to keep his enemies from locating him, he'd promised his wife that he was done with battle forever.

Never again would he fight for any cause. His only

goal was to remain home with her on her farm, in the guise of a humble human.

But the gods hadn't allowed him that peace. They'd dragged him back to their war against his will. Yet true to his word, he hadn't returned to fight for the Mavromino.

He'd reemerged as a champion for the Kalosum—the side of light. His love for his wife had proven far greater than his hatred for his father, and to please his Lilliana and save her people, he'd fought with his enemies, and protected them with every ounce of his demonic strength.

And he continued to do so even now.

Nick scowled as he looked over at his friend and saw both faces of Caleb—the demon Lord Malphas, and his loyal, if often surly bodyguard who never hesitated to put his life on the line to protect him.

Caleb looked up and froze as he caught Nick staring at him. He narrowed his dark gaze on him. *What's that look mean? I swear, Gautier, you cop a feel, and I will put you through a wall.*

Laughing, Nick blew him a kiss.

"Is there a problem back there, Mr. Gautier?" Ms. Pantall asked.

"No, ma'am. Caleb was just making goo-goo eyes at me again and staring at my chest with evil intent. Please tell him to stop sexually harassing me, as it's making me very uncomfortable." Nick clutched the collar of his shirt together and leaned away from Caleb.

Caleb choked while several students burst out laughing.

Ms. Pantall rolled her eyes. "In that case, I will remind you both of the *No Public Displays of Affection* rules that we have for the school. So behave and turn in your homework."

"Yes, ma'am." Nick pulled it out.

He'd just gotten comfortable again when the door opened to admit a new student. Something that didn't happen often in their small, private, parochial school. And it wasn't just because St. Richard's was hard to get into due to its high academic standing. But rather from the fact that the school had been set up as a place for preters to learn how to mingle with humans and not let the stress throw them into their animal states.

While there were a handful of *baretos*, or "normal" humans who had no idea that they were attending school with shape-shifters, the majority of the student body here was either shape-shifters or the children of

Squire families. Squires who had been in service to Dark-Hunters like Kyrian and Acheron for generations.

As such, the Squires usually sent their kids to private school together so that they could be watched by older Squires to ensure that no one messed with them. Especially since their enemies might want to take their kids hostage, or kill them to get back at their parents or the Dark-Hunters in retaliation for the centuries of protecting humans from their supernatural predators.

It also allowed the shape-shifter families a controlled environment for their children so that they could have playtime with humans where if they had an accident and shifted into their animal bodies, the humans wouldn't flip out and call the authorities. As Squires or their children, they understood about Were-Hunters, and they could help cover for them with the humans here who didn't know about them.

It gave the Were-Hunters a way to practice being in the normal world so that they could acclimate.

Nick had been one of those *baretos* students at St. Richard's until two and half years ago when his best friends had turned on him, and Kyrian had saved his life. For some reason that still eluded Nick, the ancient Greek had taken a liking to him and decided to give him a hand up and bring him into this amazing world.

Now he was a Squire at an age that was unheard of, since Squires were supposed to be eighteen before they could be sworn in to their oaths. But Kyrian had pulled strings and so here Nick was. The youngest Squire in Council history.

And this new guy they were introducing . . .

He didn't appear to be a Squire or one of their kids.

Nick glanced at Caleb. *What do you think?*

Caleb shrugged nonchalantly.

Ms. Pantall cleared her throat as she read his card. "Everyone? This is Nathan St. Cyr. Nathan's a new student who just moved to New Orleans from New York. I know everyone will be on your best behavior and welcome him in. Mr. St. Cyr, if you'll take an empty seat, we'll get started."

An odd sensation went through Nick as Nathan neared him. Like a wire had been touched to his spine and sent a jolt through his entire central nervous system. Not that anyone had ever done that to him, but that was what he imagined such a thing would feel like.

As Nathan neared his desk, he inclined his head to him, then sat down on the other side of Kody.

Yeah, *that* didn't endear him any. *You better not be eyeballing my girl, punk* . . .

Nick would snatch those blue eyes out of that boy's head and use them for marbles. The Malachai in him was rising up and breathing fire down Nick's neck. It was hard to leash the beast when he came calling like this. Every part of Nick wanted a piece of Nathan for daring to trespass on Kody's personal space.

Especially when he leaned over a second later and, with a charming grin, brushed his hand against Kody's arm. "Do you have a pencil I can borrow? Mine must have fallen out of my backpack."

"Sure." Kody handed him the one she was holding.

His grin turned even more debonair as he ran it under his nose and smelled the stylus as if he could still detect her light perfume on the wood. "Mmm, I'll treasure it always. Thank you for your kindness, my noble lady."

When Nick started to rise, Caleb caught his arm. *Down, boy. Don't make me smack your nose with a rolled-up newspaper.*

Nick cut a glare at his best friend to let Caleb know he could be a worthy substitution as a whipping boy if he didn't let go.

Kody turned toward Nick. *Is it me or was that gross?*

And that right there saved Nathan's life. Leave it to his girl to be oblivious.

He was relieved, until Nathan turned back toward her.

Suddenly, Kody's desk slid four inches closer to Nick's, and farther from Nathan's. She turned an indignant glare at Nick for his audacity.

At the sharp scraping that made most people cringe, everyone in the room shot around to look for the source of the sudden sound. Nick forced himself not to cringe at the involuntary use of his Malachai powers.

Clearing his throat, he glanced at his teacher. "Sorry. My foot got caught under Kody's desk."

"Why was your foot under her desk?"

Nick shrugged. "I'm too tall for the desk and my feet have a mind of their own. You've seen me walking down the hall, Ms. Pantall. I never know where my arms or legs are located, hence all the bruises I keep."

She rolled her eyes again. "Keep your feet under your own desk, Nick. Stop disrupting class or I'll send you to the office."

Something stabbed him in the leg. Hard. Nick

let out a sharp curse and though it wasn't in English, Ms. Pantall had enough Cajun in her to unfortunately know exactly what the word meant.

"That's it! Get to the office! Now!"

"But—"

"No buts! Go!"

Growling low in his throat, Nick got up to retrieve the pass from her hand. He glanced back to see the sad pout on Kody's face and as his gaze went to Nathan . . .

For the merest instant he could have sworn he saw his eyes flash red. But that would be an impossibility. If Nathan had demon in him, Nick would see it.

He'd sense it.

For that matter, he'd even glimpsed Acheron's true demonic form and Ash had more than enough power to camouflage himself.

From anyone.

But not a Malachai. Nothing and no one could hide themselves from Nick. He was the Geiger counter of preternatural species. It was both his gift and his curse.

Which got back to the weird sensation on his spine. He needed a serious consultation with his fellow Power Rangers. But that wouldn't happen until after he figured out how many hours of detention this little miserable morning was going to cost him.

*Maybe I'll get lucky and when I go after Zavid something will eat me and I won't have to finish detention.*

A boy could dream.

Taking the slip from Ms. Pantall's hand, he headed for the door and took one last look at Kody. Instead of watching him, she was saying something to Nathan.

Nick's vision darkened in such a way that he had to catch himself before he let loose his own demonic eyes and freaked out half his class. His breathing ragged, it took everything he had not to blast the door from its hinges.

*Okay, stop!*

Aeron would be the first to warn him off his anger. This was the gateway to a place he didn't want to go. It was what had forced his father to live out his "free" life in the human realm incarcerated in a maximum security prison. That had been the only place Adarian could stay where his frequent violent outbursts that resulted in the flying entrails of whoever had annoyed him could be contained.

Every time Nick exploded into those powers, he

put a cosmic target out to his enemies. Told them exactly where to find him and anyone who was near him.

The only way to have peace in his life was to keep his temper and remain dormant.

Yeah, but he wanted that kid's throat.

And by the time he reached the principal's office, he was good and livid. His palms damp and his heart racing. He even felt his temple pounding. Too pissed to sit, he paced in front of the chairs outside Mr. Head's office and half expected to go Carrie White on everybody. All that was missing was the pig's blood.

Suddenly, a tiny light appeared in his peripheral. One that wouldn't be all that noticeable to most people. It was only slightly larger than a speck of dust in a sunbeam. But Nick knew the source of the ethereal blue light.

It was a will-o'-the-wisp. Or more affectionately, Lucky Charms Legolas.

He stopped pacing to whisper, "Legolas? What are you doing here?"

*I felt you burning them powers, and wondered if you were in trouble. Or are you trying to summon Noir? 'Cause if you are, let me know now. I need to pack some bags before I abandon your sorry hide to him and his forces to save me own arse.*

Nick released a scoffing laugh. As if. Aeron would sooner cut his own throat than hightail it out. One thing about the Celtic war god, he never backed away from a fight.

Aeron manifested into his shimmering shade body. More shadow than form, it wouldn't be visible to anyone other than Nick. Or another higher-level paranormal creature. *There now, you all cocked and dry?*

Sighing, Nick nodded. "Thank you."

*So what got you all unlaced?*

Nick felt his temper rise again. *There's a prick in my classroom making eyes at Kody. Go kill him.*

Aeron burst out laughing.

Until he realized Nick was serious. *What? You're serious, like?*

"Do I look like I'm joking?"

*Nae. You look like we need to loosen the knob on your lid before you blow your gasket and pop your fool head off.* Aeron tsked, then moved as if to chuck Nick on his arm. But since he wasn't in his physical body, his hand passed through Nick's shoulder and left a peculiar tingle there. *Sorry, boyo. But you know I can't kill a man for simply eyeing your girl.*

"Then pluck his eyes out. Bring me his male parts. At the very least snap off a finger!"

Aeron's eyes widened as Nick's voice deepened to the demonic level. *Having some trouble there, son?*

"Little bit!"

"Little bit of what, Gautier?"

Nick froze at the sound of Mr. Head's voice. Great. That was all he needed. The principal thinking he warranted a visit to the psych ward. "Sorry, Mr. Head. I was thinking about my next class. I needed a little bit more time to finish the reading for it."

"Well, come on in and let's discuss this latest event that has you darkening my doorway. I can't wait to hear your version of the matter."

Nick met Aeron's gaze, then sent his thoughts to him. *If you won't kill him for me, at least go keep an eye on the troll. And if he lays one hand on her, make it a bloody stump.*

Aeron shook his head. *Hold that temper, Malachai. It's going to get you into all kinds of trouble.*

Yeah, it already had. Sighing, he headed into the office.

Aeron tried not to be amused as he watched Nick vanish. It wasn't funny, yet he couldn't help being entertained. He'd never seen the boy get jealous before. At least not like this.

And that made him curious about the Nathan boy who'd evoked such a powerful emotion. Poor child had no idea what he was courting.

With that thought, he turned back into his púca form and headed for Caleb's old raunchy smell. Bad thing about a Daeve—couldn't miss their unique stench. Though the last time he'd pointed that out to the ancient demon and handed him a bar of soap, Caleb had gotten a mite testy about it.

But as Aeron neared the door of the classroom, he felt a peculiar presence. One that made his blood run cold.

Before he could act, he was sucked into a vortex.

# CHAPTER 3

So . . . do I have to go punch Stone in the face, or just burp in Richardson's class?"

Nick scowled at Caleb's bizarre question as he took his backpack from him in the hallway outside their next class. "Do what?"

"I'm trying to gauge how much detention I need to earn to match yours. Therefore I'm asking the severity of my grievance and who to assault for it."

Nick snorted. "I don't know. Depends on Richardson's mood. With that evil witch, you could get more detention for the burp than you would if you cold-cocked Stone and made him sterile. Which might not be a bad thing. Future generations would thank you for it."

"Very true." Caleb brushed his dark hair back. "So . . . ?"

"You'll be proud. I've finally mastered my ability to manipulate the weak-minded without turning anyone into a goat or exploding the space-time continuum. . . . I got none."

Instead of being happy that Nick's power had worked for once and nothing had exploded, melted, or summoned a terrifying higher deity or hell-beast from another dimension, Caleb grimaced. "While I am more than thrilled at the prospect of not having to suffer through another round of teenage after-school angst and drama with you, I feel the need to caution you about using those powers for something so trivial. Remember, magick comes with a cost. Even for a Malachai. Ain't no such thing as a free ride in life, my friend. Sooner or later, we all pay the piper. And when that cretin comes home to roost, he always craps right on your head and ugly, oversized shirt."

"Duly noted." Nick sidled up to Kody. "You mad at me, *cher*?"

She paused to rake a suspicious grimace over him. "Uh . . . should I be? What mischief have you wrought now that I don't know about?"

"For sending Aeron to spy on you."

That took every bit of friendliness out of her stare. In fact, he could flash-freeze fire with *that* stare, and a certain part of his anatomy crawled back into his body as she scorched him with it. "When was this?"

"While I was mind-melding with Head."

She glowered even more. "Aeron didn't come into the room."

"Yeah, he did. I sent him straightaway."

"No, he didn't," they said in unison.

His stomach knotting, Nick gave each one of them a bitter glare as they headed for their next period. "Yes, he did. Because he knows I would not be happy with him if he didn't. And an unhappy Malachai kicks his *culo loco*."

"Well," Caleb said drily, "we can stand here and argue like children until one of us sticks his tongue out at the other, or you can call him and see. But I'm here to tell you that the Celt did not step foot in that room. I'd have known it. I didn't even smell him in the building."

Kody groaned. "I wish you two would lay off the odor thing with each other. Neither of you smell. Good grief."

Ignoring her chiding, Nick pulled out his phone. "Prepare to eat those words, Caliboo. One slice humble pie coming up, piping hot." He dialed for his favorite surly war god. Then waited.

And waited.

And waited some more.

It rolled to voice mail.

Okay, that was not good. Scowling, he met Caleb's smug expression. "Why would he have left when he said he wouldn't?"

"It's Aeron."

"Exactly. He's not *you*." Nick put the phone in his pocket. "He doesn't know a lot of people here. It's not like him to run off and visit anyone. Or go trolling after loose women on Bourbon Street . . . unlike a certain Daeve I know." He cleared his throat meaningfully.

"You're just jealous you can't go into any of those clubs, baby face."

Luckily, Kody didn't take him seriously and ignored that jibe. "He has a point, Caleb."

Caleb sighed. "Yeah, he does. Two, if you count the one on his head, and I hate it. 'Cause if Aeron's missing, it doesn't bode well and I'm getting really tired of ill bodings."

Nick wrinkled his nose at the term. "Ill bodings? Is that a phrase?"

"Of course it is. I just made it up."

Nick snorted. "Fine. Whatever. We've got to find him. If for no other reason, we don't need him to do something that could out himself in public."

"Yeah," Caleb said sarcastically. "They have laws against exposing yourself in public."

Kody let out a long-suffering sigh. "I think I know now why the gods made the two of you so incredibly hot. You'd be insufferable, otherwise."

Laughing at her uncharacteristic barb that proved she'd been hanging out with them way too much, Nick paused in the hallway as he saw Nathan walking past them.

A few feet away, Nathan stopped and turned around in a slow circle as he attempted to decipher their misbegotten room numbers and his schedule.

He almost felt sorry for the kid since he still remembered his first days here when he'd been just as lost and confused. The room numbers on the first floor had been arranged by some chaos demon bent on driving the unwary to utter madness. They really made no sense in anyone's world except whatever drunken lunatic had initially placed them on the doors for some kind of sick mind game.

As much as Nick hated himself for the compassion, he found himself wandering over to the warthog. "You need help?"

"Room 114?" Nathan scratched his head. "Shouldn't it be right here, between 112 and 115?" He gestured at the red lockers where a door ought to be. "But then I can't find room 113, either."

"That's because 113 is the gym."

Nathan scowled. "Huh?"

"Exactly. Ours is not to question why. It's merely to go to class and try not to cry." Nick laughed at the truly confounded expression on the kid's face. "Welcome to St. Richard's of the Severely Dyslexic and Homicidally Crazed. Room 114 is the biology lab. Down the hall, to the right. Next to the bathroom and across from room 130. 'Cause that makes all the sense in the world, to absolutely *no*-body."

He shot one brow north.

"Yeah . . . don't ask. Logic and sanity waved byebye to this place a *long* time ago. Why you think they call it an institution?"

Nathan laughed. "Guess so. Thanks."

*"No problemo."*

He held his hand out toward Nick. "I'm Nathan, by the way."

"Nick." With a slight bit of hesitation, he shook his hand. Though now that he was close to the guy, he didn't know why he'd been so weird earlier. Nathan seemed okay, except for the fact that he was the same six foot four height and Nick rather liked towering over other people.

He had so little ego in most things that it was the one and only thing he could normally take pride in that no one, other than Acheron, Xev, and Papa Bear Peltier could take away from him. And Acheron and Papa Bear positively dwarfed his Cajun hide. At almost seven feet in height, the two of them were truly giants in the modern world.

Nick squinted at Nathan. There weren't any horns hiding in that mass of thick dark blond hair. No other warning bells went off as their skin touched. His blue eyes were clear and normal. Intelligent, not demon-esque. No diamond-shaped pupils.

No pimples, either, rank dog.

And of course, the punk was better dressed. But then, who wasn't? Since Cherise Gautier thought these tacky, heinous Hawaiian shirts of the middle-aged tourist kept her only son out of trouble—and they definitely were the best birth control ever invented 'cause no female looked at him and thought, hey, gotta get me some of *that*—Nick wore them with as much pride as he could muster.

For the record, that amount of pride would fit onto the tip of a flea's needle.

Dropping his hand, Nathan glanced past Nick's shoulder to where Kody and Caleb were waiting. "Yeah, Kody told me you were her boyfriend. Sorry if I pissed you off earlier. I had no idea. But I should have known that a girl that pretty would have been taken. I was just kind of hoping, you know?"

Nick would have felt a little better had Nathan not dropped his gaze meaningfully down to his garishly orange glow-in-the-dark shirt. But he was man enough to take it. Besides, if the school lost power, this shirt doubled as a glow stick.

Who would feel the fool then?

"Sorry I overreacted."

Nathan snorted. "It's okay. I get it. I'm the new kid in town and I overstepped. Won't happen again. I promise."

*Yeah, dang straight on that.*

The bell rang.

With a sharp, nervous twitch, Nathan shifted his books. "Down the hall? Right side? Across from 130?"

"That's it."

"Thanks again."

As Nathan left, Nick had that feeling that he'd lived this moment before. A phantom memory that hung just at the edge of his mind. Teasing and annoying. He could see the faintest outlines of it. But the harder he tried to look at it, the more elusive it became.

What was his mind trying to tell him? Why did he feel like this particular moment was a repeat?

It was the strangest sense of déjà vu.

He went back to Kody and Caleb. "Is it me or is there something oddly familiar about this day?"

Kody nodded. "I keep thinking that, too. And the same with Nathan. I feel like I've seen him before, somewhere."

Scratching at his chin, Caleb shrugged. "I have no comment. Humans all look alike to me. And all my days run together, especially the ones where we're fighting demons."

Nick knew he wasn't serious about the human comment. He was just being contrary. However . . . "So Nathan *is* definitely human, right?"

Kody pulled back. "Yeah, why?"

"I don't know. I had a strange sensation when he first appeared earlier. Kind of like my Wonder Twin powers activated for no reason. It's why I'm walking around like a cat in a Doberman factory. I can't shake the unsettled feeling I had. Makes me wish I still had Nashira in my pocket. Not that she'd have given me a straight answer. Still, I'd have felt better with her cryptic crap than being completely blind, going with nothing but a bad feeling in my gut."

Caleb groaned. "Bad feelings in *your* gut give me an ulcer."

"Tell me about it." He laughed as he went into class and checked his phone for messages.

Still nothing from Aeron.

Something was definitely up. It wasn't typical of Legolas to space like this. He didn't just drift off and vanish for no reason.

*Caleb?*

He nodded. *I'm on it. I already heard your nervous thoughts about our errant irritant.* Out loud, he got up and went to ask to go to the bathroom.

Nick wanted to go, too, but knew better than to ask. Teacher would never approve *that*. One student out, okay. Two equaled delinquents up to no good in the minds of the establishment. Dang inconvenience when the safety of the entire world was at stake.

*Maybe I should fake a heart attack?*

Nah, he knew better. Karma was a bitch, and he didn't mean Karma Deveraux, who could be quite special when stirred. Real karma had a way of delivering up nasty retribution and anytime he ever told even the smallest lie, it came back on him with interest. If he faked a heart attack, with his luck, some coronary hellbeast would rise up to rip his heart out and eat it, or worse, feed it to him during lunch. That was just how Nick's luck went. He was the type of guy who could buy a lottery ticket, scratch it off, and it would be a bill he'd have to pay.

As Nick started taking notes another thought occurred to him.

Where *was* Nashira? He hadn't heard from her in a while now, either. Nor Dagon, for that matter.

His Power Rangers had abandoned him. They didn't normally do that . . . Definitely weren't *supposed* to do that.

As his generals, they were under his direct control and were supposed to stay near him at all times. Not just because he could come under fire from Grim and his forces at any heartbeat, but because they were not used to the modern world. All of them had been kept imprisoned in alternate dimensions for centuries and had no idea how to really function in current society.

Other than Caleb and Kody. Caleb because he'd been the right hand of Nick's father and had been out in the world even longer than Adarian had, and way longer than Nick. And Kody because she'd never been sequestered from people. Not to mention that unlike the others, she actually *liked* humanity and didn't want to see them die screaming in agony, inside a fiery pit of demon hellfire.

Nashira could function alone a tiny bit, due to the fact she'd been able to hear and see from the confines of her book enchantment.

But Xev, Dagon, and Aeron . . .

They did not need to interact with the general public without direct and intense supervision. At all times.

*Ever.* Heavy emphasis on the *ever* part.

Yeah, his ulcer was growing like a radiated lizard in a Godzilla movie. And if he didn't hear from one of them soon, it was going to have a baby the size of the Empire State Building.

*Will this day ever end?*

Nick cringed as the thought went through his head and he quickly glanced up at the ceiling. *Yo, up there? I said day end. D-A-Y. Day. Not world. Daaaay. Please, do not get those two words confused or mistake my request, 'cause I know how you get . . . when you want to prove a point to me. I don't need that lesson today. Really. Thank you, PTB. Peace, out.*

Now if he could just keep the bad-luck fairy parked for a bit, he might be all right.

Caleb came back into the room with a look on his face that added a good six feet to the ulcer.

Nick arched his brow.

*No sign of him.*

Nick made a sound of distress. Which caused the other students to turn and stare at him. He flashed a bashful grin. "Puberty. It's so embarrassing."

"Excuse me?" his teacher asked.

"Everyone was staring at me like I'd grown another head so I was trying to lighten the mood."

"How about you lighten it on your own time, Mr. Gautier?"

"Yes, ma'am." Nick dropped his gaze to his textbook and pretended to study so as not to get into any more trouble. Last thing he needed was another trip to the office. That would get him suspended. While he could pull the mind trick once, he couldn't erase the records that said he'd been up there less than an hour ago. So unless he committed a crime, which he wasn't willing to do, he had to calm his nervous body down.

Releasing a zen breath, he sent his thoughts to Caleb. *Did you learn anything else?*

When he didn't get a response, he glanced over to his bodyguard. *Caleb?*

He acted as if he couldn't hear him.

Okay . . . Had he pissed him off? Nick turned toward Kody. *Are you two talking right now?*

Like Caleb, she didn't so much as blink in response to his question. Now that was really odd. Even when they were fighting, she at least gave him dirty looks.

*Kody? I can see your bra strap.*

She definitely didn't hear him, because even if she'd been mad at him for something, she would have checked to make sure that it wasn't showing, since it was a pet peeve of hers.

Instead, she carried on with their assignment, oblivious to his comment.

What the heck?

Worried, Nick held his hand out toward his pencil and attempted to command it with his telekinesis. Normally it would fly into his grasp without any effort.

Not this time.

*No, no, no, no!*

Fear wrapped around his heart at the thought of his powers being drained. But how? He was the Malachai. No one could do that to him.

No one other than his son, and he'd done nothing that could cause *that*. And he meant *nothing*.

Impure thoughts notwithstanding. After all, he *was* a healthy teenage boy and *those* couldn't really be helped, especially not when he had a girlfriend who was exceptionally pretty and smelled really nice. But that being said, all they'd done was kiss. Nothing more.

Having been born to a teen mother, and having spent the whole of his life raising her, he wasn't anxious to start parenting someone else anytime soon. He had enough paranormal brats he was responsible for already. Running after them, and cleaning up their messes, kept him plenty busy.

And then there was Kyrian who was in a special class by himself.

So, no . . . there was no one who could drain his powers.

Yet the hairs on the back of his neck rose as he had the sudden sensation of being watched. Glancing around the fluorescent-lit room, he caught the gaze of Stone Blakemore fastened on him like he was the barely-clad centerfold of the Swimsuit Edition of *Sports Illustrated*.

Yeah, that was some major stink-eye. Not like he'd done anything to Stone, ever. He basically left the knuckle-dragging werewolf alone. But Stone had hated him since the moment he walked through the school doors. It was as if Stone had smelled the Malachai in his genes and reacted to it on some primal level.

"Nick?"

It took him a second to realize Kody was speaking to him. "Yeah?"

"Are you all right?"

He blinked slowly. Honestly? He was a little light-headed. "I think so, why?"

"The bell?"

Nick glanced around and realized the room was empty. Kody and Caleb were standing beside him with worried frowns.

What the heck? He'd just been looking at Stone . . . Hadn't he?

"Something's wrong. I was trying to talk to you both with telepathy. Didn't you hear me?"

"No." Kody knelt by his side and brushed the hair back from his forehead so that she could press her hand against his skin to test for a fever. "You are flushed and clammy." Biting her lip in an adorable manner, she glanced up at Caleb. "Can a Malachai get sick?"

Caleb shook his head. "Not once his powers come in."

Grateful for her concern, Nick caught her hand and kissed her fingers. "Could it be the Eye messing with me?"

She grimaced at Nick. "Please tell me you left that thing at home."

"It's in my pocket. I was going to use it to play the lottery after school."

She said something under her breath he was pretty sure was a major curse in one of her parents' native tongues.

"Why?" Now there was the tone an impatient parent used when their kid did something exceptionally bright, like stick tweezers in an outlet.

"It wasn't good for anything else. I figured it owed me a Powerball for the trauma it's put me through."

Spreading her fingers wide, she had an expression on her face that said if she held his Malachai powers, she'd be Force-choking him right now.

Caleb placed a steadying hand on her shoulder. "Remember, you loooove him, Kody."

"Wondering why."

"I ask myself that every time you say it out loud."

"Way to prop up my ego there, buddy." Nick brushed his hand against his forehead and squinted in an attempt to clear his vision. "You think the Eye's messing with me?"

"No." Caleb picked Nick's backpack up to carry it for him. "But you look weak . . . like your father used to get right after *you'd* visit him in prison."

Kody's jaw went slack. "What are you saying?"

"I said what I'm saying." Caleb held his hand out to Nick. "Give me your fist."

"Why?"

"Just do it and stop whining!"

Suspicious of what he intended, Nick didn't like that tone. Talk about things that didn't bode well. And when he obeyed and Caleb used his claw to slice open part of his hand, he knew why. Sheez!

"Hey! They hurt, you dick!"

Caleb ignored his words and cursed as he released Nick's bleeding hand. "You think *that* hurts? You've got *no* idea. And we have a massive problem."

His breathing labored, he retracted his claws and narrowed his gaze on Kody. "You know the cosmic laws. He's my master. I shouldn't have been able to harm him, at all. The only way for me to do that . . ." He jerked his chin toward the blood on Nick's hand. "Something's draining the Malachai out of him."

"How's that possible?" Kody breathed.

"*I* don't know. I've never heard of it before."

The color faded from Kody's cheeks. "Caleb . . . if anyone finds out about this . . ."

"Believe me, Nyria, I know. . . . He's dead."

# CHAPTER 4

A eron pressed the heel of his hand to his eye
as he tried to keep his skull from splitting
apart. Though to be honest, he wouldn't
mind it breaking open so long as it stopped aching
like this. *Please, anything, just stop hurting . . .*

He blinked open his other eye to see if he could figure out where in the blessed bog he might be, 'cause he
had a bad feeling he wasn't at home in Caleb's house.

By the crappy, moldy, pungent, stale stench of the
place, it wasn't St. Richard's, unless he'd somehow
gotten locked in the bottom of the boys' dirty laundry
chute.

And no one had bothered to do laundry in a few
dozen decades.

Maybe longer.

"Gah, I'll never complain about the Daeve's smell again." To be honest, he'd rather bury his nose in the smoking pits of Caleb's hairy arms after his football practice in August than inhale this wretched stench. It smelled worse than the Dagda's boots after he'd been chasing the Mórrígan around the bend.

The moment he sat up, he froze. Two inches from his nose was the ugliest dog he'd ever seen. It made the Cŵn Annwn look like a swan. All it needed was to have red ears and be howling and he'd know his death was imminent. "Here now, puppy. I'm sure I can find a nice slipper for you to chew on, eh?"

*If you hand me a shoe, I'll shove it up where the sun don't shine, Irishman.*

Dropping his hand, Aeron cracked a grin at the snide tone. "Not Irish, if you want to be technical. And who are you, Scooby?"

*Not Scooby . . .*

"Hellhound?"

*Mostly . . . if you want to be technical.*

"Snotty little bastard, aren't you?"

*You stay here any length of time and you will be, too.*

"And here would be . . ?" Aeron let his voice trail off meaningfully.

*Azmodea.*

Of course it was. Aeron groaned out loud. "I'm assuming we're on the bad side of the fence?"

*Is there a good side?*

"Thorn's."

*I know nothing of a Thorn.*

"And that answers that." Aeron glanced around at the dank, iridescent-black walls of his makeshift prison. They bled like an oozing oil pit. At least he wasn't bound. Not that it would have done them any good. Hard to pin a púca with shackles, and while he was still a bit chafed at his family for what they'd done to him with their cursing, there was something to be said for it.

Sitting back, he looked up at the eerie blue lights that radiated above their heads. They pulsed like a living creature.

He grimaced at the sight of what he was pretty sure were the remains of a poor beast who'd had a much worse day than his. Thank the gods his innards didn't glow after death. He'd hate to have his guts used in such a manner.

"You didn't happen to see what brought me here, did you, boyo?"

*Taahiki demons.*

Well, that explained the stench. They were the pole-cats of the demon world. It'd be weeks before he'd get *that* off his skin. "Now, I'm going to ask a ridiculously rhetorical question."

*No, there's no way out of here.*

"You could have at least given me the satisfaction of asking it. But since you ruined that, I have another. Me master has misplaced his own hellhound. Any chance you might be familiar with him? He's named Zavid."

*You serve the Malachai?*

Aeron hesitated in his answer. One thing he'd learned aeons ago—you volunteer no facts until you knew what side of the matter your opponent was aligned to, and he knew nothing of this new "friend."

"I don't *serve* anyone."

"Yet you're the one who said it was your master's hound." A low, insidious moan echoed around them from no known source.

The black wolf crouched low and began growling at the wall to Aeron's left.

"What's that?"

*Noir's servants. If you are friend or servant to the Malachai, they're coming to make you regret it.*

"And what are you?"

*I'm no friend of Noir's or Azura's. But if you can show me this Thorn, I will be the best friend you've ever made.*

Rising to his feet, Aeron stepped away as every warning in his body went off simultaneously. This was a little too easy. "And why would I be wanting to take you anywhere when you're the one who'd be knowing the way when I don't? Not like I've got a set of keys to the kingdom. You could have left here at any time. Why did you wait on me when you didn't know I was coming . . . ? Or did you?"

A flash of light blinded him an instant before the wolf became a tall, thin, male demon. "You're just all kinds of smart, aren't you? Pity that . . ."

Y ou know that won't break him, right?"
Noir turned a ball-shriveling glare toward Grim that would have sent anyone else in this dismal realm scurrying for a hole to vanish into. Almost seven feet in height, the ancient primal god held an insidious beauty that only the source of all evil could possess.

His black hair and eyes were as soulless as his actions. And there was a wicked light that flickered in the depths of those cold eyes that seemed to match his dark burgundy demonic armor. He tossed his bloodred cape back over his shoulder. "Are you trying to piss me off?"

"No, but that would be a sweet bonus."

Noir actually laughed. Something that caused all the demons around them to run away like rodents fleeing a pending explosion—which was most likely what they thought that unnatural sound portended. The ancient god reached out and grabbed Grim's pale hair.

His mouth curled into the semblance of a cruel, twisted smile before he jerked Grim against his chest and gave him a bone-shattering embrace. "I've missed you, boy." He placed a kiss on the top of Grim's head, then released him. Quicker than Grim could blink, he backhanded him so hard that Grim saw stars from it. "But if you back talk me again, I'll rip out your entrails and throw them to the slug demons to eat."

Wiping the blood from his nose and mouth, Grim forced himself not to show how much that blow had staggered him. Or the fact that he still wasn't seeing straight from it as his face continued to throb and ache to distraction.

Holy crap, for an old fart whose strength had waned, Noir could pack a wallop.

He passed an angry pain-filled glare to Laguerre

who held absolutely no sympathy for him in her cold, dark eyes.

But then, she *was* Noir's daughter.

He grimaced at the blood on his hand. He'd forgotten just how much he hated being around Azura and Noir. Now being that he was virtually trapped with them and dependent on them . . .

If he ever laid hands on that sniveling Malachai, Gautier would know pain unimaginable.

When people talked about having bad in-laws, they had *no* idea what true misery meant. They should have to spend a weekend with *his*.

These two ancient beings were a large part of why he'd left Laguerre centuries ago. As much as he'd once loved her, and as much fun as they'd had in war together, it wasn't worth tolerating her demented, psychotic parents and their volatile tantrums.

Not even for a dinner date.

And he'd forgotten just how much Laguerre favored her father. But now that they stood side by side, the resemblance was uncanny. Same coal-black eyes that held no feeling or regard for anyone else. Same patrician features, smug expressions, and dark hair. Only while

Noir's was short, Laguerre's fell to her waist in spiraling curls.

Just like her father, she'd sprang from her mother's womb, sword in her hand, ready to kill any- and everyone who happened into her path. No wonder the ancient humans had once deemed her the Fire Bitch of the Gods. Herit-Anat, Anat the Terror, et cetera. Back then, she'd gone by many names and even more epitaphs.

Ancient humans had left her untold offerings in their temples, hoping to buy her favor so that she'd leave them alone.

As if . . .

Instead, the two of them had led untold wars and conquests throughout the human lands. Everywhere they went, slaughter followed. For centuries, they'd been an invincible team. Laguerre as the goddess of war, and he as the god of death. Their army of demons and damned had torn up the entire earth.

How Grim missed those days of freedom, and bloody fun.

Now . . .

Grim pressed his thumb against the tooth Noir's

blow had loosened. He was trapped here. Useless and bored.

Worse, he was irrelevant. He, who had once so terrified humanity to the point they couldn't think his name without shaking in terror and dying of fright, was now reduced down in this modern age to a cartoon character who made appearances in video games and on birthday greeting cards. They'd turned him into a chibi!

The indignities never stopped.

Laguerre sighed. "The Malachai still has five of his šarras by his side. Removing one won't make much difference."

Noir slid an intolerant grimace toward his daughter. "Patience, Anat. Have you learned nothing out in the human world?"

"Only how much I loathe the mortal vermin and wish to see them crushed beneath my hooves again."

Suddenly, Noir leaned his head back and took a deep breath as if he were in the throes of ultimate pleasure.

After a few uncomfortable minutes, he opened his eyes and smiled at them. "Ah . . . see? That's why I wanted his šarras here. They hold a part of the Malachai's powers. As such, I can feed from them and take back some of his strength. It's why all of you were kept from me and banned from here while you served him. Now bring me the rest of his little friends. Once we have him fully weakened and me fed, we shall be able to destroy him. And I'll be able to leave here, not as a ghost in a body I invaded through possession, but as myself. Then we will rain down our will upon this world again and show them what they've missed."

Hey, Ma," Nick said as soon as he heard his mother's thick Cajun drawl when she answered the phone. "I'm sorry to bug you at work, but I'm really sick. I need to go home. Is that okay?"

"Baby Boo! You sound so terrible and sad! Oh, honey. It's right in the middle of the lunch crowd. I can't leave. Let me call Michael and I'll send him right over to pick you up, okay?"

"'Kay. I'm handing you to the school nurse to tell her. Love you, Ma."

"You, too, baby. Please be okay. You rest and I'll be home as soon as I can to check on you. Call if you need me and I will come running. I'll quit if I have to."

Nick snorted at his mom's offer. She loved her job

as a waitress at Sanctuary. Although, if she ever learned her boss was a shape-shifting were-bear, that might change. "Don't do that. I'll live." Though to be honest, he didn't feel like it at the moment.

His mom made kissing noises at him. Cringing, he made them back at her, but much more subtly before he handed the phone to the nurse and blushed, then beat a hasty retreat from her office in order that he wouldn't have to face that 'ah, how cute you are' look that so many gave him whenever he was nice to his mom.

As he moved to sit down outside to wait, he met Madaug St. James, who came into the office with a delivery for the secretary. At just under six feet, he was the son of two Squire brain surgeons—literally. Which was what had allowed him to create a mind-altering video game that demons had enchanted and used to possess their classmates.

Yeah, good times . . .

Not even a little. Nick was still having violent flashbacks from his Zombie Hunter experience. It was so bad, he couldn't even watch a zombie movie to this day. And poor Madaug couldn't so much as play solitaire on his PC after it.

Still, he was one of Nick's best friends. And it was

nice to occasionally hang out with someone who was frightfully normal, Madaug's extremely high IQ notwithstanding. After all, compared to Madaug, most people had the intelligence of a head of cabbage.

"Hey, Nick! What are you doing up here?"

"About to hurl."

Madaug jumped back. "Dude, I'm sorry. You contagious? 'Cause if you are, I want it! I have a test next period and I'm not prepared."

Yeah, right. Madaug was always prepared for tests. Even for the ones they wouldn't have until the end of the year. Kid was sick that way.

"Trust me, you don't want any part of this one."

"Yeah, you do look kind of green and disoriented. I take it that means you're going to miss band practice after school?"

Nick nodded. "Thanks for reminding me. Can you tell the others?"

"Sure, but Marlon's going to kill you. He's been looking forward to it. He has a massive crush on Duff."

"Sorry. What's his problem anyway?"

"What? Duff? I don't know. Distemper. Maybe parvo."

Nick scowled. "Isn't that a dog disease?"

"Yes, but I think our resident teen were-panther has it, too. At least he acts like it most days."

That he did. He took brooding teen male to a whole new level. The entire three years he'd been in school with them, Nick had never heard him say a single word to anyone. "Is he really mute or did he sell his voice to a wizard?"

Madaug laughed. "Neither. The correct term is selective mutism. His is an extreme case of it. Most likely caused by his . . . you are giving me *that* look."

Nick held his hands up. "Dude, it's a look of awe."

"Sure it is. And before my social anxiety kicks in, I'm heading back. Hope you get to feeling better. You need me to sacrifice a goat or anything for you?"

Nick feigned a round of really fake laughter at something neither of them found particularly amusing since Madaug was the one Nick had turned into a goat with his powers when Nick had rescued him from the Zombie Hunter demons. "Uh, no. No goats. No more game programming ever, partner."

"Yeah, lesson learned." He bro-hugged him, then headed back to class.

Nick shook his head. That boy was going to end up as a leading doctor somewhere.

Or as an evil villain mastermind, leading a horde of henchmen.

Thank goodness he was on their side for the moment.

Suddenly, a huge, dark shadow fell over Nick. He started to scramble away out of reflex until he looked up and realized it was the mountainous muscled mass also known as Big Bubba Burdette.

"Sheez, Bubba! You scared the crap out of me."

"Boy, you need to lay off the caffeine. You got the reflexes there of a scared Chihuahua."

Yeah, well, given the fact that all manner of deadly things tended to pop out of the shadows intending to eat him or enslave him, it was little wonder. But he couldn't tell that to Bubba.

"How you feeling?" Bubba put his hand on Nick's forehead.

"Pretty awful."

"You look pale." Bubba grabbed his backpack. "C'mon, I already signed you out."

"Thank you, by the way. I really appreciate it." Nick scowled as he caught a whiff of aftershave and realized that Bubba's scraggly beard wasn't so scraggly. He'd trimmed it down to one of those shadowy things that

Kody and Brynna giggled about on actors. "Did you shave?"

"Shut up."

And now that Nick was paying attention, he realized that Bubba wasn't wearing his usual uniform of bad horror movie T-shirt and ratted-up flannel shirt over it. Instead, he had on a nice button-down and new jeans. The only thing that remained of "old" Bubba was the heavy, steel-toed work boots. "Gah! Bubba! That's my mama, you know?"

He arched one jet eyebrow at Nick as he gave him a scathing glare that backed him down a notch. While Nick might be the Malachai, Bubba had been a semi-pro linebacker and was the size of a brick house with the muscle mass of a world-champion weightlifter who could put him through a wall with a single sneeze. Not to mention, he was a raw, bad-ass survivalist who went zombie hunting for fun in gator and demon-infested swamps. "Don't you even, boy. I asked you before I started going out with her and you said it was all right."

"I know what I said, but . . ." Nick shivered. "Can't I be grossed out?"

Bubba snorted. "Grow up, snot-nose."

Nick was trying, but it was hard. While he wanted his mom to be happy, he didn't want to think of her actually *dating* someone, especially not his best friend and mentor. And the fact that Bubba let his mom call him Michael really screwed with Nick's head.

Only Bubba's mama got away with that.

And Cherise Gautier.

As they left the school building and Nick headed home, Bubba stopped him. "I told Cherise I'd take you back to the shop with me so that I could keep an eye on you 'til she gets off work."

"Oh my God, Bubba! I'm about to turn seventeen. Really?"

Bubba's blue eyes darkened with tragedy.

Nick mentally kicked himself as he remembered that Bubba's wife and son had been murdered because she'd gone home from work due to illness and had been there alone when an intruder had broken in on her.

"You don't need to be by yourself while you're illing. You need someone to watch over you so you can sleep." Bubba's voice was emotionless, but his eyes weren't. They carried the full weight of grief and self-recrimination that Bubba crucified himself with. He held himself fully responsible for not going home early to be with his wife. It was why he took his zombie slaying to such extremes.

Why he was overprotective of everyone. And that was why Nick had allowed him to date his mom. So long as Bubba was with her, he knew no one would ever harm a single hair on his mother's head. Bubba would break them in half first.

"Okay. Sorry. You're right." He didn't bother to tell Bubba that he wouldn't have been alone at his condo. Xev was there. Or should be.

But then only he and his crew of friends knew that Xev was Mr. Fuzzy Boots.

As they reached Bubba's computer and gun store that was just over a block from the school, Bubba opened the door for him. "Do I need to send Mark out for soup or something?"

"No, I'm good for the moment. But pizza in an hour would be good."

"Pizza? Oh my God, Mikey. No wonder you like the boy. Sounds just like *you*!"

Nick hesitated just inside the shop at the sound of an unfamiliar male voice that was thick with a middle Tennessee drawl.

Reserved around strangers, he turned to see an average height, heavyset man at the counter who was probably in his late fifties. Even though they'd never met before, Nick knew him instantly. "Hey! It's Bubba from the commercials!" The only difference was that he didn't have on the flannel shirt or zombie tee either, but rather wore a red polo shirt and jeans, and his black hair and beard were laced with gray.

Bubba stepped around him to put his backpack down behind the counter. "Nick, meet my father, Dr. Burdette. Dad, this is Nick."

Nick moved forward to shake his hand. "Real pleasure to meet you, Dr. Burdette."

"And you, though to hear my son and wife talk about you, I was expecting an ankle-biting rug rat. Not a half-grown man who stands eye to eye with my giant beast of a son." He glanced at Bubba and shook his head with a sigh. "I swear to God, that boy's mama must have been feeding him fertilizer when I wasn't looking. Ain't nobody in my family ever been that tall . . . hers, either, for that matter. If he didn't look just like me, I'd be wondering, and eyeballing the mailman."

"Daddy!" Bubba barked in a chiding tone.

"What?" he asked, blinking innocently. "It's God's truth, and you know it."

Laughing, Mark stepped out from between the black curtains that separated the front of the store from the back room. Only a few years older than Nick, he was Bubba's sidekick and best friend, and fellow zombie-hunting lunatic. The two of them got into all manner of madness whenever Nick turned his back on them.

The ying to Bubba's yang, Mark was as fair as Bubba was dark, with shaggy light brown hair, and bright green eyes that seldom stopped laughing. Like Bubba, he'd gone to college on a full football scholarship and they'd grown up together in Tennessee before moving to New Orleans.

"Ah now, don't let Nick's height fool you, Dr. Burdette. He's still an ankle-biter." Mark smirked at Nick. "How you feeling, kiddo?"

"Sick."

"Well, don't give it to me or I'll make you wash Bubba's underwear for the next month."

Bubba snorted as he started opening the day's shipment and checking it in. "Don't I pay you to work?"

"Nah. You pretend to pay me and I pretend to work."

Ignoring them, Bubba's father came around the

counter to examine Nick. "So what are your symptoms? Sore throat?"

Eyes wide, Nick glanced at Bubba.

"He's a GP . . . general practitioner. Worse than my mama, any day, and twice on Sunday. Surrender, kid. It's just easier that way. He ain't going to let you alone until you do."

Oh great. If the doctor pulled him in for tests . . . he was still the Malachai with some unusual traits, and if they uncovered the fact that he wasn't human this could turn ugly fast.

Clearing his throat, Nick sought to avert disaster. "Not too bad. Mostly headache and tired and achy."

"Hmm, might just be a cold. Let me take you in back and get your vitals. Check you out. . . . You're the one with the preexisting heart condition, right?"

"He is."

"Bubba!" Nick snapped.

"Don't Bubba me, boy. Your mama *and* mine would skin me alive if anything happened to you on my watch. Personally, I think my mama likes you better, anyway."

His dad laughed. "Completely not true. I was once mopping the kitchen floor when Mikey came running through the house for no good reason—like someone was trying to kill him—and fell. Now a normal woman would be mad at the kid for tracking mud on my freshly mopped floor. Let me reiterate *normal* woman . . . I didn't marry normal. I married Bobbi Jean Clinton-Burdette. Ain't no normal in that family tree, I'm telling you. So faster than I could blink, his mama took that mop handle to me 'cause that boy done skinned his knee on my fresh clean floor. I'm telling you, she got ahold of me so viciously over it that I thought one of them Greek furies had done descended on me from Mount Olympus. You'd have thought that boy lost his leg the way she carried on. But he barely bruised it. Didn't even bleed, but boy howdy, *I* surely did."

"You did not." Bubba snorted. "And I was four when it happened."

"Four, nothing, it was last year!"

Bubba laughed and shook his head. "It was not." Sighing, he met Nick's gaze. "One thing to know about my daddy, he don't always tell the truth."

"Now that ain't so. I always tell the truth. I just do so creatively. Makes it more entertaining for folks that way." He draped his arm over Nick's shoulders and led him to the back where Bubba and Mark worked on computers while Bubba called Nick's mom to let her know that he'd picked him up and had him "in custody."

Dr. Burdette had him sit on a stool next to Bubba's linked computer monitors that had an interesting array of food lined up across them. He smiled as he saw Nick frowning at it. "Excuse my food porn. Bobbi Jean keeps me on so many diets, that's my sin right there. Anytime I get out of her sight, I start looking up desserts I can't eat and salivating like Pavlov's dog. You wouldn't want to smuggle me one of them beignets later, would you?"

"Don't you dare, Nick!" Bubba called from the other side of the curtains. "He's diabetic and he ain't to have none of that while he's here."

His father growled at him. "You and your mama, boy! What good is a conference in the Big Easy when I can't have none of that food here? You might as well shoot me and put me out of my misery!"

Bubba carried a box of parts to the back to put them on the shelf. "I don't want to shoot you, Daddy. But I would like to keep you around for a little while longer. So would Mama. Don't break her heart. You done promised her you'd behave and stay on your diet."

Nick patted him on the shoulder. "I feel your pain, Dr. Burdette. You should meet my mama. She forces me to eat vegetables." He shuddered. "And other girl foods. It's terrible."

Bubba laughed. "He's right about that, but Cherise is a great cook. I swear that woman could turn ketchup packets into a gourmet meal."

His dad got a strange expression on his face at that. "I think he has a fever. You mind if I take him up and get my kit?"

"Sure. I was going to let him rest in my bed anyway 'til his mama gets off work." Bubba narrowed his gaze on Nick. "I mean that, too. Don't let me catch you surfing porn on my PC up there, or playing no games. You can watch TV, but I want you resting."

"Yes, sir. Bubba, sir." Nick scooted off the stool and headed for the stairs that led up to Bubba's two-floor condo above his store.

As he walked up, it struck him just how familiar he'd become with Bubba over the last few years. In weird ways, he was like his father.

For that matter, he was the only father Nick had ever really known. Even though his birth father had lived with them for a time, Adarian had never felt fatherly. Never felt like he belonged as part of their family. To the day he died, he'd been a surreal stranger.

From the moment Nick had wandered into Bubba's store to rent time on a computer for a school project, Bubba had been different.

Like Kyrian and Acheron.

Nick felt as if he'd always known them. As if they were family from aeons ago, and they had spent lifetimes of history together. Acheron would say it was because lives were a tangled tapestry of overlapping threads that spanned centuries. Souls born and reborn, always reconnecting when they were supposed to and that Nick had met them before.

Madaug would call it inherited memory. He'd written an entire paper on it for class. In his mind, the DNA of previous generations left a permanent imprint on each person when they were born, and that when two people whose DNA had interacted in another lifetime came together in their current one, some primal part of their anatomy sparked like dormant neurons in the brain firing awake. That was why Madaug thought humans had that feeling of having met someone before or having known them "forever."

Nick wasn't sure what he thought. He only knew

what he felt. His father had left him cold. The saddest part about losing his father was that he didn't grieve over Adarian's passing. And that made him feel defective. Broken.

Vacant.

Yet he knew if he lost Bubba or Kyrian, it would be different. Their loss would devastate him. As would Mark's. Or one of his friends.

Even Zavid and he barely knew him. The thought of his friend being held and tortured . . .

He had to get his powers back and find him. In the back of his mind, he could still see the condition Zavid had been in when they met. Held without comfort or dignity. Treated more like an animal than a sentient being. It was how his father had dealt with people.

And it was something Nick couldn't stomach.

Dr. Burdette led him into Bubba's condo and went to the guest room to get his doctor's bag. Nick made a beeline into Bubba's room and grabbed a pillow from the bed and the blanket he kept folded on the chair, then headed for the couch.

When Dr. Burdette returned, he scowled at Nick, who was lying down on Bubba's faded leather sofa. "You're not going to rest in the bed?"

Nick wrinkled his nose. "Feels like I'm invading his privacy to be in there. Man's got to have his own space, you know?"

Dr. Burdette laughed. "You are a good kid . . . for a demon."

"P-p-pardon?"

He stepped back to glance at the door as if to assure himself that they were alone. "You have one shot to come clean with me, boy, and you better tell me the truth. 'Cause I'll know a lie and a lie will get you killed. What kind are you?" As he spoke, he didn't pull a stethoscope out of his bag.

Dr. Bruce Burdette pulled out a gleaming gold sword that thrummed with ancient power.

Moving faster than Nick could counter, Dr. Burdette pinned him to the couch and held him there. "You have three seconds before I take your head."

# CHAPTER 5

✳

**N**ick tried to scale up the wall like a spider monkey to escape Bubba's father. But whatever that sword was made of, it kept him locked in place, like some kind of invisible hand slapping him down. Dang those weapons! Couldn't anyone carry regular steel anymore?

He glared at the older man who was really spry for a pudgy dude. "What are you?"

"I ask the questions here, demon, not you! You have two seconds left . . ."

Just as Nick went to answer, a blur tackled Dr. Burdette and sent him slamming against the floor. He rolled and came to his feet, then swung at his assailant.

The assailant turned out to be a pissed-off Caleb who ducked and swept Dr. Burdette off his feet again before he disarmed him with a punch so hard, Nick swore *he* felt it. When Caleb moved in for more damage that appeared to be a planned beheading, Nick sprang from the couch.

"Whoa, buddy! Whoa!"

Caleb looked at him as if he'd lost his mind. "*Whoa? Are you friggin' kidding me?* He was about to pop your fool head off."

"Yeah, but he's Bubba's dad. I think . . . I mean . . . he is, right? He's not possessed? I can't tell. My powers are really crap at the moment."

Caleb angled the sword he'd taken at Dr. Burdette. "Yeah, he's human. Not that I count his breed as particularly humane. He's a demon-hunter. That makes him your enemy, Nick. Let me kill him. Do us both a favor."

"No! Again, he's Bubba's daddy. I can't do that to the man or his mama." He scowled at Caleb. "How'd you get here anyway? Or know that I was in trouble?"

He gave him a droll stare. "Seriously? I can't let you out of my sight without you getting, and I quote *you* on this, *Nicknapped* by something that wants to eat you, cage you, or possess you. So I've learned to keep an eye on you and I've been trailing you since the second you left school. 'Cause I knew you were going to find trouble. And look," he said, his voice dripping with sarcasm as he gestured at Bubba's father, "lo and behold, you did."

Dr. Burdette glared at Caleb. "You're a Daeve. Esme Daeve, with something a lot more powerful backing it. Otherwise, I'd have had you."

Caleb scoffed. "Hardly. Don't flatter yourself or insult me." He bared his fangs at him. "Now it's your turn for full disclosure. Give me a reason not to bleed you out at my feet."

He pulled his sleeve back to show a faint scar where a scar appeared to have been branded at one time. "I was a Hellchaser."

"Was?"

"Earned my freedom." He slid his gaze to Nick. "But you're right. I have the blood of a Necrodemian, too. That's what you're reacting to."

"A what?" Nick asked, trying to follow what was an impossible discussion.

Caleb glanced at him, over his shoulder. "Bubba isn't quite as crazy as we thought, Nick. Well, he is, but you know, zombie hunting notwithstanding. . . . Reason why he does some of what he does, and why the things that chase you also chase him? He's a natural-born Hell-Hunter. But like you, and unlike his father here, his blood is dormant, which is why I haven't cut his throat—something I assure you, I would have done had I known he was one of *them*."

Well, that wasn't even a little bit useful to him. Cay was still hogging all the information and Nick was as lost as a three-year-old in a snowstorm.

Caleb lowered the sword and held his hand out to help Dr. Burdette to his feet. "Which line are you part of?"

"Michaelson."

Caleb let out a scoffing laugh. "Should have known. That explains *so* much about Bubba."

Nick scratched at his ear. "Glad someone knows what's going on 'cause I'm all kinds of clueless over here."

Ignoring him, Caleb held the sword out to Dr. Burdette, hilt first. "Keep that in your pants. We're on the same side. Nick's girlfriend is an Arel."

His jaw went slack. "How's that possible?"

"I ask myself that every morning when I get up and she hasn't killed him. Not so much for being a demon as for being an idiot, but that's another discussion."

Nick sputtered indignantly. "Thanks, Cay. Way to bolster my teen ego."

"Yeah, right. There's nothing wrong with the ego of anyone who'd dare wear that shirt in public and not die instantly of mortification. Or bad-taste poisoning." Rubbing a hand over his face, Caleb let out a tired breath and turned back toward the doctor. "So, you're the real reason Bubba's wife and son were murdered?"

Dr. Burdette winced as he straightened some of the items they'd knocked over. "Yeah. It was an old enemy after me. I'd just left town and thought I'd covered my tracks, so that none of them could follow me. Somehow, the demon tracked my scent to Michael's and found her there alone, with Little Hank."

Tears welled in his eyes as they filled with utter misery and guilt. The kind that left a mark on the soul, forever. "She was completely unprepared for what I unknowingly led to her door. And you've no idea how much I hate myself for what I did to my child and grandchild. What I did to Melissa. I should have told Michael long ago what we were. But I never thought the blood would taint him."

"He doesn't know?" Caleb asked.

"No. How could I tell him after that? He'd hate me forever for not warning him, and I can't blame him for it. I hate myself enough for both of us."

Nick saw the same pain play through Caleb's dark eyes. No doubt, he was thinking about his own wife and what had happened to her when he'd left her to fight in a war he'd wanted no part of. An ageless war he was still having to fight, that had cost him everything and left him with nothing, except physical scars, and memories so painful he couldn't stand to think of them.

Not that Nick didn't understand himself. It was the same fate that would eventually claim his beloved mother at the hands of his own enemies if he didn't find some way to derail a future that left him screaming in his dreams as much as Caleb's nightmares from his past.

Caleb stepped closer to Nick, as if to protect him. "How long were you a Hellchaser?"

"Ten years."

Nick frowned. "Wait, what?"

"Yeah, I'm agreeing with Nick. How's that possible? No one gets a term that short."

"You do when you sell your soul for someone else's benefit and not your own personal gain."

Nick cleared his throat meaningfully. "All right, back the train up, conductors. I need some explaining.

I know when we freed Zavid, there was a Hellchaser after him who wanted to drag him back to his prison realm . . . But that's the extent of my knowledge on this subject matter—y'all are making me feel like I'm in Chem class again with them weird doodads on the board. I take it there are different kinds of Hellchasers?"

"Sort of," Caleb finally explained. "Hellchasers are damned souls that Thorn, for whatever reason, believes can be redeemed. He makes a pact with the Mavromino to salvage those souls, if he can. And if everyone agrees to the terms, those souls are allowed to work off their debt to Thorn. If they keep their noses clean and behave, at the end of their term, they're set free to live out normal, happy lives."

"That doesn't sound so bad."

Dr. Burdette let out a bitter laugh. "You've no idea the things the other side sends after us to reclaim us. They know every thought, every fear. Every desire. And they use it all against you. It's the worst hell you can conceive. They're completely unrelenting and highly imaginative."

Caleb nodded. "Yeah. They *are* bad. I'm on a first-name basis with a large number of them." He rubbed at his temple. "So how did you end up in Thorn's clutches?"

"I bargained my soul for my son's life."

Nick's jaw went slack as he finally understood at least part of this. "When Bubba had that really bad wreck with Hank in college?"

Hank had been Mark's older brother that Bubba had named his son for. Bubba's lifelong best friend who'd been killed in the crash. It was something no one talked about, but it haunted both Bubba and Mark, and was why Bubba was so protective of his "side-kick," and why the two of them had become as close as brothers.

Why they might fight like an old married couple, but if anyone so much as lifted an evil eyebrow in Mark's general direction, Bubba would lay them out cold.

His father nodded. "Michael almost died that night, too. It didn't happen exactly the way he remembers it . . . that was part of my bargain. I didn't want my boy to have any worse guilt from it than what he already does."

Dr. Burdette paused as if his emotions overwhelmed him. When he spoke again, his voice trembled. "They'd already told us to pick out funeral clothes for Michael. Said he wouldn't make it through the night." A tear slid from the corner of his eye. "You've no idea what it feels like to hear those words about someone you love. . . ."

Caleb laughed bitterly. "Yeah, I do. Trust me."

He wiped at his face and sniffed back his tears. "Anyway, from the moment Michael was born and I saw those aged, celestial eyes of his, I knew he carried the bloodline, and that he was one of the chosen who might be called on one day to fight the unspeakable horrors no one should know walks in the daylight with us. I did everything I could to keep him as far away from all of it as I could. Moved him away from my family, kept him shielded and ignorant of the things we deal with daily. Yet somehow, evil like you always seeks him out, no matter where he goes."

"Excuse me?" Nick asked. "I do have feelings, people!"

Rolling his eyes, Caleb shook his head. "Yeah, Nick's not the one you need to be fearing. . . . But go on."

He let out a tired breath. "A part of me always believed that it was why Michael had that wreck. It was them trolls going after him that night, either to get to me or him before he became active and aware of his powers."

"Probably." Caleb shook his head in sympathy. "Who'd you summon for your bargain?"

"Kaiaphas."

He made a noise that said Dr. Burdette had chosen poorly. Either that, or the demon had mutated into a hen and was about to lay an egg.

With Caleb, just about anything *was* possible.

Groaning and covering his face with his hand, Caleb stared at Dr. Burdette from between his spread fingers. "Why in the name of all unholy would you summon that jackass?"

"He answered and no one else did," he said simply. "My blood wasn't even dry on the contract before Thorn showed up, screaming the deal was invalid and that it went against whatever it is they have for a code. For whatever reason, he took up my cause and was able to negotiate a reprieve because I'd done it with noble intentions."

"You're lucky. Thorn doesn't often do that."

"Yeah, I know. It's why I still hunt for him, from time to time. I feel like I owe him that much."

"If you knew what he has to bargain with, you'd realize you owe him a lot more than that."

"What do you mean?"

"Nothing." Caleb returned to Nick's side. "You feeling any better?"

"Nope and I'm a lot worse with all this confusion. What's a Hell-Hunter?"

Caleb growled deep in his throat. "Like a dog with a mangy, old bone. You never know when to let it go and bury it."

"How is it that he knows so little?"

"He's part Sephiroth."

Dr. Burdette went stock-still for several seconds before he shook his head. "That's impossible."

"And yet here he stands. A total contradiction of everything a Malachai should be, because he carries the blood of a half-Sephiroth mother."

With a scoffing laugh, Dr. Burdette crossed his arms over his chest. "And that makes as much sense as my existence does, so I'll shut up about it."

Turning around, Caleb finally took mercy on Nick. "To answer your question, you've actually met some Hell-Hunters, you just didn't know it, and luckily, they didn't know *you*, Mr. Mortal Enemy, bane of their entire existence."

"Okay. . . . Where did they come from?"

"They were a necessary evil after the Bellum Magnus. Your great ancestor had unleashed so many demons during the first war and corrupted them that we couldn't corral them all back into their respective holes. Much like Artemis and her Dark-Hunters, the Kalosum designated warriors who would be charged with hunting them down and either returning them to their prisons, or killing them. The first group was hand-selected from volunteers. They'd been among some of the best warriors and heroes of the Bellum. And because they knew the inherent dangers of the creatures they were pursuing, they understood that their lives would be short. You don't hunt that level of bad-ass for long, without losing a fight and your life. The Kalosum knew there wouldn't be any way to maintain a constant supply of warriors with their same skill set and strength. No way to adequately train replacements in time."

"So like a Malachai," Dr. Burdette said, picking up the explanation, "they agreed to have their *ouisa* and souls bound to Seraph medallions and swords. Upon their death, those medallions call to another family member the medallion deems worthy to pick up their swords and fight. Their lure is undeniable and once you take the medallion in your hand, you're screwed."

Caleb gave a bitter laugh. "You don't get to back out of it. The only way is if Gabriel refuses to let you fight. He, alone, has the ability to call the Seraph out of you and return it to the medallion before your death."

*Oh, goodie. That didn't sound like fun.* "So after they possess you, what happens to the person you were?"

"It's not possession," Caleb said quickly. "Again, it's like you with the Malachai. They gain the memories of their predecessors so that they can call on their knowledge and strength to fight the demons they have to go after . . . you know, Nick. It's a cheat code to take the big monster at the end of the game without having to bank experience points."

"The more demons we defeat, the stronger we become."

"Yeah," Caleb said with an odd half laugh. "And if one of them can put down a Malachai, he'd be the hum-daddy of them all. Which is why, kid, we need to keep you far away from them."

"Duly noted. Avoid Hell-Hunters, pointy objects, and any hell realm, hell mouth, and babes wielding swords . . . except for the one I'm currently dating."

"You're really dating an Arel?" Dr. Burdette asked again.

"Yeah."

"The world makes no sense." He glanced at Caleb. "It's the End Times, isn't it?"

"That's what we're trying to avoid."

Now that Nick was sure his death wasn't imminent, he sat down on the couch. "You're not going to try and exorcize me or anything while I rest, are you?"

"You sling holy water on him, you'll be extremely disappointed. I'm rather sure his mother fed it to him in his baby bottle."

"No, she didn't, Malphas. That was frankincense oil. Learn the difference."

"Oh, excuse me. I didn't mean to confuse them." Caleb rolled his eyes.

Dr. Burdette gave them a look that said he was having a hard time imagining them in their true, respective roles. "How is it a Malachai knows so little about demons?"

"He screams like a girl if he has to watch a horror movie."

"Hey!"

"Well, you do. I tried to watch *Child's Play* and you

ran off to hide during the opening credits. And then he had to go sleep with his mom in her bed for three days because he was so scared."

"Dude! You promised me you weren't going to tell anyone about that."

Dr. Burdette gaped. "You're not kidding?"

"Of course not. I have to change his jeans whenever he wets them."

"Cay! That's it! You're banned from watch duty. Don't I have someone else who can guard me? Where's Xev? At least he doesn't speak to anyone. Never mind tell them horrifying truths about me. Except for the pants wetting . . . for the record, I quit doing that."

"Yeah, last year."

"Caleb!"

Dr. Burdette laughed. "You two are not the norm I'm used to running across in this job."

Caleb snorted disdainfully. "That's because you hang out with loser classes of demons. You should party with me and my friends sometime. Leave the weaponry at home, though. You pull something on one of us, and we will return it to your possession through your least comfortable orifice."

Nick cocked his head as a weird vision went through

his mind. Funny, he never really thought about what Caleb did when they weren't together. Who he hung out with. Since Caleb didn't talk about it, he'd assumed that he went into demon limbo or something.

Although, Caleb had been really familiar with all the creatures on the other side of the Veil when they'd gone into the Shadowland to rescue Nick's mother the night his father died.

In his head, he saw Caleb in a peculiar bar, laughing and joking with a group of demons who weren't disguised as humans. They were fully demoned-out. Even Caleb had let his freak demon fly.

"I didn't know you had pointed ears like an elf. You're the one I should be calling Legolas instead of Aeron."

Caleb turned toward him with a sharp frown. "What was that?"

Nick blinked. "I had an image of you with friends in the Veil World. You were in your normal skin, so to speak. Since we've always been one step from death whenever I've seen you in your demon form, I never noticed your ears."

"Yours are pointed, too, FYI."

"Really?"

Caleb nodded. "Teeth, too. You're totally sick when you go Malachai."

"Great. Good to know. Don't do that in front of a girlfriend I want to keep."

Caleb came forward to squat down in front of Nick with a fierce frown. "This is so strange."

"What?"

"It's like . . . but it can't be."

"Like *what*? You're scaring me."

"Told you," he mumbled under his breath. "Frightens like a three-year-old girl." Then louder, he spoke to Nick. "You have all the symptoms Adarian would show anytime you came near him. I swear it's like there's another Malachai here. But there can't be. It's not possible." He glanced at Dr. Burdette. "What tools are you carrying?"

"Nothing that would drain a Malachai. I have my sword. Some holy water. Nothing too powerful. I wasn't planning on stalking anything while I was here. Michael would be better stocked for that than I am."

Caleb tilted his head up to look at the sigils and symbols Bubba had inscribed on his walls and windows for protection. "Yeah, but he's not. Other than some salt, which doesn't affect kid supreme, there's nothing he's used that would touch him. We're over here all the time with no ill effects. Bubba has invited us in so we're safe. . . . It doesn't make sense."

"How does Michael not know what you are?"

"Not something we spread around. And Nick's mother has no clue, either. We intend to keep it that way."

"Yet she's part Sephiroth?"

"And has no clue about that, either. Again, long story."

"It'd have to be," Dr. Burdette said with a laugh. "But in all seriousness if he's lost or losing power, then there's something here that's dark. Something that's found a way to channel his power for its own use."

"That's what I'm thinking."

"You know if it's able to do that—"

"It's not here to make friends."

Nick didn't like the direction their conversation was headed. "So what are you two thinking?"

Caleb gave him a long, hard stare. "That whatever has you, knows what you are. Knows that you're not adept at your powers and that who or whatever it is has a plan to take you down. And take the rest of us with you."

"That's normal. We can stop them. We always do."

"There's just one problem."

Nick couldn't imagine what. "And that is?"

"We don't know who. We don't know what. We don't know how."

"That's not one. That's three."

"No, punkin'. That's one big, bad-ass entity with serious skills who's going to mop the floor with us."

"But you said that I couldn't die now."

"Yeah, as the Malachai. But if they take the Malachai out of you . . ."

"I can die, after all."

Caleb nodded. "Yeah. In the past, it's only been the Malachai's son who had the ability to weaken him. But if someone or something has found another way to do it . . ."

"I'm finished."

"We all are."

"You think that's why Aeron's gone?"

Caleb shrugged. "I don't know. I wasn't able to find a trace of him earlier. It's like he's vanished from the face of this earth. I don't know what's happened to him."

A bad feeling went through Nick, but he refused to let it take root. Aeron wouldn't be behind this.

He wouldn't. That was the Malachai voice that wanted to hate everyone around him. To trust no one with anything.

But this was coming from somewhere. As usual, he was being targeted for extinction. The problem, though, was he had no idea where to begin looking for this enemy. If it was Grim, he was doing a great job hiding.

If it was something else . . .

He was screwed, because they wouldn't see it coming until who or what made its move. And the one thing they'd all learned over these past few years— whenever that happened, it left a mark.

Nick only prayed that this time, it didn't take his head. Or worse, the head of someone close to him.

# CHAPTER 6

✖

"See, hon, he's fine. Told you I wasn't going to let anything happen to your young one."

Nick glanced up as his mom and Bubba came through the door. As tiny as Bubba was large, Cherise Gautier had blond hair and vivid blue eyes that filled her angelic face. Still dressed in her black Sanctuary T-shirt from work, she rushed past Bubba to the couch where Nick was sitting with Kody.

Faster than he could move, she latched onto him with her ninja mom moves and octopus-like tentacle grip. Dang, for a tiny woman, she was stronger than all get-out. Forget toddler strength, his mother could match Hercules.

"Ma . . . can't . . . breathe! You're choking off my

airway. Counterproductive move. Release the choke hold on your sole progeny before you kill him."

Laughing, she ruffled his hair before she kissed his forehead to check for a fever. Unlike a normal mother who would use her hand or a sanitary thermometer, his mom had never once done that.

Nope, Cherise Gautier always checked with a kiss and a tickle, which made him jump and let out an undignified noise in front of his girl and best friend— something he did *not* appreciate. But all Caleb did was make a face while Kody laughed.

Meanwhile, his mom didn't care that her son had no measurable dignity or ego, hence his most hideous wardrobe. And her need to cup his face like he was still three and pinch playfully at his cheeks until he flashed a dimple at her. "You do feel a little warm, Boo, but not bad. How are you feeling?"

"Better 'til you pinched me. Kody brought my homework." He held his English book up for her to see. "I'm almost done with my assignments."

His mom patted Kody's knee. "Thank you, Miss Kody."

"My pleasure, Ms. Gautier. We can't have our boy

flunking. They might move my seat next to Stone. Then, I'd have to shoot myself."

She laughed as she rose to her feet.

"You want some pizza?" Nick gestured toward the box on the coffee table.

His mom wrinkled her nose. "No, and you need to lay off eating so much of it. You're going to turn into one if you're not careful." She stepped back to take the bag from Bubba's hand. "I brought you some of Jose's chicken noodle soup from Sanctuary. He made a batch just for you. And Mama Lo sent over some gumbo for you and I think Papa Bear snuck in a bear claw, even though I told him not to."

Thanking her, Nick took the Sanctuary bag and opened it, then laughed. "That's not all they snuck in here." He pulled out a Styrofoam cup. "Mama Lo done sent me some bread pudding!" Flashing a grin, he protectively cradled it in his hands so that his mom couldn't confiscate it. "And I'm not sharing this. But there is plenty of other stuff if anyone else is hungry."

With an irritated noise, his mom met Bubba's amused smile. "I don't know what I'm going to do with that boy."

"What you always do . . . tolerate him and love

him. But as you can see, he's fine. So are we still on for dinner?"

She bit her lip and turned back toward Nick with an arched brow.

"I'm fine, Ma. Kody and Caleb can babysit me. You know they're both responsible adults, and I won't be alone. We can have Aunt Mennie or Mark check in on us."

"You're not going to work tonight, Boo?"

"I already called Kyrian and told him that I caught Rosa's ick. He wasn't happy, but he's not going to kill me for it." Thank goodness Rosa had gotten sick and it'd given him a good excuse for not going in.

She glanced at Caleb and Kody. "Your parents are good with you both staying a little later than normal? I don't want either of you to get in trouble. Do I need to call them?"

His poor mom had no idea that Caleb was thousands of years old and that his parents had literally kicked him to the curb three minutes after his birth.

As for Kody . . .

Right now, her father was imprisoned on a Vanishing Isle in the Greek Underworld, and her mother was frozen in an immortal sleep as a statue in the

Atlantean heaven realm. It would still be a few years before her father was released, and a lot longer before Styxx would be able to reclaim her mother.

And since the only reason for Kody's father's initial reprieve would be for him to open a hell-gate by killing Ash and unleashing a whole group of demons into the world in an attempt to raise the goddess of destruction . . .

They were better off not asking his permission about anything. Styxx just wasn't in the best frame of mind at present. He would need a few decades to zen so that he could forgive Acheron and humanity, and realize that the world didn't need to come to a screaming, horrific end.

"We're good, Ms. Gautier," Caleb said in that kind tone that he only used with her, and Nick appreciated it more than Caleb would ever know. It meant a lot to him that his friends took as good care of his mom as he did.

While the two of them might not always get along or agree on things, his mother was all he had. And Nick would skin alive anyone who harmed her or hurt her feelings.

"Okay. If you're sure. Like I said, I don't want either

of you in trouble with your parents. And I definitely don't want your parents worrying about you. There's nothing more terrifying than not knowing where your child is."

"No fears, Ms. Gautier." Kody smiled. "We'll see Nick home and make sure he's taken care of. You two go and have a great dinner. Don't worry about anything."

"Not a puppy, people. I can walk and tie my own shoes and everything."

"I wouldn't take that bet," Caleb mumbled under his breath. "Your shoes have been untied all day."

"That's called a fashion choice."

"It's called a broken leg waiting to happen, but far be it from me to correct your delinquent behavior. I can use the laughter when you trip and fall, and bust your . . ." Caleb glanced at Cherise as he barely caught himself before he spoke profanity, "rump."

Bubba laughed at them.

His mom just shook her head at Caleb before she spoke to Bubba. "Give me an hour and pick me up?"

"We can go now, if you want."

She smiled sweetly. "Michael, I'd like to take a shower and get the smell of fried grease off my hair and change out of my work clothes."

"Why? I think you smell real good, and look even better."

Nick groaned. "Hello! Do you mind? Son is present and choking on my own bile! Gah! Old people. Y'all are so gross!"

His mother glared at him. "Eat your pudding and shush. . . . And I'm *not* old! I'm barely over thirty. You'll be here before you know it!" She turned back to Bubba. "See you in an hour." When she went to kiss him, Bubba pulled away.

She gave him a stricken look.

He jerked his chin toward Nick. "Trying not to antagonize the most important man in your life."

"I'm not looking," Nick groused. "I already threw up in my mouth. And Ma, I don't want no grief from you the next time you come into a room and I'm innocently leaning too close to Kody. 'Cause I *know* we're not doing anything, and I don't want to know what you two do or don't do, and you better not be doing nothing. That's all I'm saying."

She shook her head and sighed. "I have raised a rotten child."

Bubba grinned. "Nah, he's a good one. It's why I've let him live this long. Though drowning is still an option if he ever gets too lippy. I do know how to dump a body in the swamp where no one will ever find it. . . . gators got to eat, and all that."

Laughing, she paused at the door. "You want to come on home with me, Boo?"

"Can I finish my food?"

"I thought you were sick?"

"I am sick. You know the saying—starve a fever. Feed a cold. So I'm feeding it this bread pudding while it's still warm."

She pressed her hand to her forehead. "Thank goodness I work for a restaurant and a kindhearted boss who doesn't mind it when I take food home, otherwise I'd never be able to afford groceries for that boy. I swear his legs are hollow."

"My mama always said the same thing about me. That and that I was a reincarnated tapeworm. But it's all the football drills your boy runs, Cherise. You've gotta feed that metabolism."

"Just don't let me forget to bring home leftovers for him after dinner."

Nick groaned at her. "Again, not a puppy, Ma. I don't need a doggie bag."

"Says the boy who will be starving by the time we

get back tonight." She gave Bubba a quick peck on the cheek. "I'll see you shortly. . . . Nick, behave!"

"You, too."

As soon as she was gone, Bubba scratched uncomfortably at his jaw. "You sure you're okay with this?"

Nick hesitated. Honestly? He was a lot of confused about it. His mother was a sacred entity where he was concerned, and he didn't like sharing her with other people. Ever. He never had. Even as a kid, it'd bothered him to see her holding another baby, even at church.

But he was getting old enough to appreciate the fact that his mother had never dated, and that he'd selfishly taken up her entire life since the moment he'd been born. Like she said, she wasn't old. But he'd hogged every day of her youth.

She deserved to be happy and to find a decent guy who would treat her like the queen she was.

When all was said and done, he couldn't think of anyone better than Bubba, except Kyrian. But Nick knew from Ambrose that Kyrian had another destiny waiting.

Another woman he was meant for.

And Bubba deserved another chance to find a woman who could love him. Since the day he'd lost his wife and son, he hadn't dated, either. He'd been locked up in this business and zombie hunting with Mark. A lost, lonely soul.

Yet whenever Bubba was around his mom, a light came on in his eyes. His cocksure friend lost a lot of his composure. It did Nick's fragile ego good to see that he wasn't the only oversized male his tiny mom cowed and unsettled. Besides, he really did admire Bubba.

"Yeah. I'm just busting your chops, Triple Threat."

Bubba grinned at his old football nickname that only Nick used these days. "All right. I meant what I said, Nick. You're both important to me. And you're definitely the most important thing to Cherise. Last thing I want to do is cause problems between you. Say the word and we go back to how we used to be."

"It's all good. Really. Now, go get dressed. Don't keep her waiting. She can't stand that. Trust me. I've still got the hand prints on my butt to prove it."

He snorted. "Your mother's never laid a hand to you and we both know it."

"Not true," he whimpered playfully. "Her harsh words singe my soul."

"Okay," Bubba said with a laugh, "fine. Mark's

watching the store tonight. If you need anything, he can get right over to you. My dad is out with his friends, but he should be back before much longer. And you know if you need anything, me and your mom are just a quick call away."

"Yes, sir. But unless Caleb gets frisky with the stove, I'm not anticipating any problems."

"Frisky with the stove?" Caleb scowled. "What fresh lunacy is this?"

"You know? Your house? I saw your kitchen. Looked like Mark came through it with his flamethrower."

"Mark *did* come through it with his flamethrower, chasing demons!" Caleb said indignantly. "Dang near burned it down. Remember?"

"Oh yeah. Never mind." Nick grinned at Bubba. "We'll be better off without Mark, I'm thinking."

"Considering the fact the boy almost fried himself to God with his cell phone cord and burned his Jeep completely up with it . . . yeah, I'm thinking you're right. Don't call Mark, on second thought." He jerked his head toward his bedroom. "I'm going to change clothes. I'm taking your mom to Brennan's if you need us."

Nick made the sound of agony at the thought of

them going there without him. He was already salivating. "Bring me back some dessert."

Bubba laughed. "A'ight. Will do."

As soon as he was gone, Nick slid his gaze to Kody. "Menyara's?"

"Yes. I'll get Xev."

Caleb made a sound of total disgust. "Why?"

"This concerns him." Then, Nick froze as he realized something. "Holy crap, Caleb! You're my uncle."

He curled his lip in that surly way only Caleb could manage. "No!"

Kody laughed. "It's worse. He's the half-brother of your *great*-grandfather."

Caleb glared at her. "You're not helping."

"No, but I'm entertaining myself at your adorable expense."

Nick snickered. "Yeah, y'all are missing the important fact. To a Cajun, that makes him my uncle."

"Great. I always wanted to be a monkey's uncle. Nice to know I finally succeeded."

"Now, why you want to go and hurt my feelings?"

"Mostly 'cause I can't break any of your bones or feed off your blood." He got up. "C'mon, sport. Let's go see if Menyara has any insight into this."

"Sure thing, Uncle Cay."

"Ah gah," he groaned. "Don't call me that. It could cause an involuntary reaction."

"Such as?"

"Repeat stabbing."

"When did this escalate to violence?"

Caleb arched a brow. "Remember our earlier encounter with Bubba's father? He called me an Esme Daeve?"

"Yeah. What of it?"

"They're the rage Daeves, Nick." Kody stood up. "Much like a Malachai, they live in a state of perpetual ire, and are always looking for a fight or are trying to start one."

Caleb nodded.

"That explains so much about your personality."

"Yeah. I'm just like you. Irritating from my first breath to my last." Caleb clapped him on the back so hard, Nick stumbled. "Good to be alive."

"I really need a book on this. I miss my grimoire girl."

Kody frowned. "Where's Nashira?"

"Don't know. Both her and Aeron have abandoned me. I haven't seen either one in forever."

Caleb passed an irritated grimace to Kody. "Define *forever*. Three hours or three days?"

That tone pissed him off. "Two days on Shira. And you knew about Aeron."

Caleb cursed. "I didn't know he was the second one to go missing."

"Third if you count Dagon."

Caleb literally froze. He was so still that for a moment, Nick thought someone had cast a spell on him.

But after a few heartbeats, he blinked and turned toward the two of them. "Let me get this straight. Dagon, Aeron, *and* Nashira are all AWOL? At the same time?"

"Yes."

"And you just now thought to mention this?"

"Didn't think it was that important. I assumed they'd be back."

At least Kody appeared as confused by Caleb's overreaction as he did. "What is it, Caleb?"

"Aeron wouldn't have just taken off. Not if he had an assignment. Same for Nashira. She doesn't have family or friends here. It doesn't make sense that they'd head out alone like that. I would have been more vigilant going after Aeron, but I don't dare leave Nick alone while he's like this, because you and I know what happens when he's left to his own defenses. As for Dagon . . . Dagon's a bit more flaky. He might be visiting family on Olympus, but it's still not like him to not check in."

Kody bit her lip as she turned back to Nick. "Are you still having visions?"

"Kind of, but they're weird. Not like the usual ones."

Caleb ground his teeth. "Get Xev," he said to Kody. "Meet us at Menyara's shop."

Inclining her head, she vanished.

Nick was about to ask what Caleb was thinking, but before he could, Caleb took his arm and flashed them to Menyara's lapidary on St. Philip.

For the first time since his powers had come in, the trip nauseated him. Badly.

No sooner had they appeared in the back courtyard than Nick had to make the mad dash to the nearest bush and fertilize it.

Caleb made his own set of noises in response. Unlike Kody and Nick's mom, Cay had a sympathetic gag reflex. Which made no sense whatsoever to Nick given the fact that Caleb was a battle-hardened demon overlord who'd marched his army over the crushed bones of his enemies. Entrails, blood, brain matter, none of that bothered Caleb.

But you let a little bile up, and it was over.

Nick was on his knees, gasping for air and unable to control himself.

Still making a face at Nick, Caleb looked like he was about to join him at any second. "You okay?"

"Yeah. Whatever I got into I want to return. This is crap."

"Just make sure you keep it over there."

Nick rolled his eyes. "You're such a baby."

"Don't make me zap you while you're sick, Gautier. You know I will."

He would threaten to zap him back, but right now, he wasn't sure he could make good on that threat. So he kept his mouth shut and stumbled toward the door.

No need to aggravate the devil when all you could do was upchuck on his shoes.

And speaking of . . . a part of him was still angry at Menyara for binding his Malachai powers when he was born, and lying to him for the whole of his life . . . never mind setting up his innocent mother to incubate another Malachai without her permission. Because of that, his mother's life was, and would forever be, in danger.

It didn't matter that Menyara was an ancient god who claimed she only did it to protect others. No one should play with someone else's life like that. Nor should they make those kinds of decisions for them, without at least *consulting* them.

People weren't pawns. Or a means to an end. They were sentient creatures who deserved to be made aware of their choices and allowed to decide if they wanted to be jerked around or not.

Or used like broodmares.

Yet that being said, Menyara was the closest thing to a family Nick and his mom had ever known. She'd stood by them when no one else had, and had always made sure they had what they needed.

That alone allowed him to continue to speak to her.

After all, family was family. You didn't have to always agree with each other's point of view or actions to still care about the other person as a whole.

Not to mention, Menyara had taken his mother in and helped birth him on her own sofa. So it was hard to stay angry at her all the time. No matter what came, she would always be his Aunt Mennie.

Even when they were fighting.

It took several minutes before a tiny woman came to the back door and opened it.

She scowled at Nick who scowled back at her. "Can I help you?"

"Uh . . . you must be new. I'm Nick. Just here to see my aunt Mennie."

A slow smile curled her lips. "Ah, Nick. I've been waiting for you." Her expression turned dark.

Sinister.

Then the sclera of her eyes turned completely jet. "Malachai."

Before he could move, she attacked.

# CHAPTER 7

N ick threw his hands up to counter and fight as the mortent demon came at him with its messy, sloppy jaws snapping. Was it too much to ask for his telekinesis to be left intact?

Of course it was.

Or for a napkin so that the creature could clean up after itself and stop demon-drooling all over him? It was so gross! Made him *never* want to have a teething child. He'd done his time in the crying room at church.

Nick slugged the demon, causing the mucus to go flying.

Gah, his mom would have a fit if this was in her house. They'd have to fumigate. Defunk and do who knew what to make it livable again. Just once, couldn't they get an attractive succubus after him?

No. Way too much to ask of the universe at large.

Nick hit the demon with a blow that slimed his whole fist and left his entire arm numb.

D-i-s-g-u-s-t-i-n-g.

His stomach churning with revulsion, he felt another visit to the bushes coming on. Which was definitely not something he needed to do in the middle of being attacked by demons. That would probably *not* work out well for him.

Them either, really.

Unless he wanted the demon to keel over laughing at him. But hey, he had the tacky shirt for that. It had happened before. There was something to be said for being a demon laughingstock.

He ducked a punch the demon aimed at his head and twisted away from it.

"Caleb! Stop napping!" Nick head-butted the demon. "I need a little hand over here. One not covered in demon snot."

Sliding in from the left, a colorful blur caught the demon in front of him, and slammed it to the side. Ah, he knew that blur and never had he been more grateful for that mass of mismatched hair, and almost seven feet of immortal fury.

While Xev continued to battle in his stead, Nick turned to find Caleb on the ground, oozing his black blood all over the pavement. Pale and shaking, his friend could barely breathe.

What the heck?

Terrified, he ran to Caleb.

Kody had already peeled his shirt back to expose an ugly, jagged wound where Caleb had been stabbed in his side, to the left of his navel. She was trying to tend it. She held Caleb's balled-up T-shirt to it in an effort to stave off the bleeding.

"What happened?"

Caleb grimaced. "Demon came in behind me while I was distracted. Stabbed me before I killed it."

Nick scowled. "You don't get distracted."

Sucking his breath in sharply, Caleb gestured at his side. "You would be wrong. Apparently."

Xev came running to their sides.

Kody looked up at him. "Did you get the demon?"

With a nod at her, he grimaced at the sight of Caleb's injury. "This is bad."

Yeah. It wasn't healing and Caleb was getting paler by the heartbeat. His breathing became more and more shallow as it rattled in his chest. Even his form was beginning to fade from human to demon, which meant he was losing power and getting too weak to maintain his human disguise.

Nick froze at the underlying dire note in Xev's voice. "What's going on with him?"

"The blade was coated. I can smell the poison. They were assassins sent to kill Caleb."

"They can't kill him. He's immortal."

Xev scoffed. "We're not immortal. We're just hard to kill and immune to normal human decay, and weapons. But this wasn't a man-made weapon. This one was made specifically for Daeves." His eyes teared up as he wiped at the blood on Caleb's cheek. "And I'm not losing you, brother. Not like this!"

Caleb grabbed the front of Xev's shirt in a fierce fist. "Don't you dare!" he snarled. "Don't you *even* think about it. So help me, if you do it and I live, I *will* kill you."

"You're in no position to stop me."

"What's going on here?" Menyara rushed from the back door of her shop. No taller than his mom, she was a tiny slip of a woman who barely came up to the middle of Nick's chest.

Dressed in bright yellow, she had her sisterlocks twisted into a loose bun. "What happened?"

Nick would gesture at the bodies, but since the demons were self-cleaning and had burst apart at death, Caleb was the only thing that gave testament to their earlier presence. "I was attacked by demons."

"In my courtyard?"

Nick nodded. "One came out of your shop to get us."

"That's not possible. Demons can't get through my barriers to enter my store."

"This one did."

Nick had never seen terror in her hazel-green eyes, but he saw it today. And that did nothing to alleviate his own stress level. Rather it jacked that bad boy through the roof. He also knew what that expression on her face meant, and it wasn't "hey, Nick, how ya doing?"

"What aren't you telling us, Mennie?"

Before she could answer, he realized that her fear wasn't over what he was saying.

It was what Kody had been doing behind his back that she'd been watching.

Quicker than he could blink, Kody shot Menyara between the eyes with her bow at the same time Xev tackled Nick to the ground to get him out of the firing range. They fell a few feet from Menyara's body.

Angry, grief-stricken, and a whole lot of confused, Nick shoved at the much larger being. "What the hell, man?"

"It wasn't Menyara. Look." He gestured toward the body that Kody was now toeing while she kept another arrow nocked and ready to fly.

A body that burst apart into ashes a moment later, showing him that it'd been a demon who'd come at them again, and not Menyara, after all. The sudden wind carried the swirling embers until they were burned out and gone.

Stunned over the deception, Nick met his gaze. "My powers are gone." Perspicacity had been the first he'd developed and it'd been the only one to never fail him.

Until now.

He'd been completely deceived. No part of him had been able to tell that wasn't Mennie. Not even a hair on the back of his neck had risen in warning.

Ah, this was *not* good.

*I'm defenseless.* That thought ran through him like a freight train and sent him reeling. And with it came a new, overwhelming fear.

Menyara!

If the demons had made it into her store, what had

happened to her and her staff? It wasn't like she'd have opened the door and said, "Here, demon, come on in. Make yourself at home. Pull up a chair and have tea."

His heart rose to painfully lodge itself in his throat as he jackrabbited for the store. He slung the door open to find a battleground of shattered shelves, destroyed merchandise, and utter destruction. They had rained down a mini Armageddon in here.

"No," he breathed. How could they have gotten to Mennie? It shouldn't have been possible. She was a goddess. Her powers absolute.

Yet there was no denying the mess that surrounded him. There were even scorch marks on the ceiling and walls where they'd fought with god-bolts. The protection seals on the walls continued to glow as if trying to contain whatever evil had happened here.

"Nick?"

Unable to breathe, he turned at the sound of Kody's voice. "What did they do to her?"

"I don't know, sweetie. But we have to help Caleb, right now. He's in bad shape."

"What's Xev wanting to do?"

"Call their father."

"I thought he was being held captive like yours."

She bit her lip. "Not like mine. Even though he's enslaved, their father has the freedom to come and go."

"Then let's do it!"

As Caleb had earlier, she hesitated. "It's not that easy, Nick. You're talking about raising a major power. He won't come willingly and he holds no love for either son. There's no guarantee that he'll do anything to help them. Not without *your* cooperation."

"What do you mean?"

"You're the Malachai. Their father is subservient to you. You can control him, but he won't like it and he will fight you every step of the way. But . . . I might know something to leverage his cooperation."

"How can I command him when I don't have my powers?"

"I didn't say it wasn't risky."

But if they didn't do something, Caleb would be lost. And he wasn't willing to take that loss.

Nick glanced around at the store, and the destruction that had been wrought. Whatever had broken through Menyara's protection sigils and burst in here to take her had incredible abilities. In the past, they'd known their foes. Known what they were up against and how to fight them.

*That's not true.*

*Shut up, mind, I'm trying to give myself a pep talk. Last thing I need is you crapping all over it, and throwing logic and truth at me.*

'Cause honestly? He was terrified about this, and getting more so by the moment. Logic and truth would only serve to scare the bejesus out of him. The less sense and facts he had, the braver he'd be.

His breathing ragged, he met Kody's worried frown. "What do we have to do?"

"We'll have to leverage the farm for it, but . . . I know the one thing their father wants that you can use to bargain with. The one thing he'd never say no to."

"My soul?"

She laughed. "Unfortunately, it's not as simple as that. Your soul we'd have no trouble giving him. What he wants will take a miracle and the best Cajun charm you possess."

Gah, what was she wanting? "My freedom?"

"Maybe. I don't know the price. But whatever it is . . ."

Nick would pay it to save Caleb's life. He owed him that much.

Steeling himself, he inclined his head to her. "Let's do this."

They'd just started for the door when Xev and Caleb came through it. Caleb was leaning hard against Xev's side. Quickly and carefully, Xev let him slide to the floor, then used his powers to slam and seal the door.

That, too, was concerning.

"What's going on?"

"We've got company." Xev moved past Nick to sift through the debris. "Kody, I need you to help me find hematite, malachite, bloodstone, and jet or obsidian. Quickly. As much as you can."

"On it."

Caleb cursed him, but Xev ignored him as he searched until he found a bottle of black salt and sea salt. He handed them to Nick. "Seal the doors and windows."

Nick moved to do it as fast as he could. "Do I need to say anything?"

"No. Cam's protection will return once we seal the thresholds."

"Is that how they got in?"

Xev shook his head. "Someone invited the evil in. Probably one of her employees who didn't know better." Then, under his breath, he muttered, "How many times do you humans have to be told to leave evil alone, and never, *ever* invite it into your circles?"

"Not exactly our fault, you know? It's all pretty and shiny. If it came in looking like Nosferatu, we'd know to run." Nick finished pouring the salt mixture, then returned to Xev's side.

He was laying out the crystals.

Kody frowned. "You're summoning him here?"

"We can't exactly leave. Not to scare you two, but you might want to peek through the blinds."

Nick did, then wished he hadn't as he saw the demon spectacle going on in the street. "Is that viewable to the rest of humanity or are we just cursed?"

"I think we're cursed," she said, stepping away from the glass as a giant demon came up and screamed at it.

Nick jumped away and let the blinds fall back into place. "Okay, the hell-monkeys have returned and are having a party on our block. All they need is a float and krewe, and they're ready for Mardi Gras season. Have I said today how much I don't like them?"

"I think that feeling's mutual." Nekoda cringed as they slammed against the glass, trying to break through.

Nick winced. "That didn't sound like them slinging beads at us. Think if I whip my shirt off, they'll go blind and leave?"

No one commented on his stupidity.

Instead, Kody turned back to Xev. "I didn't think he could be summoned unless it was at an oak tree with full moonlight."

Xev passed her an irritated grimace. "I'm not a demon. Those rules don't apply to me."

That was true. He'd been an ancient god, which made Nick curious. "What exactly were you a god of, anyway?"

Caleb answered for him. "He was a chaos god, Nick. The god of blood disease, fire, plagues, famine, violent death, fear, and destruction."

"Yeah," Xev said drily. "I was in charge of all the fun stuff."

Wide-eyed, Nick passed a concerned look to Kody that he'd been dumb enough to set Xev loose in the world again. That might have been a mistake, in retrospect.

"Don't give me that." Xev passed an irritated smirk at him. "Through chaos, order is born. I was the balance for a goddess whose powers negated mine. And before you judge me, need I remind you of what your role is in this universe, *Malachai*?"

"Valid point. You're right. But while I was born of destruction, I'm trying *not* to end the world in an ugly war I lead. Which is my big bone of contention. I've read the books and seen the movies. The guy in my role is supposed to be the Chosen One. The good guy in a white hat. The kid who gets superpowers and saves the world. Not the one who eats it. Who do I have to see about an upgrade of my role?"

Xev shook his head. "We are all victims of our births, Nick. And if we're lucky enough to survive childhood, then it becomes a race to see if we can overcome those roles we're assigned the moment we draw our first breath by those who judge our parents, and the labels everyone else wants to place on us. The labels we use to define and hem our own destinies with. Saddest curse of humanity is the day someone teaches you how to hate. And gives you a cause for it. You come into the world a pure, unscarred soul. And your first experience is being slapped on the ass by a callous hand, supposedly for your own good, to draw your first breath."

He winced as if some horrible memory went through his mind as he looked down at Caleb. "Sad really that people would rather focus on what makes them different than on what makes them the same . . . compassion, hope." He glanced from Kody to Nick. "Love. For all the differences between us, we're more alike than anyone wants to admit."

And with that, he began a chant.

Caleb tried to interrupt him, but he was too weak. Xev ignored him and continued.

Nick fell silent as he watched the two brothers who'd been divided by a single tragedy that had ruined both their lives.

Forever.

It made him want to seek out his own brother. The thought had occurred to him a lot, especially lately, but since his brother was also a cursed god, he'd avoided it. There was no telling what he might end up with.

Or how his brother might feel about learning of Nick's presence. Nick wasn't even sure if his brother knew Adarian was his father.

Even though his brother was a god, they didn't "know" everything. Case in point, Menyara was currently missing. And she wouldn't have been had she known demons were at her doors.

Like everyone else, gods could be fooled, too. And

if his brother didn't know he was part destructo demon, Nick definitely didn't want to be the one to drop that bombshell on him. Lesson learned, never be the bearer of bad tidings to an angry god. It just didn't pay. They tended to rip the wings off and eat those messengers.

As Xev chanted, a loud crack popped. A bright light flashed.

Two heartbeats later, something even uglier than the hell-monkeys outside rose up to come at Nick and Kody.

Instinctively, Nick threw his hands out to attack it, only to remember he was powerless. Kody stepped around to deflect it before Xev caught it and banished it back to whatever dimension it'd come from.

"What was that?"

"When Menyara wrote the protections for her store, she trapped a number of entities in the fields around it. That was one of the things she pissed off." Kody sighed. "What is going on here?"

"There's another Malachai," Caleb growled.

"Ambrose?" Kody arched a brow at Nick.

"That would make sense, but the last time I saw him, he told me to get the Eye, and reset everything.

He said he was out of juice. That he couldn't time travel anymore. He was on the verge of slipping over and destroying everything. I don't think it's him. It doesn't feel the same. This is a very different kind of power."

Caleb groaned. "I agree. Totally different essence and feel. More powerful."

"*More* powerful?" Kody gaped. "That's not possible. There's never been a more powerful Malachai than Ambrose."

And speaking of . . .

Nick's pocket began to burn him. Hissing, he realized it was coming from the amulet. "Why's the Eye hurting me?" When he started to reach for it, Kody grabbed his hand.

"Your powers keep waning. We don't know what's going on. If you touch that right now . . ."

It could kill him.

"She's right. You need to get that off you without touching it."

"How?"

"Drop your pants!" all three of them growled at once.

"Flipping great!" he yelled back. "Woman finally gets me out of my pants and it's humiliating. Only my luck!"

Unbuttoning his fly, he quickly toed his shoes off and pulled his jeans down before kicking them off. Thank goodness he'd worn boxers this morning.

Worse? His mom was right. It paid to always have on clean underwear.

You just *never* knew.

Lesson forever imprinted on his psyche for all eternity. Especially when Kody glanced down, looked up, and started snickering.

"Kody!" he snapped. "Do you mind?"

"Sorry. It's just adorably cute."

"Cute? Really? That is not something a guy wants to hear the first time his girl sees him without his pants on. Dang, woman. Could you make this any worse on me? You know I have no ego as it is."

"Sorry. So sorry." And still she laughed. Pressing her lips together in an adorable expression, she batted her eyelashes at him. "It's just . . . how Cajun are you that even your underwear is the New Orleans Saints? Seriously? I guess I should be grateful it's not purple and yellow with masks and beads."

Caleb snorted. "You should just be grateful it's clean and that he's actually wearing some that doesn't have holes in it."

Nick glared at him. "Shut up and die already! I thought you were on your last breath an hour ago! Shouldn't you have bled out by now?"

Just as Caleb opened his mouth to retort, another bright flash almost blinded Nick. He expected it to be a new hell-monkey.

It wasn't.

No, this varmint was far worse. Far more sinister.

Tall, dark, and terrifying, it was something that hell itself had spawned and spat out. Forget the Malachai. This made Nick's father look like Mickey Mouse up against Godzilla.

They had bantered about the term *primal power*, but until now Nick hadn't understood what that meant.

Yeah . . . if this was the good guy, he dang sure didn't want to meet the bad ones.

Ever.

His head was bent low like a vicious predator that smelled fresh meat as he met Nick's gaze. He had one eye that was a vibrant green and the other a dark, earthy brown. That stark contrast was as unnerving as it was startling. Shockingly enough, his features were almost identical to Caleb's whenever Caleb was in human form. Same sculpted jaw. Same aquiline nose and arched brows, tawny skin, and jet-black hair. They were even the same height and build.

Only difference was the height and length of hair. Whereas Caleb's hair was short, his father's brushed his shoulders. There was also something even deadlier about his father's demeanor. Colder.

Far more sinister.

Nick wouldn't have thought *that* possible.

And when he turned to face Xev, his eyes blazed a vibrant red. The green amulet around his neck glowed with an ethereal fire a moment before he blasted Xev so hard, it lifted him from his feet and sent him slamming into the wall behind him.

"I warned you!" He snarled at Xev as he closed the distance between them. "This time, I will rip out your worthless heart and feed it to you!"

# CHAPTER 8

Nick tried to reach Xev to help him, but some unseen force held him in place. He couldn't move or speak.

*Kody?*

She could only move her eyes. *I'm frozen, too. Jaden's got me locked.*

Horrified, he couldn't do anything other than watch as the ancient god grabbed Xev by the throat and held him against the wall. Cut and bleeding, Xev appeared to be as helpless against his father as they were.

His breathing ragged, he fearlessly met his father's gaze. "Kill me if you must, but help Malphas. He carried your banner and paid the highest price of all for it. The least you could do is save his life. Cam needs him in this fight. Without him, Jared dies. If you have any feeling for anyone besides your own selfish hide, save them."

Raw fury and hatred twisted Jaden's handsome features as he snarled at his son. "What did you do to him this time?"

Xev laughed bitterly. "Why ask when you won't believe a word I say?"

In that moment, Nick saw the strangest image in his mind. Since he no longer held the amulet, he had no idea where it came from, but he saw Xev with Myone. Tall and lithe, she was absolutely gorgeous.

The epitome of feminine perfection. No wonder Xev had lost his head to her.

Graceful and elegant, Myone had long black hair that fell in soft, thick waves to her waist. It was the kind of hair that a guy wanted to sink his hands and face in.

With the round face of an angel, she had large eyes and a pert nose and full lips. Her skin had a golden cast to it, as if it were made of gold or brushed with it. Even her wings appeared to be made of spun gold. Though barefoot, she was dressed in a thin red gown that left one gold-kissed shoulder bare.

Xev wore ancient bronze chain mail that moved like articulated dragon scales, and gold greaves buckled over burgundy boots that matched his cloak. The center of his bronze breastplate had the head of a hideous, terrifying chimera. With solid jet-black hair that matched his iridescent wings and normal blue eyes, he looked like an entirely different person. Nick barely recognized him.

Xev's is pale eyes twinkled with devilish joy as he snuck with her into the small room of an ancient temple. An oracle chamber of some sort that was lit with wall sconces that threw their flickering shadows up on the wall behind them.

"You're not supposed to be here," she admonished him. "What if someone were to see you?"

Completely unrepentant, Xev gave her a kiss so hot, it made Nick uncomfortable to witness it. He pulled back with a soft moan. "I had to come. I've information about my mother's battle plans you need to know."

Biting her lip, she cupped his face. "Dary . . . you must stop spying for us. They'll kill you if they find out."

He shrugged her concern away. "What are they going to do to me?"

"Cut out your heart and feed it to you."

He cupped her hand in his and pressed it to the

center of her chest. "My heart is here, beyond their reach."

She opened her mouth to protest, but he silenced it with another tender kiss.

After a minute, he pulled back to smile down at her. "They're planning to attack at dawn on the north gate, where you're usually weakest. I'll slow them down as best I can to give you as much time as I can to fortify your positions."

Fear and concern lined her brow as she stared up at him. "Be careful."

"You, too." He lifted a lock of her hair to rub against his lips so that he could savor the softness of it. "One day, Myone, I hope to have more than just a kiss from your lips."

"You know better. We both do. Even this is more than either of us should have allowed. Now go before someone sees you. And don't come here again!"

Xev's eyes showed the depth of his heartbreak. The depth of how much he loved her and how much those words cut him.

"Sorry I bothered you, *ägna*," he said, using the submissive demonspeak term for owner. The agony of her rejection was tangible as he dropped her hair and stepped back. "I will trouble you no more."

The moment his back was turned, silent tears fell from her eyes. She covered her mouth and sobbed where he couldn't see or hear. And when he closed the door without looking back, she flinched as if she'd been struck.

"I love you, Daraxerxes. I do." She whispered the words under her breath. "I'm so sorry."

She turned to walk in the opposite direction.

"Stop him! Don't let him escape!"

She gasped at the sound of a sharp voice that was followed by the clashing of swords and the sound of fierce fighting in the main temple room. Wiping at her eyes, she flew to the door and threw it open to find Jaden there with Xev, surrounded by guards.

On his knees with his hands and wings tied, Xev was cut and bleeding where they'd outnumbered him twenty to one. Two of the guards held swords at his throat.

"What is this?" she demanded.

"We captured a Mavromino spy." Jaden gestured at his guards. "Take him and lock him up."

She paled at Jaden's cold words as they brutally hauled Xev away, making sure to cause him as much harm as they could while they did so.

Trembling, she approached Jaden slowly. "What are you planning to do with him?"

"He'll be interrogated for information about their army and intentions."

"You mean tortured?"

Jaden didn't respond. "We're at war, Myone. Don't underestimate our enemies."

"He's your son."

"Who came here of his own free will to gather information for his mother to use against me. You think that deserves my mercy?"

"And if he didn't? What if he came to give us information, instead?"

Jaden laughed. "Do you know how he was conceived? Through lies and deceit. He was meant to be a tool to be used against us from the very beginning. And that's what he is. Don't *ever* be fooled by him. He was born of a lying beast and suckled on the breast milk of demons. Trust me. I made the mistake of trusting him once, when he was just a boy, and it almost cost me my life. It's a mistake I won't ever repeat. Keep your heart hardened where he's concerned, or else you'll pay dearly for your mercy."

Nick flinched as the memory faded and he watched Jaden pull Xev by his hair toward Caleb.

"Are you the one who did this to him?" Jaden snarled in Xev's ear.

Xev refused to speak. He merely blinked slowly and said nothing.

Pale and shaking, Caleb glared at his father. "Told you to let me die. Next time I tell you not to call someone, brother, maybe you'll listen."

Those bitter words took the fire out of Jaden's eyes. "You side with our enemy?"

"Against you?" Caleb let out a scoffing laugh. "I'd side with Lucifer."

Jaden took those words like a slap. Apparently, they stunned him enough that he loosened whatever hold he had on them.

Kody stumbled forward while Nick hung back, unsure of this new being who didn't appear to be the most stable of creatures.

The one thing his psychotic father had taught him was to lie low out of a striking range until they either calmed down or went away.

And to be prepared for any attack.

"Caleb was poisoned," Kody said.

The moment Jaden saw her, he cocked his head and frowned. "Bet?"

"I'm her daughter."

"You can't heal him?" Jaden asked her.

"I don't have her powers. My father was a Chthonian."

He nodded. "I need lapis lazuli ground with red jasper."

Kody went to gather them and crush the stones for him.

"You're not asking payment for this?" Xev wiped at the blood on his lips.

At first, Nick thought Jaden wouldn't answer. Or that he didn't hear.

But after a few seconds, he spoke. "You are my sons, regardless of how you were conceived." He glanced up at Nick. "Lesson to you, boy . . . beware of any woman who comes near you with a tongue laden with flattery. And twice as wary of anything she hands you to drink." He scowled. "Where are your pants?"

"Uh . . . over there." He pointed toward them.

"Why?"

Xev almost grinned. "Our latest Malachai isn't quite as competent as his predecessors."

Jaden went completely still. "He's the Malachai?"

Nick nodded. "I had much the same reaction, only with a bit more screaming." He paused as he remembered the day Ambrose had told him his destiny. "And a lot more cursing and denial."

Aghast, Jaden glanced from Caleb to Xev. "That idiot killed Adarian?"

Caleb laughed, then choked and groaned in agony of his wounds. "Yeah, he did. Don't underestimate him. He kicked Grim's butt, too."

"And Noir's," Xev added.

"*Him?*"

Nick pouted at the insulting tone. "Wow. My ego is taking one serious butt-whipping today. Anyone else want to pile on, and I don't mean the hell-monkeys outside?"

Kody returned with the stones Jaden had requested already crushed inside a granite mortar. "And before you say anything more against our Malachai . . . you should know, Jared's his grandfather."

Jaden would have dropped the mortar had Kody not caught it from his slackened grip.

Time hung still. It honestly felt as if something had sucked the air from the room as Jaden stared at him with those eerie bicolored eyes.

"How is that possible?"

Xev sighed. "Cam orchestrated it. He's the Malachai of prophecy. Born of light and darkness. The most powerful one ever."

"Standing here with no pants on." Nick grinned and winked at him, then clicked his tongue and pointed with both index fingers at the ancient being.

Jaden wasn't charmed . . .

Or amused.

"Okay . . . I'm going to put my pants back on now." Nick cleared his throat and headed toward them.

"Un . . . believable." Jaden took the mortar from Kody's hands and returned to treating Caleb while Nick carefully picked his pants up, making sure to slide the amulet out of the pocket without touching it.

Well, the good news was that lack of belief had saved Nick's neck more than once. So while Jaden's reaction didn't help his ego, it did serve to spare his life. He'd take it.

Kody came over to brush his hair back from his face. "You okay?"

"Sure, *cher*. I know what I am. His rejection don't bother me none. There's only a handful of people whose opinions matter where I'm concerned. And I don't give him permission or power to hurt me."

Smiling, she pulled him into her arms. "Love you," she whispered.

"*Moi, aussi.*" Nick fisted his hand in her hair and ground his teeth at the realization that she was one of the handful of people who could completely destroy him. While he honestly didn't care what Jaden or his enemies thought, he did care about Kody.

And in the back of his mind was the image of the day he killed her. It haunted him constantly now.

Even with his eyes open. It forever played like a game day slow-mo clip.

From across the room, he met Jaden's gaze as the ancient god watched them curiously. He didn't speak while he worked on Caleb.

And Xev . . . he had turned away to give them privacy.

He always did. Nick didn't need his powers to know why. Xev still mumbled Myone's name in his sleep. Half the time, he woke up whispering it under his breath as he reached for her in the bed only to curse once he realized he was no longer in the past, and that she was gone.

His heart broken for him, Nick stepped away from Kody and took her hand to lead her closer to Jaden and Caleb.

Once Jaden had Caleb's wound packed, he stared down at him. "I can't believe that wound didn't kill you."

"Yeah, especially since you dragged your feet tending it."

Jaden rolled his eyes. "Same Malphas. Ever cantankerous." He moved away from him. "Since you were maintaining your human form, I knew you weren't overly dire." He manifested a cloth and wiped his hands off. "You could thank me, you know?"

"For what? Being a father for once in my extremely long life? Well then, thank you." Yeah, there was no sarcasm in those words at all.

Ignoring it, Jaden scowled at the mess around them, and the sounds of the demons still trying to break in. "What exactly is going on here, anyway? Where's Cam?"

"Missing," Xev and Kody said simultaneously.

"Again?"

Caleb sat up with a grimace. "We don't know what's

going on. Hence why Rainbow Pony over there decided to call you in against my better sense."

Crossing his arms over his chest, Xev glared at his brother. "Go ahead and insult me, but we need information. The one thing I know about the other side . . . they're a chatty bunch, especially my mother."

Jaden nodded. "He's right about that. Discretion's not her valor. But in terms of this . . . I know nothing. *This*, they haven't talked about."

Irritated, Nick growled low in his throat. "Well something isn't right. I've lost my powers. I can't use the Eye. My generals are missing. We got hell-monkeys at the door and mortents disguised as Aunt Mennie, who's now missing, too."

"Aunt Mennie?"

"Cam," Xev said. "His generals are Dagon and Aeron."

Jaden gaped at Nick. "Why would you pick them for your generals? Have you lost your mind?"

"Up until they vanished, it was working."

Jaden pressed his hands to his head as if he was developing a migraine.

Or a brain tumor . . .

Strangely, it was the same look Kyrian got whenever

he had to deal with too much Nick logic. Bubba, too, for that matter. Well, at least he had one superpower that was still working. He could frustrate full-grown adults past rational speech without even trying.

Bully that.

Nick grinned at him. "And lest I forget, there's still the matter of my missing Aamon demon named Zavid."

"That one, I know."

They all turned to Jaden.

"Pardon?" Nick stepped forward. "You've seen him?"

"Noir has him."

Kody placed a comforting hand on Nick's shoulder. "So it's true. He isn't dead."

"Well . . . he is dead. But Noir took custody of his soul. Poor bastard."

Xev cursed. "You just had to add that last bit, didn't you? You couldn't leave well enough alone." He made a sound of supreme disgust.

"What?" Jaden asked innocently. "What did I do?"

Caleb joined his brother in making the noises of IBS. "Isn't it enough I've been poisoned and almost killed? Gah! I don't need the Eye to see this next act of blatant stupidity that Nick's about to hurl at us."

The two brothers gave Nick an identical droll stare of utter contempt and irritation.

"Well, don't give me that look. Obviously, you know me well enough to know what I'm going to say and do. So it's not going to be any surprise to either of you."

Caleb hooked his thumb at Xev. "*He* can't go. His blood is what's holding them down there. If he steps foot into Azmodea, it'll blow those seals wide open and set them free. And if you go, little Malachai, they'll never let you out. You are their power source. Daddy Dearest Hernia, tell him."

Jaden nodded. "He's right. You don't want to know what they did to Adarian. There's a reason he was psychotic. Even I felt bad for him, and pity doesn't come naturally to me."

Xev snorted. "The poster child for *I Need Serious Parenting Classes* isn't lying about that."

"Yeah, Nick. And it's not hard to know why." Caleb jerked his chin toward his father. "You met his parents during our last fun-filled Disney adventure."

Nick scowled. "I did?"

Kody leaned in to explain what they were hedging around. "Tiamet and Chronus."

His jaw went slack at the reminder of two of the

scariest things they'd been up against in a while. And with Tiamet as a mother, it explained a lot about Jaden.

About everything.

He didn't know who to feel worse for—Jaden or his sons.

"Those were your parents?"

"She birthed all the original monsters," Xev muttered as he cut a pointed and meaningful glare toward Jaden.

Jaden arched his brow at the less than subtle innuendo. "Pardon?"

"Oh . . ." Xev blinked innocently and spoke with utter sarcasm. "Did I say that out loud?"

Jaden narrowed an evil glare on him. "Yeah, you did, and need I remind you that she didn't birth the Malachai?"

"Oh, pardon. There's one she didn't birth. How forgetful of me. Must be all the centuries I spent in hell being tortured. Tends to take a toll on one's memory." Xev rolled his eyes.

"What's that supposed to mean? Need I remind you of where *I've* been? Where your brothers are . . . because of *you*?" Jaden snarled.

"I had *nothing* to do with that!"

"Yeah, sure you didn't!"

"I didn't betray my own army!"

While they continued to argue and Caleb blatantly ignored them, Nick's mind spun with what they'd just inadvertently disclosed.

"Hold on! Wait with the family squabbling for a sec." He scratched at his head as he ran through what they'd said.

Yeah . . . *that* was what they'd said.

He met Jaden's freaky gaze. "Your father is Chronus, right? That's what you said. As in the god of time?"

"What of it?"

"Is there any way you can get me into the future to talk to Ambrose?"

Kody turned pale. "Nick, that's a profoundly *bad* idea."

Caleb sat up. "She's right. No one should know too much about their future and you already know way too much about yours. It's why it keeps getting screwed up."

"True, but I need to ask him one more thing. Please?" Nick turned his puppy eyes to Kody. "You said you could help me barter with Jaden to get what I needed, right?"

"I didn't mean *this*."

Xev shook his head. "Listen to them, kid. Don't do it."

"Maybe. But all of you, except Jaden, know how stubborn I am. You really think you can stop me?"

Caleb lay back down with a groan. "You know you can't stop King Stupid from blatant acts of supreme idiocy. Believe me, I've tried everything. He wears you down with it and always wins. I've learned just to go with it and save my strength for battling whatever nightmare is unleashed by his failure to listen to good advice."

Nick cleared his throat. "You know, Caleb, I am standing right here."

"Yeah, and I'm laying right here, *bleeding* from the last time you didn't listen to me."

While he might have a valid point, Nick refused to concede—which was exactly what Caleb was arguing. But he was too old to change his ways now.

Besides, this was the best shot they had.

"Look, Ambrose hasn't failed us. He's been honest from the beginning." At least for the most part and they didn't need to know about the few lies he'd told himself.

"You said yourself that he was slipping," Kody reminded him.

"True, but we could go back before Ambrose goes nuts and kills everyone. Right?"

Jaden hesitated before he answered. "That's one unstable theory."

And still the only thing they had to go on. Nick glanced around at them and at the destruction that told them nothing about whatever power or entity they were up against. "Fine, I'll go alone. Risk only me. The rest of you can stay here until I return."

"No!" they all shouted at once.

Jaden cast his gaze around at them. "Take it you've all had a bad experience?"

"You don't want to know," Caleb said bitterly. "He's the only one I know who could find trouble waiting for him at the bottom of a Rice Krispies box."

Nick would be offended if it wasn't true.

Xev stepped forward. "I'll go with him. I'm the least likely to screw something up."

The look on Kody's face said she wanted to argue, but after a few minutes, she relented. With an irritated glare, she turned toward Nick. "Are you set on this?"

Nick nodded. "I have to see it through."

She glanced at Jaden. "Can they get back here?"

"Returning's not the issue. They just have to make sure not to bring anything back with them."

Nick held his hands up. "Not a problem."

"See that it isn't." With that warning spoken, Jaden let out a long, tired breath. "We'll work on the dramonks outside. I trust you know how to return?" he asked Xev.

Xev nodded. "So long as my curse doesn't prohibit it."

For the first time, Nick saw guilt in Jaden's eyes. "Let me see your arm."

With an emotionless stare, Xev loosened his sleeve and rolled it back to expose the ancient words that bound him to eternal slavery, and limited his powers.

Jaden examined it for several seconds. "Now your side."

Xev hesitated as his gaze went to Kody.

"I won't look." She turned around to give him privacy.

Still, there was shame in his hazel eyes as he dropped his gaze to the floor and lifted his shirt for Jaden to see where the rest of the curse had been brutally seared into his flesh on the day they'd ripped his wings from his back and condemned him to this existence. His muscles were absolutely taut from the rigidness of his stance.

Nick wanted to comfort him, but how could anything do that? He'd lost his wife, his son. His wings.

His freedom. All he'd done was try to help and they'd coldly taken everything from him for the effort.

Yet in that moment, Nick understood why Jaden didn't trust him.

He saw Xev as a young teenager. Probably no more than sixteen or seventeen—his age.

While Jaden had slept, Xev had crept into his room and swapped amulets on him. Not the green one he currently wore, but another that had drained his powers and left him at the mercy of Xev's mother and her demon horde.

The moment he'd discovered his son's treachery, Jaden had declared his hatred and enmity. "I welcomed you into my home! Why would you do this to me?"

Xev had returned his glower without flinching or shirking. "For all the years you didn't welcome me, Father. For every lash and insult I've been given in your name, and for all the years I was forced to serve them as an animal because you refused to acknowledge me as your son. I do this for her, and I go free. You owe me this!"

"I owe you *nothing* save my hatred."

"Then we are even, after all."

Worse? It'd been a trick. Azura had still refused to

release Xev even after he'd handed Jaden over to her. Instead, she'd laughed in his face and slapped him for being stupid and gullible enough to believe her lies.

So as a final act of defiance, he'd freed his father two days later. Rather than return the favor, Jaden had left him behind, locked in his cell as punishment, even while Xev had begged his father for mercy and forgiveness. Even while he'd begged his father for death.

"You can't leave me here . . . you can't conceive what she'll do to me for it!"

"Like I care? Rot here with your mother and her demons. I never want to lay eyes on you again, you treacherous bastard! You are no son of mine!"

And so Xev had been left to face his mother's unreasoning wrath.

Nick flinched as he felt the nightmare Xev had barely survived.

Jaden had no idea what he'd condemned his child to. Any more than Caleb understood the nightmare that had been Xev's existence. It was why Xev still lashed out and trusted no one. Why he had a hard time accepting kindness of any sort. While Lil had saved Caleb, it was nothing compared to what Myone had done for Xev.

Xev swallowed hard as Jaden finally stepped away from him.

"You'll be fine to return."

Lowering his shirt, he cut a suspicious grimace toward Jaden. "Can I trust your word, this time?"

"He's not lying to you, Xev, and you know I won't leave you behind. Not for anything. They come for you, they deal with me."

His gaze softened as he reached out and pulled Nick to his chest so that he could hold him. He clutched his fist in Nick's hair so hard, his hand trembled. It was weird and awkward, but Nick tolerated it by reminding himself that Xev didn't see him as a boy-toy.

He saw him as his child. His great-grandson. His last link to Myone and to the son he'd been forced to give up in order to keep that child safe from being treated the way he had. Rather than watch his child be raised in the same environment he'd known, he'd returned to the shadows to live alone and watch from a distance as the woman he loved more than his life took another husband who believed Xev's child to be his.

So long as she'd lived and their son had been protected and safe, Xev had been leashed and content.

But the moment she was gone and their son enslaved . . .

He'd been an insane, suicidal monster ever since. Not caring who he harmed or what happened to the world or himself.

Until now.

Everything had changed the moment he'd learned what Menyara had done and that Nick's mom was his granddaughter. Since then, Xev had become a worse Velcro Nick-don't-skin-your-knees monster than his mother was most days. He was lucky Xev hadn't bubble-wrapped the bathroom to make sure Nick didn't injure himself whenever he went in to brush his teeth.

Xev had even modulated the water pressure and temperature to barely more than a lukewarm drip, because *you just* never *knew* . . .

Sighing, Nick patted him on the back. "You good? 'Cause, no offense, you're freaking me out, Gramps."

Laughing, Xev kissed him on the head before he let go.

Nick ran his hand through his hair to settle it back into place. "We really need to get you your own pet or teddy bear or something."

"No, we just need to make sure you don't get hurt."

Nick nodded, then turned around to face Jaden. "So what exactly's involved in doing this? We sacrifice a Lego? Bathe under the light of a full moon? Eat nachos? Yank on Acheron's coat and run before he catches us?"

Jaden wore that same pained expression his teachers often had whenever they saw him in their room on the first day of class and realized he was there to stay and not dropping off books for a friend, especially his English teacher.

Like they were nursing an ulcer.

He glanced at Kody. "Is he always like this?"

"Yes."

"Poor you."

Kody screwed her face up. "You know . . . a lot of people say that to me."

"Yeah, it's beginning to give me a complex."

Laughing, she kissed Nick's cheek. "Don't listen to them. I think you're wonderful. Just the way you are."

"I really appreciate that, Kode. And I love and adore you. But the mere fact that you go out with me and continue to do so brings your entire ability to reason and judge into question."

Laughing, she wrapped her arm around his waist

and buried her face against his shoulder blade. Nick sucked his breath in sharply, savoring the warmth of her body pressed against his back. She had no idea what that embrace did to him. What it meant to his sanity.

Then again, she was his anchor. Maybe she did know and that was why whenever he needed her most, she was here to keep him grounded. For all the preternatural abilities and magic he normally wielded, they paled in comparison to the sorcery of her touch. She alone could tame the Malachai inside him and bend it to her will.

He was completely helpless where she was concerned. And he couldn't imagine a world where that would ever change.

Sobering, she peeked up at Jaden. "Don't let him get harmed. Nick better come back whole and healthy or else you're going to meet the Bathymaas side of me."

Jaden's eyes widened. "You're threatening me?"

"I'm promising you." She gave Nick a fierce hug before she rose up on her tiptoes to whisper in his ear. "Please stay out of trouble."

"*Cher*, you know how hard I try. But when the devil be wanting a *fais do-do*, what's a po' boy to do?"

"Stay out of trouble," she repeated. "I mean it."

"I will do my best."

Her eyes sad, she nodded and let go of him. Then she went to Xev to give him a hug. "Be careful, especially since you're hauling the trouble magnet."

Nick clapped his hands together. "All right. What—"

A bright light cut his words off.

One second they were in the remains of Menyara's store and in the next, he was standing outside of St. Louis Cathedral.

At least that was what it looked like it used to be.

His heart pounding in terror, Nick turned around slowly to see that he was definitely in what remained of Jackson Square. But it was currently on fire. The Pontalba Buildings and Cabildo . . . even the Café Du Monde were all ablaze. This was a hellacious inferno. Bodies were strewn like contorted dolls in the street. Cars were twisted, burned-out chassis, interspersed with military equipment that included the remains of tanks and even downed helicopters.

Bile rose in his throat to choke him. He felt the color drain from his face as he realized that Jaden had dropped him straight into ground zero of his worst nightmare.

This wasn't before Ambrose had lost his mind.

This was at the height of him and his army destroying the world.

Xev appeared as stunned as Nick was while they both turned in slow circles to stare agape at the unholy destruction around them. "How is this possible?"

Nick swallowed hard at the devastation. "This is what I've been seeing in my visions. It's what Ambrose has been warning me about."

Suddenly, a loud pterodactylesque scream sounded. They turned in synch to find a huge red-fleshed demon bearing down on them from the sky. Closing the distance between them, Xev grabbed Nick to shield him with his body.

Just as the beast would have reached Nick with its claws, it burst apart with an ear-splintering cry. Blood and entrails rained down everywhere, along with hot fire that luckily Xev used his powers to deflect.

Straightening, Xev loosened his hold. Disgusted by the mess, Nick lifted his head as the smoke around them swirled and dissipated a bit.

Out of the darkness stepped the last person he'd expected to see.

It was his lunatic demon friend, Simi. Only she appeared older than the teenaged shopping, diamond-eating Goth he knew and adored. Dressed in gleaming armor and with her black hair braided, she was the best sight he could imagine in this madness.

Until her eyes turned bloodred and she nocked an arrow for his throat. Then, he realized that things between them weren't quite the same.

"Simi . . . it's not what you think."

"I'm not Simi. I'm her daughter. And you're the worthless bastard who killed her. Now I'm going to kill you!"

# CHAPTER 9

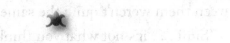

That was not what Nick had expected the girl in front of him to say.

*Ever.*

Too shocked to move, he was an easy target for her.

Thankfully, Xev wasn't the idiot he was. He grabbed him as she let loose another arrow for his head and jerked him out of the way of it, just in time.

When she went to release another, Xev used his powers to disarm her. He sent her bow flying, skittering across the burning pavement. "He's not the Malachai who did this!"

"Yeah, right." She manifested a sword to come after them.

Xev did the same. But he hesitated at using it on the demon. Instead, he protected himself from her attacks, but didn't go on the offensive. "I don't want to hurt you, especially if you're a daughter of Simi's. But I can't allow you to harm him, either. He has to live."

Her breathing ragged, she stepped back to angle her sword and circle them while debating whether or not to reengage Xev. Or maybe she was looking for a better way to attack him.

Wow, she looked just like her mother. Virtually identical. Nick couldn't get over it. Same height. Same build. All she needed was a bottle of barbecue sauce, Goth clothes, Doc Martens, and a coffin purse, and she'd be the spitting image of the demon who'd kept him amused until his sides ached from laughter over her insightful truths and antics. Not to mention her never-ending quest to find an all-you-can-eat buffet that didn't throw her out after half an hour of her powering through a month's worth of their groceries.

How could he have ever harmed Simi? He loved her. She wasn't just one of his best friends. Simi was family.

This didn't make sense. He knew himself. Nick Gautier didn't hurt the ones he loved. Ever. Malachai or no Malachai. It wasn't in him to be like that.

Was it?

Could he really be *that* treacherous and not know it?

As he tried to understand, his head began to career as a thousand images tore through him at once and drove him to his knees. How could life change anyone *this* much and turn them into a monster?

How?

And in that moment, he saw the pained expression on Kyrian's face the night he'd asked him what it'd felt like the first time he'd gone into battle as an ancient warrior and taken someone's life.

More than that, he saw and *felt* Kyrian the day he'd actually done it. It wasn't just a vision. It played through him as if it were his own memory. As if he were there in Kyrian's place. Feeling and seeing everything his boss had.

For some reason, he'd thought Kyrian was older when he'd gone off to war.

But his stalwart boss had only been nineteen or twenty at the Battle of Prymaria. More skinny than muscular.

Practically Nick's age . . .

Back then, Kyrian hadn't been the fierce, competent general Nick knew and respected. Like him, he'd been nothing more than a scared kid, trying to make

sense of a world that really was random and nonsensi-
cal most of the time. One that seemed a whole lot cru-
eler and more merciless than it needed to be. And that
was the hardest part of puberty. Those daily, often brutal, slaps in the face that let him know adulthood was
nothing like he'd thought it would be when he was
little. That it didn't work the way it was supposed to.

You didn't get to eat dessert for dinner, even though
you were now the one in charge of ordering your own
food. Your money didn't go to buy all the video games
you wanted. Instead of answering to a teacher, you answered to a boss who made you ache for the days when
your worst dread was the school bell. You still had to go
to bed at a reasonable time and get up early, and do chores
you hated, rather than hanging out with your friends.
And bullies didn't get the comeuppance they were supposed to, nor did they get left behind on the playground.
Now they were your boss and if you punched them in
the face like they deserved, you didn't go to the office
for suspension or alternative school, you went to jail.

The people willing to stand up for you became far
fewer or were nonexistent. And more days than not,
you were left feeling alone and abandoned. Unwanted
and worthless.

But that being said, life still had a way of taking you by surprise. Just when you were willing to give up on it entirely and throw in the towel—just when you thought people weren't worth the trouble, something or someone would come along and reorient your entire way of thinking.

Some tiny miracle would give you hope in the midst of the darkness and carry you through it, and you would see the beauty of the world anew.

Those were the moments that made life worth living. And they were what everyone clung to in those dark, desolate hours.

Closing his eyes, Nick saw one of those life rafts that stayed with Kyrian to this day . . .

Exhausted from the grueling march to the town and sickened from the sight of the slaughter that had greeted them, and from the fighting earlier that day, Kyrian had removed his armor to help build funeral pyres and move the slaughtered bodies to them.

Against orders, training, and protocol, he'd left his sword and shield on his horse. Honestly, he was too disgusted by war at this point to look at them. The last thing he'd wanted was the weight of what he'd done on his chest, and the reminder of the lives he'd taken earlier to save his own while he laid these innocent civilians to rest.

And as each hour passed and he carried another child or its mother in his arms, it was taking everything he had not to run to his horse and ride home to his father and admit that his father had been right.

He wasn't a soldier. War was horrible and awful, and all the things his father had warned him of. Kyrian wanted nothing to do with a soldier's life, after all. He wanted nothing more to do with the slaughter and brutality. All he craved now was his old bed and the comforts of home.

Only his wounded pride kept him from running. That and the fact that his father would never let him live it down. Never see him as anything more than a petulant, spoiled boy who had failed to stand by his hotheaded decision that he'd made because he'd thought only of the fame it would bring him.

*How could you ever stand and lead a kingdom if you aren't man enough to see your decisions through? Good or bad, once you decide, the consequences will always be yours, alone, to live with. So think through all outcomes, son. And make sure you understand the course it will force you to walk, and that you're willing to make that journey and see it through to the end. Good, and especially bad.*

And so Kyrian forced himself to swallow his gall and bile, and continued to prepare the dead even though he feared he'd never sleep or eat again.

"Boy!"

Kyrian had frozen in place as he reached for the body of a young girl.

Dimitri, their burly second-in-command had stormed toward him. "Where's your armor? Your sword?"

Straightening, Kyrian had tried to think of a reasonable explanation that wouldn't result in a whipping for violating their orders. Unfortunately, there wasn't one.

"Did you not hear me?"

Swallowing hard, he gestured toward their pitched tents. "It's with my horse, sir. On the edge of camp."

Furious, Dimitri grabbed Kyrian's crimson exomis in a tight fist and snatched him forward. "We're at war, boy! You do not abandon your equipment to a place where you cannot reach it should we come under attack, or where thieves or enemies could steal it. Is that your desire? To arm your enemies so that they can cut your throat with your own arms? I'll have you whipped for this! Maybe next time you'll remember."

As Dimitri dragged him toward the tents, a deep resonant commanding voice rang out. "Halt!"

Kyrian almost wet himself as he recognized Julian of Macedon's restrained fury. As their commander and the famed son of a goddess and legendary Spartan hero, he was the warrior no one wanted to cross or anger. Even though Kyrian's father had placed him under Julian's direct protection, Kyrian had done his best to stay out of his sight, and away from his notice as Julian was the one person in this army who could kill him with impunity.

For that matter, his comrades would probably applaud Julian for his murder since they couldn't stand Kyrian anyway.

But he refused to let Julian know he was intimidated as he closed the distance between them.

Forcing himself to lift his chin, he met his commander's gaze without flinching. After all, he was a prince of Thrace. Whatever punishment he had coming, he'd take it with every fiber of regal bearing he possessed.

Julian didn't even glance in his direction as he came

to rest a few feet away. His ire was for Dimitri. "Release him. There's been enough blood spilled today. Let the boy alone."

"Seriously, Commander? Prince or not, he needs to learn his place."

Julian's expression turned to stone. "Are you questioning my orders, soldier?"

That sent Dimitri scurrying away in terror, out of Julian's line of sight, and more importantly, his reach.

His throat tight, Kyrian bravely met Julian's gaze. "Thank you for your mercy, Commander. I won't leave my armor off again, I promise."

Julian had inclined his head to him. "If it makes you feel better, Highness, I threw up in battle my first time, too. I even pissed myself, and I was Spartan born and trained. Don't let the others get to you. You showed a lot of courage on the field today, and stood your ground at times when I've seen far more experienced soldiers fall or worse, turn and flee."

Ashamed, but grateful for Julian's uncharacteristic compassion and unexpected understanding, Kyrian had looked away. "Does it ever get easier?"

Julian had further stunned him by offering him a drink from his own wineskin. "Yes. But the day you can walk into battle and coldly take the life of another without feeling anything for that man and the future you've just robbed him of is the day you should dread most, not one to be anticipated. What we do, while necessary, is an evil, young prince. And it is a course that should never be taken lightly or served with glee. Rather, one always walked with reverence and full knowledge of the cost to every soul it touches. For the one truth of all fights, no matter how small, is that everyone walks away forever mired by it, and with bloody hands."

Those words echoed in Nick's head as he saw the sickening devastation around him.

It was a lesson Kyrian forever harped on with him.

Now, he understood why. But he didn't understand why he was seeing it *right now* when he needed to be attentive elsewhere. Any more than he comprehended what was causing the visions to come to him in the first place.

There was something important about them. That much he knew. His brain wouldn't be coughing them up otherwise. It was some part of his residual Malachai powers trying to warn him of something.

Yet they were more frustrating than Nashira's old

riddles. And they made even less sense. Something he would have never thought possible.

Shaking his head, he focused his sight on Simi's daughter and Xev. She was still staring at Xev as if debating whether or not she should battle him. Which would be a huge mistake. As powerful as she was and even though Xev had a lot of his powers restricted and bound, it didn't alter the fact that he remained one of the best fighters Nick had ever seen.

He'd put Xev up against anyone.

Even a fully charged Malachai.

She lifted her chin and sniffed at the air. "You're of the Source? Why would you protect *him*?" She jerked her chin toward Nick and used a tone that implied he hadn't bathed . . .

Ever. And that he'd recently fought and lost a match with a herd of polecats.

Though actually, that might be better applied to Xev since he was the one she could supposedly smell.

But Xev ignored the obvious insult. "Because he's not the one you're after and we're here to get answers."

Suddenly, another demonic screech sounded.

She glanced up at the dark sky, then disengaged Xev and ran toward the smoldering remains of the cathedral.

*Oh, that can't be good.*

If whatever made that sound sent her into flight on foot . . .

It had to be a winged Godzilla heading for them. Or something even worse. And if it was worse, Nick definitely didn't want to meet it out in the open.

Not without some kind of supercharged weapon.

As more screeching sounded, Xev took his arm and pulled him after her.

His heart lodged painfully in his throat, Nick followed the path Simi's daughter had taken. He saw her just up ahead.

"What happened here?" he called out to her as they ran down the alley and jumped over large broken pieces of pavement.

She cast a menacing glare at him over her shoulder as she dodged someone's charred body, and kept moving. "You should know. Your army did this."

"Not. *My.* Army." Frustrated, Nick groaned out loud as he saw even more flaming wreckage and bodies that turned his stomach and made bile rise in his throat.

New Orleans had been turned into an all-out war zone.

Ambrose hadn't been kidding. This was unlike

anything Nick had ever imagined. No wonder he'd been so freaked out that he'd sought to go back in time to stop it from happening.

His head spinning, he glanced at Xev who was pulling up their rear. "What makes me do this?"

It didn't make sense. At this point in time, his mother would have been dead for centuries. Malachai temper or not, he should have moved past it. "What's my catalyst for going hog wild on the world?"

Something profoundly bad had to have happened to make Ambrose strike out like this. Why would he continue to think it was his mother's death that caused his anger and wrath to break?

It just couldn't be that simple.

Could it?

As they headed down Pere Antoine Alley toward Royal, a huge demon rose up from the smoke with blazing eyes. Letting loose a fierce war cry and burst of blue hellfire, it flew at them, snapping and sizzling in the air that was rife with static electricity. The stench of sulfur and smoke hung thick in Nick's throat, making it hard to breathe.

More demons exploded from the air around the first, ready to attack and eat anything they saw.

As did a group of heavily armed humans who came spilling out of the old Ethel Kidd Realty building. Between the ages of eighteen and thirty-five, and armed with flame-throwers and demon-grenades, they all appeared to be graduates of the Bubba and Mark's School of the Zombie Apocalyptic Survivalists.

It wasn't until Simi's daughter ran to the humans to fight with them and half the demons turned to be caught between the humans and a group of demons behind them that Nick realized this had been a staged trap that she'd led them into.

Strategic explosions rained down searing debris and shrapnel over the demons that forced him and Xev to take cover in the shelter of the church's crumbling alcoves. Bubba would definitely be proud. And Nick was most decidedly impressed with their ingenuity.

Until they began to attack him and Xev. Then he lost his respect for their abilities.

Xev pulled him back to protect him. "Whoa! Allies! We're on your side."

They didn't buy into it.

Not until the largest demon on Team Humanity went for Xev's throat and one of the humans grabbed his arm to stop him from taking Xev's head. She held him back with a determined grip. "Lucy! Stop!"

Hissing, the red-and-gold-fleshed demon glared at the attractive young woman who was probably a year or two older than Nick. His red eyes telegraphed fury and another emotion that appeared to be concern, which made no sense whatsoever.

With long, wavy dark hair, the woman reminded Nick of Caleb for some reason.

"Are you insane?" the demon snapped between his clenched fangs.

Her breathing labored, she gestured at Nick with her sword. And she stared at him as if he were some forgotten memory that she'd buried because it'd been too painful to remember. "That's not Cyprian come for us. He's my father . . . it's . . . it's Ambrose."

# CHAPTER 10

O kay, forget how shocking the Simi-had-a-daughter declaration had been . . . *this* was absolutely *the* last thing Nick had expected a girl to say to him.

Ever in his entire lifetime.

He couldn't have been more stunned had she declared herself pregnant with his child.

Never mind the fact that she was physically older than he was, and he'd only been driving a car for a year on his own. And not particularly well, he might add. Or that he'd never slept with a woman, period, so the concept of being anyone's father was just a little weird and impossible on every level imaginable.

For that matter, his mom barely allowed him to watch R-rated movies. And even when she did, she guilted the snot out of him, and then made him go to confession for it.

Only to have Father Jeffrey laugh at him for confessing something so mild.

Yeah, his future therapists would thank her mightily for that psychological damage.

Still . . . why should he allow logic to interfere with this bizarre reality? 'Cause he was *really* freaking out right now . . . like a hyperactive squirrel that had just awakened in a dog kennel of T-virus-infected hellhounds hyped up on Red Bull and steroids in the heart of Raccoon City.

"I'm the who, what?"

A slow smile curved her lips. "You're my father."

The demons shot fire-bolts at them.

Cursing and dodging, they turned to rejoin the fight.

His "daughter" shot a blast at her assailants, then rushed to Nick's side with a laugh before she practically tackled him with a hug. "I can't believe it's you! That you're finally back. I've missed you so much!" Tears swam in eyes that were identical to his.

Eyes that he realized were identical to his mother's now that she was closer to him.

"You said you'd find a way to return. But dang, Dad, you're only half grown and about half the muscle mass of the scary demon I'm used to. Where's Mom? Did you find her?"

Nick's mouth worked, but no sound would come out as she hugged him again. She'd struck him speechless, which was a hard, hard thing to do. "What's your name?"

Releasing her hold, she took his question like a slap in the face. She even recoiled from him. "You don't know me?" A tear fell down her cheek before she glanced back to the others who continued to fight the demons, oblivious to what he was saying.

He felt terrible for having hurt her feelings. But . . . he was still in shock over this.

Xev ran back to them. "Nick, we've got a *huge* problem."

"Yeah. You could say that . . ."

With a fierce growl, the demon his daughter had called Lucy landed on the ground in front of Nick and blasted him with his powers.

The blow would have sent Nick careening, had his daughter not blocked it.

Furious over her actions, the demon tucked his

wings down before he assumed a human body. Tall and well-built, he was as fair as Simi's daughter had been dark. With bright green eyes and wavy blond hair, there was something strangely familiar about him. Yet Nick couldn't quite place him.

He stalked toward them with a tic in his jaw that said he wanted to mop the alley with Nick's blood and use his eyes for a game of marbles.

"That's not your father, Charity. You know that. It's another trick of the Malachai to weaken and divide us. Our fathers died together in battle. We were there and saw the Malachai drive his sword through him. I don't know who or what this prick is, but he's not Ambrose."

Biting her lip, she shook her head. "Somehow it's him. I can feel it, Lus. His blood speaks to me."

The tic picked up rhythm as he eyed Xev with venom. "Declare yourself."

"A god suckled by Inari."

"That explains the stench."

"And yours?" Xev asked in a tone that was either really brave, or incredibly stupid.

The demon snorted. "Charonte."

"You're not just Charonte. There's something a lot more powerful in you. And it's not Kalosum blood."

"Yours either. . . . Which is why you don't need to know anything about us." He glanced at Nick's *daughter*. "Cherry, we've got to go while we have an opening. Otherwise, we'll be trapped in the city without reinforcements."

"Take Amara and the others and go. I'll be right behind you."

"*Cher*—"

She cut his words off by gently brushing her fingers against his lips. "Lucien, please. I have to pick up Annabelle, anyway. I'm not about to leave her behind. She'll need help to carry supplies."

Nick saw the love and pain in Lucien's gaze as he debated what to do. "You don't delay. Understood?"

"Understood."

A long-legged beauty armed with a silver-tipped whip came forward to clap Lucien on his shoulder. There was something about her that reminded Nick of a blond version of Tabitha Devereaux—the lunatic vampire slayer who "helped" them out from time to time at home. Only thing missing was Tabby's zoo crew and her androgynous Ziggy Stardust boyfriend.

"I'll stay with her, Lucy. You know I won't let anything happen to your girl."

"Thanks, Marissa."

Two men stepped forward. "Me and Drystan'll stay behind and pull point for them."

Lucien handed his grenade holster to the dark-haired man who'd volunteered. "*Pax*, Val, and thanks."

Securing the holster to his hips, Val inclined his head. "*Pax tecum*."

Lucien gave a light, lingering kiss to Charity. "Don't break my heart. I've lost too much in this fight already to lose you, too." Then he and the others took flight.

Nick passed a baffled stare to Xev. "I'm so lost."

"Yeah . . . And for what it's worth, Marissa is Kyrian's daughter."

Eyes wide, Nick's jaw went slack. "Whaaat?!"

She arched a teasing brow at him. "Don't you remember bouncing me on your knee, Uncle Nick? Teaching me how to burp my alphabet with chocolate milk while my mom and Rosa had fits? How to eat beignets without inhaling powdered sugar up my nose? Or the jitterbug and two-step, and sing 'Iko Iko,' and play the spoons and accordion? Any of that ring a bell?"

Charity gaped. "Wait, wait, wait. . . . Are you kidding me? After the way he used to get on to me for belching at the table? Telling me it wasn't ladylike? And he taught *you* how to do it? That's so wrong!"

Another shadow materialized beside Nick and sniffed at him. Cocking his head, he manifested from werewolf to a blond human. "He doesn't know any of us. He didn't even recognize your brothers, Rissa."

Drystan grimaced. "That's just hurtful. And here I thought I was hard to forget. Not like you meet an addanc every day."

"*Ca c'est fou, mon nonc!*"

Nick gaped as Val said, "That's crazy, my uncle" in Cajun. It was obvious that before Ambrose had lost his mind, he'd been a major part of their lives.

They weren't lying.

This *was* his daughter.

And these were the grown children of his friends.

"Xev?" Nick turned to him as he struggled with it all. "What's happening?"

"Jaden sent us too far into the future. And yet," he paused to let out a bitter laugh, "I think we were *meant* to be here. To meet them."

"I don't understand. . . ."

Xev rubbed at his arm where his curse was hidden by his sleeve. "Yeah, I know. I'm having a hard time with this one myself."

Nick pressed his hand to his forehead as he tried to comprehend why they were here. "I'm not the one who destroys the world?"

Charity scowled at him. "No. . . . How can you not remember *any* of us?"

"He's still in high school," Xev said quietly. "None of you have been born yet."

Marissa passed a concerned look to Val. "That means our parents haven't met."

He went pale. "Then why's he even here?"

The werewolf let out a foul curse. "Don't you see? It's a trap! The Mavromino's behind this. By sending him here, it could jeopardize all our lives. Stop our parents from ever meeting . . . *us* from being born! He's here to screw it all up. It would change everything. Alter history as we know it!"

Nick held his hands up. "No. That's not why I'm here. I mean, yes, it is, but not to change *your* history. To protect your lives and mine. I came here to stop *this*"—he gestured at the debris—"from happening. I was told *I* did this. That *I* ended the world."

"Who told you that?" Marissa scowled.

"Ambrose."

Charity arched her brow. "But *you're* Ambrose."

"I know that."

And then they stared at each other in mutual confusion. Until another thing hit Nick. "Wait a second . . . All of you know me. Yet you don't seem to know my Šarru-Dara. Is it me, or is that weird?"

Arching a brow, Val scowled. "What are you sniffing?" He jerked his chin at Xev. "That's not the Šarru-Dara."

Nick exchanged a scoffing laugh with Xev.

"Yes, I am," Xev said firmly. "I've been the Šarru-Dara since the very beginning. There's never been another."

Marissa shook her head. "You're wrong. The demon Livia's the Šarru-Dara."

Nick sobered instantly at what that would have to mean. "Uh, no, she isn't. I kicked her rotten butt out of our clubhouse the minute I took over."

Xev held his hand up to stop them from commenting. "Wait. Who are the ušumgallu right now in this time period?"

Charity counted them off on her fingers. "Bane, Livia, Grim, Laguerre, Yrre, and Kessar."

He cut a gimlet stare to Nick. "Don't you get it, kid? For her to have my position, I'd have to be dead or seriously incapacitated and if they'd succeeded in eliminating me, then they would've opened the Kiazazu—the gates to Azmodea. Noir and Azura are out. This *is* the end."

"Yeah," Nick said, stretching the word out, "but we stopped them. I chose a different set of generals. You were there. You know I did."

"Yes. But something else must have happened at a much later time." Xev gestured at Charity. "You said that Ambrose isn't your Malachai?"

"Correct. Cyp—" Her words were cut off by a blast that struck her in the chest and knocked her backward, away from Nick.

"No!" Nick shouted as she hit the ground, hard, and rolled to her side.

The others scrambled to return fire as more demons flew in to engage them for a fight.

Ignoring them, Nick ran to his daughter. He gently turned her over to find that she was covered in blood from the wound that had opened up most of her side.

Her breathing ragged, she stared up at him with tears glistening in her pale eyes as her lips trembled from the pain of the gaping injury the demon had left her with. "It's the Cyprian Malachai," she whispered.

Nick tightened his arms around her. "Stay with me, Charity. I'll get you some help."

No sooner had he spoken those words than he felt that horrible, familiar tugging sensation. He was under attack from another entity. An unseen force.

Nick stood to confront it.

But the moment he did, he was sucker-punched. Air violently left his lungs and everything went dark.

# CHAPTER 11

Nick jolted as he slammed into the floor of Menyara's shop, facedown. What the heck? How had he come back home? They hadn't been ready yet. He had questions he still needed answered.

"No!" He pushed himself up and looked around for the others, hoping that maybe they might have come with him.

Kody rushed to his side. "Nick, what is it?"

Xev fell to the floor, a few feet away.

"Why did you bring us back?" he asked him.

Shaking his head as he pushed himself into a seated position, Xev appeared as bewildered as Nick felt. "I didn't do this. I was in the middle of fighting and trying to help them."

Frustrated and furious, Nick raked his hand through his hair as he tried to use powers he didn't have to get back there. "What about Charity? Will she be okay?"

"I don't know." Xev rose and headed straight for Jaden. "What the hell is going on?" he snarled at him. "Did you do this to get back at us?"

"What?"

"Don't you dare, '*What, me?*' like you don't know."

If Jaden was feigning ignorance, the man or demon or whatever he was should win an Oscar for the performance. 'Cause he looked completely innocent and oblivious. "What did you see there? Did you find Ambrose?"

"No." Xev gestured at Nick. "There's another Malachai who reigns after Ambrose. He's not the last one!"

Utter silence rang out in the room.

Caleb sat up slowly. "I beg your pardon? Are you on meth?"

Xev turned slowly toward his brother. "You heard correctly. It's confirmed. I saw it myself. Nick saw it. Ambrose falls to another Malachai. And that Malachai is the one who opens the gate to Azmodea. Not Ambrose." He faced Kody. "But it doesn't mesh with *your* memories. At all."

Nick's head pounded. Though whether it was from trying to sort this out or from the time travel or being slammed around on hard concrete repeatedly, he didn't know. "Could Kody be from an alternate future? Would that explain why she doesn't know about this other Malachai?"

Jaden narrowed his gaze on them. "There's one way to find out for sure."

Xev threw his hand up to his father to put an invisible wall between Jaden and Kody. "Don't you even! You take one step toward her and I'll rip out your heart."

Jaden gave him a look that dared him to try it. One that said he'd feed Xev his own heart if he attempted it. "Don't you want an answer?" he asked bitterly.

"Not at *that* cost."

Kody bit her lip. "What's the cost?"

Xev glanced at her over his shoulder. "A blood donation that would tie you to my father. Forever."

"That doesn't seem so bad."

"Noir and Azura would be able to use it to track Nick *and* you through him."

"Oh."

"Exactly. We can't afford to let them near either of

you. Not until we know who the mother of his son is. It could be you or another—we were pulled back before we could ask that, or how this new Malachai comes into being." Xev moved toward Nick. "What did Charity say to you?"

"Only the name of the Malachai. Cyprian."

"Her brother?"

Nick shrugged. "I assume. I mean, he would have to be, right? He has to be a son of my bloodline, too."

Kody gaped at Nick and the disclosure they'd just blindsided her with. "Wait . . . what? Back this up. Charity was *your daughter*?"

Nick held his hands out in hopeless despair, not quite sure how to explain it to her without really making her mad. Not that he blamed her since he had no way of knowing when he'd fathered his children or with whom. "Believe me, no one's more shocked about this than me, especially given how a Malachai is *supposed* to be conceived. I can't imagine *any* circumstance where I'd hurt someone, especially a woman."

"Unless he wasn't."

They all scowled at Jaden.

"Come again?" Xev approached his father slowly.

Jaden pressed his fist to his lips. "C'mon, you two

remember how Grim and Laguerre were cursed to become the šarru-namuš and the šarratum-ippīru."

"*They* might, but it was a few hundred thousand years before either Nick or I was born. So would you please explain for us?" Kody asked.

Jaden let out a bitter laugh. "It's ironic really. I think it's why you can't kill Nick, little Kody. Even though you were ordered to. Even though you know it will ultimately cost you everything you'll ever have or love. You just can't. Because, over and over, no matter how hard the gods keep trying to come between you, the two of you find each other in spite of all obstacles."

Kody's scowl matched Nick's. "Pardon?"

Caleb sighed heavily. "He's right. Remember how I reacted the first time I saw your bow and realized you were the daughter of Bathymaas?"

"Yeah?"

"Kody?" Nick breathed as his head began to swim. He stumbled back away from her, and fell.

"Nick? What's going on?"

Something about Caleb's words had triggered a seizure in his brain. Worse? It'd snapped the Malachai fury and returned his powers with a vengeance.

They were taking him over in a way they hadn't

done since the early days of when they'd first become unlocked. And he was powerless against them.

No longer in control. He felt his breathing turn frenetic as that familiar heat burned through him and his black wings snapped out of his spine. His vision darkened and his heartbeat pounded in his ears like a war drum. Fast. Furious. Thumping. Rolling, he came to his feet, head down to glare at his friends in the manner of a rabid dog trying to decide whose throat he was going to rip out first.

Fangs filled his mouth and the blood craving whet his appetite . . .

Kody swallowed hard as she saw Nick's eyes change over. No longer blue, they were all demon black now. His skin changed to that deep bloodred that was marked by ancient black symbols so that it formed an elegant, swirling pattern all over his body. Strangely beautiful and at the same time, terrifying. Black lines cut across both of his eyes and down his cheeks into sharp points. And the same bloodred laced through his black hair, just as it did his eyes, until they glowed in the dim light.

The Malachai was a creature of exquisite death.

And when those blood-streaked eyes met hers, she

trembled, but not in fear. Somehow she knew he wouldn't hurt her. Even though the Nick she knew had receded behind the monster in front of her, there was something about him that said she was safe.

"Ambrose?"

His black wings fluttered, stirring the air around them and sending dust and debris rattling.

Jaden took a step toward her.

Hissing, Nick grabbed her into a tight, protective embrace. He literally wrapped his entire body around her and lifted her from the floor. He held her cradled against his chest with an ease that was truly, truly terrifying. With his wings flapping in a slow, rhythmic arcing motion, they hovered in a far corner of the shop.

Nick closed his eyes and pressed his cheek against the top of her head. He held her as if she were unspeakably precious. As if he'd lost her and had finally found her again. She had the impression that he wasn't going to allow anyone to come near her or remove her from his arms.

And while he held her like that, she saw why . . . .

They were no longer in New Orleans. Rather she was in an ancient Hurrian city, on top of a hill that overlooked the capital where people were in the pro-cess of rebuilding structures that had been damaged by a savage war. Even the temple where she stood hadn't been spared. The walls around her still bore the charred scarring of god-bolts and one of the pillars had yet to be replaced that had collapsed under a fierce assault.

Oblivious to it, she stood on the balcony with a Charonte demon who reminded her a great deal of a taller Simi, except her skin was a swirling prism of red and white. Dressed in black armor, she wore her ebony hair braided with red feathers and gold beads. She even had gold tips on the edge of her pointed, pixie ears.

"I've a bad feeling, Rubati. You should do as Monakribos wants and run with him."

"I'm not afraid, Xi. His mother will protect us. Braith won't allow her child to be harmed. It was the promise the other gods made to her and his father when Kissare gave up his life so that Monakribos could be born. They swore that they would never ask for her to sacrifice more of her blood to them." She cupped her stomach that was just beginning to show the signs of her pregnancy. "We're safe from their wrath."

Suddenly, the sky grew dark overhead. Thunder clapped so hard, it shook the building around them.

Rubati stumbled, then extended her white wings to catch her balance so that she wouldn't harm her unborn baby. "Are we at war again?"

"I'm not sure, but I'm being summoned. You should hide!" Xiamara leapt from the balcony to fly down toward the city.

Just as Rubati started to leave, she saw Monakribos come into the room, through the doors.

Relief flooded her. "My love!" She rushed to him only to have him backhand her so hard that the blow lifted her from her feet and sent her skittering across the floor.

Stunned senseless, she barely remained conscious as he seized her.

He lifted her up in a cruel fist. "Damn you for what you've done!"

She grabbed his hand in both of hers and tried to loosen his grip. "Kri? What's wrong with you?"

But her words didn't seem to register as he set upon her with a warrior's vengeance.

By the time the drug he'd been given cleared his blood and he came to his senses, it was too late.

Rubati barely clung to life.

Monakribos pulled back in horror as he took in the

whole scene and saw what he'd done to the female he'd loved above all others. He saw his bloodstained hands and her battered body. "Ru?"

Her breath rattled in her chest as she stared up at him, too weak and broken to move. Tears fell from the corners of her eyes, leaving streaks in the blood on her face. She swallowed hard before she spoke in the faintest of pain-filled whispers. "I was going to tell you about the baby I carry. But it's too late now. You've killed us both."

With those words spoken, she expelled one final breath. And the light that had always shone so bright in her eyes, faded and left them glassy and hollow.

Empty. Devoid of the only love he'd ever really known.

Throwing his head back, Monakribos bellowed in rage and grief. Unimaginable pain shredded every fiber of his soul.

He pulled her against his chest and held her there as tightly as he could. In that instant, his heart and soul shattered.

Damn them! They'd told him the price of the cessation of war. That all of his army would have to be put down.

For peace, he'd done it. Without question. Without fail. He'd callously killed friend and foe alike.

But he'd refused to harm his wife and he'd told them as much. Her life had been the one he'd warned them to leave alone. Like his mother, he was a creature of great fury and bitter destruction. They all knew this to be true.

And they should have heeded his warnings.

His plan had been to take his wife and run from this place. To hide somewhere they couldn't find them.

Rather than let him go, they'd tricked him.

Now . . .

"You will pay for this!" he snarled up at the ceiling above. "So help me, if it's the last thing I do! Every last one of you will taste my vengeance as I ram it down it your throat!"

He ran his fingers over Rubati's lips until they were coated, then used her blood to paint binding sigils on his body—they were identical to those that marked Nick's Ambrose form. "By the blood of my wife and unborn child, I swear that my sons shall all remember this and that they will carry forth my powers, my strength, my hatred, and my wrath. Each one will know you for what you've done here this day. We will never forget and with each generation we shall grow stronger until we have enough power to put you all down and reign over you! We will not rest, will not falter until the day comes that we are avenged for this wrong you've done us. Let our wrath rain down on you! So mote it be!"

And as he continued to chant and call for vengeance against the gods who'd wronged them while he held her, he felt something striking against his stomach.

With a fierce grimace, he pulled back to see that her blood had begun to spin and twist with his. More than that, the winds picked up his cries.

Suddenly, a piercing light erupted from her body, tearing through her chest where her heart had once fed life to her.

Monakribos shrank away and held his hand up to shield his eyes. The light danced and spun, coming together until it formed a beautiful young woman. One who bore a striking resemblance to his wife.

Only where Rubati had been fair and pale, this creature was her darker counterpart.

A perfect shadow creature of his beautiful wife.

With the grace and dignity of a fully grown goddess, she rose to stand before him. Yet for all the appearance of a woman, she glanced about in utter confusion and bewilderment. She was a lost child who knew nothing of the world she'd just been born into.

Monakribos rose slowly to his feet. "Rubati?"

She frowned at him as if she understood nothing he said.

When he reached for her, she shrank away.

"Step away from her . . . she's not your wife."

With a heated curse, he turned toward Cam, intending to kill her. But she wasn't alone.

She stood in his mother's temple with the rest of her pantheon.

With her gold and pearl skin gleaming, Cam approached him slowly. "She has no heart, Monakribos. She's merely a shell conjured by your grief. A physical manifestation of all the emptiness you feel inside."

"Then let her be called Bathymaas. For she shall be my promise of a plague of unending misery on this earth. As you've all damned me, I curse you in return. None of you will know peace or love or happiness. Ever. Not until the day you do right by me and make amends for what you've wrongfully stolen. Damn you all! Damn you!"

With those words spoken, he manifested his

Malachai sword and descended on the gods with his full fury. One way or another, he wasn't leaving the room until he'd slaughtered them all!

Not until the floors ran red with *their* blood.

They had thought the war was over. But it was only just beginning . . .

# CHAPTER 12

Kody gasped as she felt Nick's memory fading away from her until she was again aware of being inside Menyara's store, and in his arms.

With a ragged breath, she finally understood why she felt so connected to him. "My mother is Bathymaas reborn," she whispered.

Caleb nodded. "She's the empty shell. When she met your father, he gave her the heart she was missing and completed her. Which allowed you to be born as her completed whole . . . the part of her that was Rubati. It's what makes you the anchor for the Malachai. Even when he's like that, he feels you for who and what you really are."

Kody laid her hand on Nick's cheek. "Can you understand me?"

Nick blinked slowly before he nodded. Still in his Malachai form, he slowly lowered them to the floor and set her on her feet.

"Better?"

"I have my powers . . . for the moment. So I think the answer is yes." He narrowed his gaze on Jaden. "But you didn't explain what Grim and Laguerre have to do with this."

"It was their daughter who drugged Monakribos," Jaden said quietly. "Needless to say, he went a little crazy."

"And you have a hole in your memory, Nick." Xev slid a glance to his father. "No Malachai before you has ever known what happened to Monakribos."

He scowled. "Yeah, you're right. I know the fate of all of them. But his is missing."

Xev nodded. "Because my father and his friends ripped Monakribos apart."

Jaden sputtered. "*I* had nothing to do with that. If you recall, I was against it since I didn't know what Monakribos's death would do to Jared. I was the one who risked everything to bring him back!"

"So you were."

Nick felt his powers waning again as dread washed

over him. This had disaster written all over it and catastrophe as a master seal. "Bring him back how?"

Jaden sighed heavily. "A new Malachai—Jeros—sprang out of Monakribos's blood, in much the same way that Bathymaas had done with Rubati's. I foolishly thought he'd be the same exact way that she'd been. Innocent and ignorant. Harmless."

"Boy, were they all surprised," Caleb said sarcastically.

Xev let out a bitter laugh. "True to Kri's curse, he came back all kinds of pissed off and wanting vengeance. His first course was to hunt down Grim and Laguerre's daughter and exact an ugly revenge on her."

Nick could see where this was headed. "So they killed him again."

"I'm sure they wanted to," Xev said. "But no. They weren't allowed. So they cursed him to die by the hand of his own son. Which is the part you know, as it falls to you now."

Caleb saluted him. "And so when *Jeros's* son, Evander, was born and killed Jeros, then realized that one day his son would do the same, Evander decided the best way to exact revenge for that juicy little curse was to capture the two creatures who'd put it on his bloodline and to make them subservient to him and his progeny for all eternity. Better still, he decided to use their powers to feed his own and make them his generals, to serve him and his army."

"Well, that explains Grim's nasty attitude toward me." No longer a god of death, he was now completely dependent on the will of the Malachai for his duties. Yeah, Nick would have a bit of a wedgie over it, too. "He told me when we first met that he was an angel of death."

Caleb snorted. "In a manner of speaking, he is. Even as a god, he wasn't a major deity, but rather an escort of sorts. Over the centuries, after the degradation of what Evander had done to him died down, he realized he had a better gig under the Malachai's banner. Still, the role reduction was always a bit of a rub."

Nick was finally in control enough to return to his human body. "And I pissed him off even more when I slighted him."

"Yeah, you did," Caleb said belligerently. "But pissing people off is what you do best, Gautier."

"Thanks."

"S'okay. It's what I do best, too. Why we get along."

Nick snorted, knowing Caleb was right. And still

his head was reeling from information overload as he tried to sort through it all. "Is there any way to go back and help Charity and the others? I don't like leaving her wounded."

Sympathy darkened Jaden's freaky eyes. "That's not your battle, kid. Sorry."

"But, if you change what happens . . . if we find out what went wrong, that won't be her world anyway."

Nick considered Xev's words. "All this time we've been trying to stop Ambrose."

Xev nodded. "And it wasn't Ambrose. You were right the whole time. *You're* not the problem."

"Doesn't really make me feel better to know it's my kid."

Jaden stiffened at those words. Too late, he realized that his own sons had seen his involuntary reaction.

They exchanged a silent, bitter glare of mutual sibling resentment for their father. While Nick was glad to see them getting along for once, he hated that it was hatred for their father that bonded them and gave them common ground.

Kody cleared her throat in an effort to distract them. "Did you learn anything else from the future?"

"Learn's a bit of a stretch, but we did meet Kyrian's daughter. And Simi's two kids."

Instant tears welled in Kody's eyes. "Oh my God! Lucy and Amara were there!" she breathed. "They were alive?"

Well, that was as shocking as their initial discovery. "You knew about them?"

Crying even harder, she nodded. "I never mentioned them to you because I assumed they were long dead. So there was no need." She let out a sharp, hysterical laugh. "I can't believe they survived the attack! I'm so happy they made it out."

"And did you know Lucien hooks up with my daughter?"

The shock of that stopped her tears instantly. They ended in one sharp, stunned hiccup. "Seriously?"

He nodded.

Sniffing and laughing, she wiped at her eyes. "Well, since I had no idea that *you* had a daughter, no, I didn't know about that."

"Do you know who their father is?" Caleb asked.

She nodded.

"Care to share?"

Biting her lip, she dabbed daintily at her eyes with her sleeve, then cleared her throat. "Given who they are and the way they get together, I think sharing that with present company would be a profoundly bad idea . . . that knowledge could alter the future. 'Cause I'm pretty sure, knowing you as I do, that one of you would do something to stop it."

"Kody—"

"Trust me, Nick. I know what you in particular would do."

He would argue, but she did know him better than anyone else. "All right. I surrender to your superior common sense."

But that didn't alleviate the ache in his chest. He turned toward Xev. "I feel like we need to do something. We left them under fire. Charity was hurt. Can't we send some kind of help?"

His eyes sad, Jaden shook his head. "Sorry. Doesn't work that way. Their future is their own."

"It doesn't seem right."

Jaden glanced at each of his sons. "Life isn't about fair. It's about survival training. What doesn't kill you makes you stronger."

Caleb let out a sigh of disgust. "There are some people who should *never* procreate."

"Amen, brother. Sing it to the choir." Xev did some kind of odd hand gesture with him that must be the demon equivalent of a fist bump.

"So, Captains?" Nick asked in his best *Star Trek* Bones McCoy impression. "How do we fix the space-time continuum?"

"Ambrose said that the Eye of Ananke was the key." Kody gestured to where Nick had left it on the floor. "We should start there."

"Wow!" Jaden cut Nick's path off. "What exactly did the Malachai tell you?"

"That he'd screwed everything up by trying to stop it. He told me to use the Eye as my guide and do everything the way it was supposed to happen to make sure that nothing else got screwed up."

Caleb curled his lip. "Oh I know that expression."

"Yeah." Xev breathed. "It makes me sick to my stomach."

Nick arched his brows. "What? Clue us in."

"He knows something vital, Nick, that he's not sharing." Caleb cut a look of absolute contempt at Xev.

"Remember that battle we went into where he conveniently forgot to tell us that our powers weren't going to work?"

"And that our enemies would be twice as strong? Yes, I remember. I still limp from it."

"That's the look, Nick. Memorize it for future warnings."

Jaden gave both of his children a droll, irritated stare. "I'm thinking how best to explain it, since you two jackals neglected to tell the child what the Eye was."

"It's a Fate stone."

He rolled his eyes at Caleb. "It's more than a Fate stone." He took a deep, annoyed breath, then went to the Eye and picked it up. "Nick? Do you know who Ananke is?"

"Primordial goddess of fate. Roughly the same as Tiamet."

That answer appeared to give Jaden an ulcer judging by the grimace he made. It was nice to know his stupidity didn't just annoy and offend his mom and teachers.

Jaden set the Eye down on a broken shelf. "Ananke is compulsion. She's the goddess of inevitability." He placed three more stones beside the Eye. "Think of her as a fixed point."

"He knows what pith points are," Xev said from between clenched teeth. He's not an . . ." He glanced at Nick. "Well, he can be an idiot, but he's a highly intelligent, high-functioning moron."

"Thanks. Please, don't attempt to bolster my ego. I can't afford the therapy."

Jaden cleared his throat to get their attention. "Again, not just a pith point. She is the formless, unseen force that pulls you to your inevitability."

"So she's like gravity for fate."

"Exactly. She holds the time sequence together. She's the order to the chaos."

"But . . ." Nick paused as he considered what Jaden was saying. "Gravity has an escape velocity."

"And so does Ananke."

Nick's jaw went slack. "Are you saying what I'm hearing? Or am I hearing what I want to because I want to believe it?"

"With the right application of force and counterbalance, even a pith point can be altered. Everything, and I do mean *everything* is subject to free will. But shifting a pith point can have devastating, unimaginable consequences."

"As in unravel the fabric of the universe," Kody

said from behind him. "It's what the zeitjägers guard against."

"She's right."

"Yeah, I don't want to do that. I unraveled my sheets once. My butt still stings from the beating my mother gave me. That taught me about messing with things I need to leave alone."

Pressing his hand to his head, Xev groaned. "Tirade aside . . . it sounds to me like Ambrose came to that conclusion and screwed up something he couldn't fix."

"Maybe that's what gave us this Cyprian?" Caleb scratched at his chin.

"Or maybe the Cyprian was always there." Jaden jerked his chin at Kody. "Think about what an Arel is. What they do."

Kody screwed her face up at him. "They track and record human history."

"And?"

"They're the powers who defend and dispense justice."

Jaden nodded and rolled his hand as if they were all following along, but Nick felt as off-the-tracks as Kody appeared.

Once he realized they were all stumbling in the woods, slamming into trees, including Caleb and Xev who sent extremely rude gestures back at him, he made a sound of supreme exasperation, then extrapolated for them. "Sraosha's original role as Arel was to set things in motion for that history that he kept, to ensure that it moved forward correctly and on time. He was also the judge of the dead, and one of the primary warriors who'd chase away the demons of violence and anger who preyed on mankind."

"Hence his overwhelming love and adoration of *me*," Caleb muttered.

Jaden ignored them as he used his powers to lift the stones around the Eye so that they hovered. "We've been assuming that Ambrose failed. But what if he didn't? What if he succeeded?"

He set the stones down in different positions, then looked at them.

"Sraosha would still go crazy." Kody breathed. "Because the order would be upset."

Jaden nodded. "Especially if there was a second Malachai and Ambrose had found a way to break that curse."

"You're speculating."

Jaden glanced at Xev and shrugged. "So I am. You have a better conjecture?"

"We don't have enough evidence for any kind of conclusion right now."

"True."

"But I like where his head is." Nick bit his lip as his mind whirled with the possibilities of it. For the first time, it gave him hope. "In his version, I'm not the jerkweed who destroys the world."

"No, your son is."

He rolled his eyes at Caleb. "Go stand in the corner until you learn to be more positive in your thinking. You need an attitude adjustment, Mr. Daeve!"

"My attitude is fine. What I need is an environmental change where I'm not locked in a hovel with an ass"—he cut a gimlet glare to Jaden, then Nick—"and a pimple."

Nick scowled at Xev. "Why are you smiling?"

"I'm reveling in the fact he left me off his hate list."

"So . . ." Kody spoke in the most diplomatic of tones to get their attention off the matter. "Can we use the Eye to reset the future like Ambrose wanted?"

"See . . . that's what baffles me most. The Eye doesn't really work that way and Ambrose had to know that. I'm sure Nick's already been experiencing some of its side effects."

"Are you talking about my spirit channeling?"

He nodded. "So you have been communing with it?"

"Oh yeah. And I don't like it at all. It's like dreaming with my eyes open."

"Yes, but they're not dreams. They're important insights that relate directly to the matters you're trying to understand. The reason why it's called the Eye of Ananke is that it shows the why of a matter or a person."

Nick felt so stupid as he finally got it. "It doesn't show the future."

"It can, but it shows the past. The present or whatever it deems necessary to give you understanding."

Kody crossed her arms over her chest as she studied the Eye from a distance. "You're right. It doesn't make sense that Ambrose would send us after it, given that that's what it does."

"And it shows all futures," Nick muttered. "Which I truly despise. It's like having my mom on steroids. . . . Don't do that, Nick . . . I had a friend in high school who did that once. And I'm telling you, you could fall, skin your knee. Get a compound fracture. Break the bone and get blood poisoning. Funky cancer, or rabies, and *die!*" He finished in a mocking, deep voice. "She always has to go to the most morbid and horrendous conclusion imaginable." He jerked his chin. "So really I didn't need *that*. Already had one from birth that walks around behind me all the time doing it."

Caleb laughed. "Cherise would kill you if she heard you say that about her."

"Probably, but it's the truth."

"You know the one thing it can't do, though, is lie."

Nick turned back to Jaden. "Come again?"

"I'm thinking . . . Unlike a person, or a memory that can become distorted by time and emotions. It doesn't fabricate or lie. It never gets misled or misinterprets events. It always gives the cold, unvarnished truth. What you see is what happened or will come into being. Your little tirade on your mother is what made me think about that. Our memories are always faulty. They're tainted by our emotions and perceptions. We filter everything we take in by our experiences. I mean, you said yourself a few minutes ago. Did I say what you thought I did or did you hear what you wanted me to say? It doesn't make me a liar or you a fool. It's just human nature. People see what they want to see and they hear what they need or want to hear. The Eye doesn't do that."

"Ambrose wanted you to know the truth, whatever

it is." Kody met Nick's gaze. "I think someone other than Ambrose is tampering with the timeline."

Caleb cursed. "That's what brought out our ugly friends. They were looking for whoever did it. And they thought it was Nick because of Ambrose."

Kody nodded. "But while he did tamper with the time sequence, it wasn't egregious enough to warrant punishment."

"They were after the real culprit, whoever it is."

"Yeah." Covering her mouth with her hand, she looked as sick as Nick suddenly felt. "What are we dealing with?"

"Same thing we've been dealing with. The end of the world. Only we no longer know how to stop it." Nick walked around the shattered remains of Menyara's store. "I mean, look at this place. If they could come in here and do this to Mennie . . . how are we going to stop them?"

Caleb glanced at Xev. "You're up."

"Not me . . . Kody."

"I'm on it." She went to Nick and wrapped her arms around his waist. "Breathe deep and focus. Shh . . ."

Nick was having a harder time than normal with his panic attack. He opened his mouth to tell Kody that she wasn't there—that she hadn't seen it, but luckily caught himself before he was that stupid and insensitive.

She'd not only seen it. She'd died there with her family.

And that made it worse for him.

His breathing turned more ragged.

"Beware the seeds that are planted, even in the most fallow of fields. For those we lay with callous hands, might very well prove to be those of our ultimate destruction."

Nick blinked at Jaden's words. "Pardon?"

"It's something Bathymaas used to say." Caleb's voice was tight as he spoke. "Those words were often carved on her temple walls as a reminder to use restraint and good judgement in all things. For whatever you plant today, you will ultimately reap tomorrow. Whenever you bring evil into your life or do evil to others, the universe will spit it back at you with a vengeance."

And if Nick wasn't on edge enough, two seconds after Caleb finished speaking, something hit the front doors so hard, it caused them to rattle.

Worse, blood ran beneath the doors, pooling around his feet. . . .

# CHAPTER 13

✦

**H**ellooooo? Akra-Menyara Cam lady, quality goddess, you in there? Why you gots all these nasty uglies circling outside your door anyways? Can the Simi eat some? 'Cause they just gonna drive away your good business people and they kind of scaring the tourists. If you ask me, it's just a public service to let the Simi eat them. Hello? Akra-Mennie? You in there? Can you hear me?"

Laughing nervously, Nick almost fell over in relief at the sound of Simi's singsongy accent as she pounded on the doors with enough force to rattle the hinges. It was a wonder she wasn't shattering them.

Dang, that demon was strong to be so thin. She could double as a wrecking crew.

Kody went to the door to unlock it, while being

careful not to step in the bloody demon mess that Simi had left behind on her arrival.

She carefully opened the door after first peeking outside to make sure all the other demons were gone.

Or eaten.

Though to be honest, Simi usually asked permission before she chowed down on things that could converse.

"That is you, right?" Kody asked.

"Well, there better not be nobody else pretending to be the Simi or else the Simi going to have to get some barbecue sauce and eat them heads 'cause I ain't going to have no one else sleeping in my bed or hanging out with my akri in my stead, pretending to be me. The Simi don't cotton to no imposters. Nor do she share, unless forced to against her will and loud complaints. You can ask my akri and he will tell you this is quite true. Don't know what you heard, akra-Kody, but you were badly misinformed if you think otherwise."

Yeah, that was definitely the adorable Goth demon Nick knew so well. All six feet, striped leggings, leather purple corset, and short, black frou-frou skirt of her. She had her black hair pulled up into two pigtails that fell in twisted cybergoth falls from just above her ears.

Her coffin-shaped bag was slung over one shoulder and she wore a crystal vampire-bat choker.

Cocking her hip and head, Simi frowned, pouted, then frowned again at them. "Well, what all happened in here that has y'all looking so sad and irritable? Party? Bomb? Bomb party? Did someone get a little too excited and burp a chaos demon who ran amok and did all this?"

Then she saw some of the entrails on the floor and she bowed up at Caleb. "Oh no! No, you didn't! You done had a buffet and you didn't invite the Simi, for shame on you akri-Caleb! You a mean demon boy! You off the Simi Christmas list for that! No oven mitt for you! Bad, bad demon, bad!"

Caleb laughed. "There was no buffet, Simi, I promise. We got here after it. I mean, not after the buffet. After the fight that made this mess. You didn't miss anything, other than a battle."

"Oh, okay." She grinned adorably. "I'll put you back on my happy list of mitt deserving quality demons, then." She waved at Jaden. "Hello akri-demon-dealer-god-man! Been long, long time since I saw you last."

"Hi, Simi. You still hanging out with that loser with a surfboard?"

She gasped. "Akri-Savitar is the bestest. He makes

the hottest diamond barbecue sauce this side of the Sunken City. You should try it sometime."

"Yeah, I'll pass, I rather like my intestines not on fire. But thank you for the offer."

She sighed and patted her coffin-shaped handbag. "Your loss, akri-Jay-Jay. The Simi telling you that it fully enhances all the flavors of the innards, and can kill the ones you don't like." Pursing her lips, she looked around the store. "So where's akra-Mennie? She promised the Simi some new sparklies!" There was something about Simi's enthusiasm and happiness over the simplest things that was infectious and made being around her such a joy.

Provided she wasn't sizing you or your entrails up for her dinner pot.

"We don't know." Nick gestured at the mess. "It was like this when we arrived."

"Um, people." Xev paused as he moved toward the doors. "Anyone else realize that the demon Simi killed is still on the ground over here, bleeding and not self-cleaning the way we like our demons to?"

"What's that mean?" Nick asked.

"That it's crossed into this realm and has its own corporeal body." Caleb paled.

"And Xev's right. We don't like when that happens." Kody turned even more ashen than Caleb—which was impressive given that her skin tone was darker.

"Why?"

It was Jaden who responded. "It's a whole new level of wet–your-pants evil. More powerful. More brazen. And when you kill them, you risk a jail sentence because you leave behind a body for the authorities to use for a murder charge."

Nick's stomach shrank at those words.

"It's what your father went to prison for killing. As you so eloquently once told Bubba, no one buys the old he-was-a-demon-who-needed-killing-Your-Honor plea." Caleb pulled the body into the store and used his powers to clean up the sidewalk. "Teams of them have been known to set us up and get the humans to come after us for centuries."

"Yeah." Jaden stepped forward to examine the body. "They've razed entire villages. Dark Ages were a bitch. . . . Or a lot of fun, depending on your perspective."

Caleb gave his father a disgruntled gape.

Jaden scoffed. "Please. Like you've never toasted

marshmallows over your enemies' corpses. You forget, I've seen you . . . no wait, those were their brains you toasted, weren't they?"

"Their hearts, actually," Xev said under his breath. "Then he ate them."

Nick choked on that as he passed a concerned, wide-eyed stare to Kody. *Note to self, don't piss off Caleb anymore.*

She gave him a droll smirk, but didn't comment.

"Speaking of them munchies . . . can the Simi have the body? Akri won't let me eat no people. But ugly demons nobody likes are usually on the menu." She passed an eager, hopeful, and extremely adorable look at them.

"I got no problem with it." Caleb glanced around at the others.

Nick cringed. "As long as I don't have to witness it, I guess I can live with it."

Clapping her hands together in instant joy, Simi jumped up and down in excitement and made a sound in the back of her throat that vaguely sounded like a happy dog panting.

Suddenly terrified by that amount of enthusiasm, Nick put a little more distance between them.

"Before you go, Simi . . ." Kody caught her arm. "I have a favor to ask. We need to find Aeron. Can you help us track him down?"

She was already digging her barbecue sauce from her purse. "Sure. But his friend would be better at it than the Simi. His nose is made to go a'sniffing."

"Friend?" Nick scowled. "He doesn't have any friends."

"Uh-huh. And that's just mean, akri-Nick! He gots that very nice wolfie friend what comes up to play with us when akri-Caleb at school. Sometimes we even goes out for eats."

"Did you know about this?" Nick asked Caleb.

Caleb shook his head. "I had *no* idea."

But the look on Xev's face said that he might have a clue about it.

"You know who she's talking about, don't you?"

His jaw worked for several seconds before he finally spoke. "I didn't think he'd go back for him. But it shouldn't surprise me, either, I guess . . . given their relationship. I'm extremely curious where they're hiding him, as he doesn't blend. *At all.* Ever. I can't imagine where they could put him that he wouldn't attract a *lot* of attention . . . in either form."

"Well, aren't we Mr. Dark and Cryptic . . . shall we call him?" Nick pulled out his phone.

"I doubt he knows how to work that. I'm sure he'd sniff it and eat it if you gave him one." He glanced at Simi. "Do you know where they're keeping him?"

She nodded like a bobble head. "You know how akri-Caleb's house is up off the ground and gots all that room under it for storage?"

Caleb screwed his face up. "Oh dear gods, he's in my wine cellar? Seriously?"

She kept nodding.

Caleb groaned irritably. "I'm thinking I should have made amends with my brother sooner and moved him into my house to watch the púca." He glanced from Simi to Xev and back again. "What kind of mutant life form do I have living in my cellar? And do I need to fumigate my house?"

"He doesn't particularly stink unless you get him wet. But you might want to spray for fleas and ticks . . . and he does like to chew on things. . . . He's a feral Cŵn Annwn. With an extremely heavy emphasis on the feral part. As in he makes Zavid look like a hand-fed Pomeranian. Back in the day, he was Aeron's primary general. They're a scary pair when they get together. And whatever you do, don't give them alcohol of any kind. In *any* quantity. You liquor them up and that, my friends, is what really happened to the Picts. *All* of them. And why the Romans never got over Hadrian's Wall."

Caleb laughed sarcastically. "Oh, goodie. He must be having a ball in New Orleans, chasing down all the lost and blackened souls, and unchristened people here."

Xev nodded in agreement. "No doubt."

"So why's he here?" Nick asked.

"You shall have to ask Aeron." Crossing his arms over his chest, Xev sighed. "But Simi's right. Kaziel will hunt him down and get him back, and if Aeron didn't go of his own volition, I wouldn't want to be *that* guy when Kaziel lays fang to him. He is a battle cŵn. Fiercely loyal. Trained by Scáthach, the Lady Shadow, herself at her home fortress. And I can tell you from personal experience, he's a pistol load of fun."

"Can't wait to meet him!" Nick said with a fake amount of enthusiasm. "All righty everybody, let's go get Scooby!"

When Jaden started after them, both Xev and Caleb faced him with questioning brows raised.

He returned their stares with an equal amount of unspoken defiance written in his expression.

"Where do you think you're going?" they asked in perfect unison.

Jaden blinked nonchalantly. "With you."

"Why?"

"I have a vested interest in how this plays out."

"Since when?"

Even though Caleb had spoken the question, Jaden cut a killer stare to Xev. "Since the day I sold myself into slavery to save the life of *your* son. Contrary to what you think, I didn't betray you. I was trying to save you both."

With a slack jaw, Xev staggered back in disbelief. It was the same sensation Nick felt at that unexpected disclosure.

"You knew about Jared?" Xev whispered.

"Of course I knew. How stupid do you think I am? I knew it the moment I first held him in my arms."

"Yet you never said anything? Why?"

"The same reason you didn't. It would have destroyed both Jared and Myone." Agony burned deep in Jaden's eyes. But beneath that was a deep, undeniable love. It was obvious that he did care about his sons and their well-being. That he wasn't the heartless ogre they accused him of being. "In spite of what you and Caleb think, I've always loved you both. You are my sons. I just can't trust the blood inside you. I know the call it makes. How hard it is to resist. What do you think the Verlyn is? An unstoppable force *I* have no control over. Forget the blood of your mothers . . . you both have *that* beast inside you."

Xev shook his head. "I still don't understand . . ."

"What? That I loved him as my own? That I protected him and raised him in my home?"

"Yeah. Let's start with that, given how much you always hated me."

Jaden winced. "Not trusting you isn't the same as hating you. You never could understand that. And I never asked to be at war with you. But every time I tried to reach out, you looked at me as if you could go through me. As if you wouldn't hesitate to cut my throat. And if I ever gave you the chance, you did betray me. So yeah, I've been cold in response to what I've felt. That's my nature. I never knew what to do with either of you, given your attitudes. Ironic, isn't it? My greatest fear was that your mother would use you to control me. Instead, it was your child who put me under her thumb completely.

Had I done right by you and embraced you as the father you needed me to be when you were born, I wouldn't be forced to serve her now. Jared wouldn't be enslaved and we wouldn't have lost this war. I screwed everything up because I was blind and afraid."

Nick stepped back as those words echoed in his head, and smacked eerily of what both Ambrose and Acheron had said to him.

"We manifest our worst fears."

They turned to stare at him.

"Sorry, I didn't mean to intrude on your moment. I was just thinking over something Acheron said about how the worst things in his life happened because someone tried to circumvent his destiny. Had they just left it alone and allowed it to play out as it was intended, he and the world would have been a lot better off." Rubbing his hand over his face as he grappled with that, he glanced at Kody. "Is that the key to this? Should we stop trying to fix it? Just let it run as it's meant to?"

But even as he asked the question, Nick knew it wasn't that simple. Not when the cost of doing nothing meant his mother would die.

Maybe that was selfish.

The world or his mother. If you were to ask anyone, they'd choose the world. To them, the choice would be simple. One life for billions . . .

Yet his mother *was* his world. And he was willing to sacrifice a billion strangers to save her. Because living out his life, knowing there was a chance he could have prevented her murder and didn't at least try . . .

He understood the source of Ambrose's madness.

God help him for that.

Kody wrapped her arms around his waist and leaned her head against his shoulder. "I know, Nick. I do. Remember, I chose you."

"Woman, you chose poorly."

Laughing, she kissed his cheek. "Let's find Aeron and we'll work on this puzzle once we have more pieces."

He liked that plan. "Okay. As we all know, procrastination is my middle name."

"The Simi thought it was Ambrosius."

He laughed at her baffled tone. "Ambrosius Procrastinatius."

She pursed her lips. "Hmm, that be as hard to say as Parthenopaeus. How you fit all that on your driver's license?"

"Very carefully. And with a lot of practice."

Winking at Simi, Nick teleported to Caleb's huge, sprawling mansion of a house. He popped into the living room and was quickly joined by the rest of his crew.

He didn't move as he waited for all of them to appear. Though to be honest, it was eerily quiet like this. Nick had never been over when there wasn't loud, obnoxious music playing or demons attacking.

"So . . ." He cocked a brow at Simi once everyone was there. "Where do we find this mysterious hellhound?"

"Follow me." Caleb led them to the kitchen where the cellar door was. He passed an annoyed glance at Simi and Nick over his shoulder. "I'm really hoping my houseguest wasn't so inconsiderate as to invite a guest of his own. But I'm thinking I've been played."

Turning on the light and opening the door, Caleb headed down the narrow spiral stairs.

They followed him into the "cellar," which was an illusion since it was technically the first floor of the house built with tiny windows where they used to keep perishables back in the day before they had real refrigeration.

At first, it didn't appear anyone was here. But as they neared the southern corner, there was no mistaking the presence of something highly powerful attempting to mask itself. The air literally crackled with the paranormal static of emanating power. Most creatures wouldn't be able to detect it.

The Malachai wasn't most. Whatever was there lit up every bit of his psychic sense and had it singing a soprano chorus. Nothing could hide from Nick's breed.

Or Jaden, apparently. He stiffened and reached out to stop his sons. "Don't move."

Nick heard the subtle growl off to his right. It was low and powerful, and only registered on the demonic plane. Yet it was enough to let him know that the beast was ready to come for his throat. The sound rippled in the air like low thrumming thunder, with enough energy that he had no doubt the growl, alone, could be weaponized. "What exactly are these things again?"

"Watch and learn, akri-Nick! The Simi will shows you." She flounced around him to kneel a few feet away. "Here, here, akri-Kaziel. No one gonna hurt you, the Simi promises and you knows you can banks it all day long." Clicking her tongue, she held her hand out.

The growling subsided. A slight rustle sounded

before the largest wolf Nick had ever seen came out of the shadows.

"Holy mother of God!" Nick involuntarily crossed himself. If he'd had holy water, he'd have flung it at him, too. Not that he thought it'd do any good.

Just for good measure.

As it was, Nick could barely refrain from holding up two fingers in the sign of a cross against the beast.

Yeah, it was *that* scary.

Give him a demon, a hell-monkey . . .

Anything over *this* monstrous thing. Even on four legs, it had to be over four and half feet tall from paws to haunches. Completely snow white, the hound was all muscled sinew and furry beast. That would be scary enough. Add to that unholy bloodred ears and matching demonic, glowing, flame-red eyes and fangs that showed even when he closed his mouth, and yeah, that wouldn't blend on the street no matter what you tried. Especially given that every other breath shot flames out his muzzle. What it would do, though, was give you nightmares and send you to a psych ward, especially if you were dumb enough to try and tell anyone what you'd seen.

"What did they use those for again?" Nick asked in a voice that came out a lot squeakier and in a much higher octave than he'd intended. One that sounded like he hadn't quite reached puberty yet.

Yeah, it'd just sucked out a whole level of testosterone he wanted back.

Xev stepped around his father. "Messengers of the gods. They guarded the gates of Annwn. Were sent to hunt down the dark ones and Children of Llyr, and unchristened souls. They were also used by the gods in battle. It was said anyone who heard their baying would die. So in a way, they were like banshees."

Nick cleared his throat and intentionally dropped it an octave before he spoke again. "And the gates of Annwn are what?"

"Celtic Underworld." Xev moved slowly toward Kaziel. "You remember me, old friend?"

The way he eyed Xev with those freaky glowing eyes, Nick half expected him to take a bite out of him. But he held himself perfectly still as Xev approached him to present his hand so that Kaziel could sniff the back of his fist.

Only then did the hound shift to his human form.

Crouched low, and wearing jeans and a black leather jacket, he unfolded himself slowly to emerge as an even more impressively giant, muscled beast.

Nick crossed himself again. Though this time, he did manage to withhold the verbal expletives. Yet he still exchanged a wide-eyed gaping stare with Kody.

Standing a good two inches taller than Nick, Kaziel had long pale blond hair that fell to his shoulders. Tiny braids interlaced with beads and feathers held it back from his face. That wasn't the nonblending part so much as the facial tattoos that curved from his chin up and over his cheeks like tusks, to come to a sharp point under eyes so light and green they glowed with an ethereal, fey light.

There was also an additional tattoo in the center of his forehead that appeared to be the stylized symbol of some god.

More Celtic birdlike tattoos that were almost identical in form to the ones on the Dark-Hunter Talon, covered the left side of his well-muscled torso beneath his leather motorcycle jacket.

And none of that took in his lethal aura that said, *yeah, I'm an ancient warrior who can kick your butt and not care.*

Nick frowned. "Are those symbols for the Mórrígan?"

Snarling, Kaziel started for him, but Xev caught him and forced him back. "It's okay, Kaz." Over his shoulder, he scowled at Nick. "How do you know that? You *never* know that kind of thing."

"Talon of the Morrigantes. He has markings like that, in the same place on his body. He's also an ancient Celt. And though his hair is short, he has similar braids, too."

That seemed to calm Kaziel.

Xev released him. "In the case of Kaziel, his have to do with Brân the Blessed. And the sun marks him as being aligned to the children of Dôn."

Kody pursed her lips. "I thought she was a moon goddess like Artemis."

"But aligned to the side of light."

"So he's like us," Caleb said. "A creature torn between light and dark?"

Xev nodded. "Born of both sides. Forever lured between them. Never trusted by either, and cursed by both."

"That explains it."

Jaden scowled. "Explains what?"

Caleb gave his father a cold grimace. "Why he hides

in the cellar and they get along." Then he turned to Kaziel. "Nice meeting you, brother. Welcome to the family. . . . We should start making T-shirts."

Without a word of comment on that, Kaziel stepped away from Xev to approach Kody. She slid an uncomfortable look to Nick who didn't like the sudden light in those creepy green eyes as Kaziel circled her.

Yeah, he didn't need his powers to guess what thoughts were in the horndog's mind.

Before either of them realized what Kaziel intended, he stepped closer to Kody and nuzzled his face against her hair.

"Okay," Nick snapped. "Dude, enough of that. She's *my* girl. And you don't go sniffing on other guys' girls. I don't know about the time and place you come from, but it's considered rude here."

When Nick closed the distance between them, Kaziel growled at him.

Nick didn't flinch or back down. "Check the attitude at the door, 'cause I'm about to open up some fresh whoop . . . ass."

"We don't need to escalate this to violence." Kody wrapped her hands in Nick's baggy shirt and attempted to push him back a bit, only to learn he had no intention of budging. "I'm sure he didn't realize he was trespassing."

"Does he speak?" Nick asked Xev.

"Can and does are two different things."

"Meaning?"

"Yes, he *can* speak. He just seldom chooses to do so."

"And I can respect that. Just as I'm sure Lassie can respect the fact that Kody is *my* girl, and while I try not to be *that* jealous boyfriend, it is purely a self-serving act I put on so as not to offend her. Inside, I am *that* jealous boyfriend, and any public pawing of said girl-friend is subject to an uncontrollable fit of rage I may or may not be able to stop, hence the uncontrollable pre-viously promised ass-whooping."

Kody shook her head and sighed. "You really are a basic, cave-dwelling beast, aren't you?"

"*Cher*, you're lucky my knuckles don't drag across the floor when I walk." He winked at her.

Jaden scowled. "He is not like the other Malachais, is he?"

Caleb clapped his father on the back. "We blame your screwed-up genes on this, all the way around." He wrinkled his nose. "Can't wait to find and meet that next generation of screwed up."

Xev snorted. "Ain't that the truth."

A hurt look passed over Kody's face. "I know I can't be the mother. I'm too young."

Nick bit his lip. "As a Malachai, I have the power to look ahead and see who the mother of the next Malachai is. Right?"

Jaden nodded.

"I wouldn't advise it." Caleb met his gaze.

Xev concurred. "I'm going to weigh in with my brother and Acheron. Just because you can, doesn't mean you should."

Yeah, maybe, but for now . . . "Kaziel, we have a problem. Aeron went missing and we can't find him."

His green eyes darkened to the same red they were in his wolf form.

No, that wasn't spooky or creepy at all. Not even a little.

His breathing intensified. "Was he attacked, like?"

Oh yeah, now there was a thick, almost unintelligible Welsh accent. It made Aeron's seem bland.

"We don't know. I sent him to watch Kody and he never made it."

Reddish-orange flames radiated from his entire body. His tattoos turned red.

"Xev? Is that normal?"

"Yes."

When Kaziel started to turn around, Xev caught his arm and stopped him. "Where is he?"

"Nether Realm. Rather, he's being held to lure the Malachai."

Jaden let out a tired sigh. "I'll get him and Zavid, and return them."

The color drained from both Caleb's and Xev's faces. "We can't let you do that."

"Like you really care. Besides, if any of you go in there, Noir and Azura will know. No one will notice me."

"Why would you do this?" Caleb searched Jaden's features with his gaze.

"I'm your father."

"*Now* you get paternal?"

Jaden shrugged nonchalantly. "I've always been a jerk. Take after my sons."

"Wait!" Xev approached him slowly. "You never told us your price for helping us."

Tears welled in Jaden's eyes. "I got to see my boys again." His gaze went to Nick. "Find out that I have a great-grandson . . . and you gave me something I haven't had in countless centuries."

"What?" Xev breathed.

"Hope. I don't need anything else."

"You know what they're going to do to you when you return?"

He shrugged nonchalantly. "What they do to me has never bothered me. What has always pissed me off is that one by one, all three of you threw away the freedom I bought for you with my blood and soul by chaining yourselves to my enemies because you were too damn hardheaded to listen!"

A tic started in his jaw as he hesitantly held his hand out to Xev. "I know sorry can't even begin to repair the damage I've done to either of you. The mistakes I made were never done for spite or out of cruelty. And if I could bring back Myone or Lilliana, I would."

Pain radiated so deep in Xev's hazel eyes that it choked Nick as he took Xev's father's hand and he pulled him in for a hug. "Thank you for coming."

Jaden didn't speak. But Nick wished Xev could see the anguish on his face as he held him and fisted his hand in his hair. Hair that turned completely black beneath his fist. And before he released him, he kissed his brow, turning his eyebrows black as well.

Nick met Caleb's shocked expression, but neither of them said a word as Jaden turned toward Caleb.

"Stay out of the line of fire."

"And you."

Jaden held his hand out to Caleb.

Tears swam in Caleb's eyes before he took his hand and they embraced.

Then in a bright flash of light, Jaden was gone.

Caleb choked on a sob. "You worthless bastard!" he growled, wiping at his eyes.

Xev cleared his throat. "Kaziel? Could you please go with him and help him free Aeron?"

Kaziel placed a brotherly hand on Xev's shoulder before he vanished.

"You sure you don't want me to—"

"No!" they shouted in unison.

"Okay," Nick said, holding his hands up in surrender. At least that broke their melancholia.

Caleb manifested a small hand mirror for Xev and held it up for him to see. "Thought you'd want to know."

He gasped as he saw himself whole for the first time in hundreds of thousands of years. "Why would he lift this portion of the curse?"

"No idea. The others will kill him when they find out."

Smiling, Kody walked over to him. "You look so strange like this. I'll miss the old you."

He laughed at her words. "You're the only one who felt that way."

"Cherise, too."

He lowered the mirror. "My two Arelim." Cupping her cheek in his hand, he kissed her forehead. "Treasure her, Nick. Those who judge only by the heart are far too rare in this world."

"Believe me, I know." Nick paused as a bad feeling went through him.

"You okay?"

Not really . . . he still felt odd. "Weird feeling just went through me."

"Weird feeling how?"

Before Nick could speak, a searing pain exploded inside him and drove him to his knees.

# CHAPTER 14

✦

Jaden fell back as he manifested near Noir's main bank of "special" rooms where he kept his most hated guests. He was rather sure his name was engraved on the door of the room at the far end of the hall.

As was Seth's.

Guilt wrenched his gut as he paused by *that* door and he did his best not to think of the horrors that were visited daily upon its occupant. And the fact that there was nothing he could do to spare the demigod his eternal suffering.

All because of Adarian Malachai.

And because of *him*.

He had so much to atone for. Wrongs made against

others for things he'd thought were the right reasons at the time. But with perspective of age and distance . . .

Jaden regretted so much of his existence. Yet nothing weighed on him as much as the gulf that divided him from his own children and the wretched fates that were theirs because of his own failure to protect them.

It wasn't like he hadn't tried. That was the bitterest pill of all. Like his sister Apollymi, he'd done everything he could to spare them from the cruelty of others. Sacrificed everyone he'd ever loved and everything he'd ever cherished, and what had it gotten him?

Hated.

Condemned to hell.

Imprisoned and tortured for untold centuries.

He'd once been a primary power of the earth, a fierce, feared primordial god. And now he was reduced to being nothing more than the punch line of jokes bandied about by slug demons or worse. A broker for lesser beings to summon so that they could commune with the brother and sister he hated beyond tolerance or measure.

A brother and sister he'd done his best to destroy the moment they'd been spat out of the farting abyss of darkness itself.

Life was never what you planned for. Never what you thought.

And he was so tired of being sucker-punched by it.

But this wasn't about him and his weary, eternal journey. He'd let his children down enough. For once, he would be there for them.

As he moved forward, he felt a powerful presence behind him.

Jaden turned, ready to battle. Yet to his utmost shock, it wasn't one of the revolting, shattered, and twisted souls that called this infernal realm home.

It was Kaziel.

"What are you doing here?"

"I'm your reinforcement, like."

"Did they not trust me?"

Kaziel snorted at his question. "They were worried." And with that, he changed into his dire wolf form.

Much more touched than he wanted to admit, Jaden took a moment to savor the miracle that had sent the wolf to him. All he ever remembered was fighting against his children. Hurtful, bitter words that cut straight through the heart and seared their very souls.

He was as guilty of it as they were.

Whatever fool had penned the nonsense that words

could do no harm should be condemned to Tophet's lowest fiery pit. For they did far more damage than mere broken bones that eventually healed.

Furious, hate-filled words spoken by a loved one left bleeding gashes that no amount of time or apology ever masked. The slightest frown or look could rip the scabs open and begin the bleeding anew as if no amount of time had passed at all from the initial injury.

Yet the most amazing thing about love was how willing you could be to let the very one who hurt you the most, who cut you deeper than anyone ever had, back into your life to do it again.

That blind, stupid trust was what he hated most.

For his sons, alone, he was willing to be the greatest fool ever spawned.

Even when they hated him.

*I am pathetic slug.*

Sighing, he headed for the cell most likely to contain Noir's latest catch.

Kaziel veered off unexpectedly.

"What are you doing?" Jaden asked between clenched teeth.

He shot fire from his snout as he lifted it to sniff at the air.

Bemused, Jaden watched as the wolf turned around to sniff at several different corridors. "Kaziel?"

*Aeron isn't here alone.*

Those whispered words in his head gave him pause. "What do you mean? Are you talking about Zavid or Menyara?"

He shook his head.

Too late, Jaden realized who else was here . . .

Gwrach y Rhibyn—the hag of the robin. Better known as Noir's alarm system. His number-one tattletale who lived to report everything to the old bastard.

Crap!

Tall and thin, she was a ghostlike wraith who functioned like an Irish bean-sidhe. Dressed in black rags, she had long, stringy red hair and dark eyes and lips. As with Kaziel, she had a tattoo in the center of her forehead, only hers was more of a dark, elongated star than the open sun symbol that marked his brow.

And just as she opened her mouth to let fly her

banshee scream, Kaziel launched himself at her, trans-
forming from wolf to man. He wrapped his arms
around her and slapped his hand over her mouth to
keep her from making that horrendous sound she was
known for.

"Shh." He breathed calmly in her ear to hold her
tight against his chest. "You let fly yours, love. I'll let
fly mine and we'll both have bleeding ears. And I know
you don't be wanting any of that, now do you?"

"Kaziel?" she whispered in her deep husky voice.

"Aye."

"What the bloody *cythral* are you doing here?"

"I've come to fetch Aeron. You're not going to be getting in me way now are you, boyo? I'd hate to be hurting
you after what all we've been through together, like. But
I won't be letting sentimentals stop me from protecting
me penlord. You get me way, like, and I will be hurting
you. Friendship be damned."

"Aeron here? Are you *moithered* or drunk?"

"Neither."

Jaden was having the hardest time following this
bizarre exchange. Never mind the fact that their
Welsh accents were thick, and they were technically

speaking English, which up until now he would have sworn he was fluent in.

But . . .

"You two know each other?"

And that got Rhibyn's attention on him, which turned out to be a bad, bad thing as she started for him like Cujo after fresh meat.

Kaziel picked her up and swung her about. "None of that. He be friendly, like."

"Now you're all coggy-headed, for sure! You're as addled as me da, after Cordelia's feast! Now put me down, you brute, or I'll take from your hide and be making meself new white, furry boots."

"Nae, I won't having none of it, now. Stop your fussing, Vawn! I mean it!"

Rhibyn bared her jagged gray, bony fangs.

"Really?" Kaziel laughed in a mocking tone. "You think to be scaring me with that patheticness o'yours? What? You going to wash your clothes at the creek, now, and cry 'bout it, too?"

"You're such a bleeding arse!"

"I come by it honestly, I do."

Rhibyn pointed at Jaden. "He'll be the one what

turns you in. Mark me words on that. He's a low-lying, worthless piece-o-work what can't be trusted no further than what you can toss him, and you can't even pick his giant arse up."

"Be that as it may, I was sent here to protect him, and you know I will."

"*Och, Duw!* You were ever half-soaked, boyo! From your first breath to your last. Never be changing your ways."

"Most likely not. Now will you be helping or are we to keep talking?"

She spoke in fast, furious, demonic Welsh that questioned Jaden's parentage, as well as Kaziel's, and all his sense, both common and otherwise.

Finally, Rhibyn calmed. "Of course, I'll be helping you. What kind of monster do you be thinking I am? But swear you'll be getting me out of here, too."

Kaziel scowled. "How is it you're here, even?"

"Was captured and traded."

Tilting his head, Kaziel looked at Jaden. "Can I be taking him from here? Would that be allowed?"

"Why do you keep calling her a him?"

He looked at Jaden as if he were the daft one. "What are you? Blind? Rhibyn's a man."

Jaden swept a skeptical glance over the lush curves of her body. While he'd never seen her naked . . . "You sure about that?"

Rhibyn rolled *her* eyes?

Kaziel bit back a laugh. "Aye, indeed. He was cursed into that body after he broke the heart of a woman, and she killed herself for him. Now he's forever damned to walk the earth in her very image, and cry out for the souls of those about to die to warn others that they will lose what they hold dearest."

"Oh, that's harsh."

Rhibyn ground his teeth. "You've no idea. It weren't even me fault. *She* preyed upon me until I was near mad with her attentions. The lass was unhinged." Gesturing at himself, he sighed. "And this was her final vengeance upon me. To make sure I'd never have another woman. Ever. I'd have rather she turned me to a goat, to be honest." He turned to Kaziel. "And one smart word from you, man, and you'll be getting it kicked from a woman, you hear me?"

He held his hands up in surrender. But his eyes twinkled with unspoken humor.

"So I take it then that the Robin is short for Robert?"

"Rhyvawn Ddu," they said in unison.

Jaden felt the urge to say *bless you*. But he refrained from saying more as he led them toward the room where Aeron should be found. "You know, Kaziel . . . for someone who couldn't talk, you sure found your tongue."

Kaziel returned to his wolf form.

"He's only silent around those he doesn't know or trust."

"Apparently." Jaden didn't miss the way Rhibyn kept one hand buried in Kaziel's white fur as if afraid the Cŵn Annwn would leave him.

They stopped as Jaden passed a door, and heard the sound of Noir's voice coming from inside the dungeon room.

"How can I be weakening? We know who the Malachai is. I sent my siphon. How can I be *weaker*?"

"It must be something Cam did to protect him. She's been soft toward their bloodline since the day we demanded the life of Kissare for his sacrilege."

Noir snorted. "Longer than that. She's wanted our deaths since the hour of birth. But for Braith, we'd have never survived the other three gods, and well you know it. They'd have wiped us out centuries ago."

Someone stumbled and hit the ground.

"Kadar!"

Jaden froze as Azura used Noir's oldest name. It had to be bad for her to make that slip.

And for Noir to allow her to get away with it. No one was allowed to call him Kadar. To call the dark ones by name gave you power over them. It allowed you to bind them.

Most importantly, it allowed you to banish them. Hence why Noir and Azura were currently imprisoned in the Azmodea—a Nether Realm that existed between dimensions. Forever held out of time and place by Xev's blood.

There had been a time when this plane had been readily accessible by regular portals. But that was long ago. Before war and punishments.

"I need you to summon Thorn," Noir groaned.

"He won't feed you. You know that."

"Yes, he will. Or we will war. More to the point, I will war against his child. And that he won't tolerate. Tell him, he has one hour before I open my gates on Cadegan."

Jaden's mind spun over what Noir revealed. Noir, like Nick, was weakened. Drained.

Could it be from the same source?

A Malachai would strengthen Noir. Not weaken him. He always got a huge boost whenever a new Malachai rose to power. Those raw, untapped powers added to his.

Nothing should be able to drain them both. Simultaneously. It made *no* logical sense. There was no such creature or device that would do that.

No sooner had that thought gone through his head than a phantom wind whistled down the hallway with enough force that it slammed him into the wall and pinned him there.

Kaziel and Rhibyn were slammed and held across from him. That was Azura leaving this area to carry out her orders.

And it allowed him a chance to see Noir's condition firsthand.

Pale and shaking, the ancient god was on his back, flat on the ground. Jaden had never seen him like this. Not even in battle.

Azura was right to be terrified. This *was* abnormal. The things that could do this to a god of their magnitude were few and far between.

The Malachai was one of them and he wasn't here.

Nor would Nick know how to do that without being shown.

Jared would be the other, and he wasn't here, either. The two of them had specific weapons that they wielded with their powers that could lay low the primals. But those had either been destroyed or were well hidden in the world of man so long ago that no one had seen them in centuries.

Provided they still existed.

And Jaden ought to know as he'd been searching for them as a way to gain his freedom. They were some of the few things he'd give a demon anything for. Break any rule to possess.

But so far . . .

Demons were a worthless lot.

"What are *you* staring at?"

The doors slammed shut in his face, and Jaden and his companions were instantly freed from whatever was holding them immobile.

Thankfully, Azura was preoccupied and didn't consider them enough of a threat to think them behind this. That, alone, saved their lives.

Jaden straightened his clothes with a tug as he met

Kaziel's gaze. "This is bad. If Grim and Laguerre have found a way to kill Noir . . ."

*They could unravel the fabric of the universe.* Kaziel sent that thought to Jaden.

Jaden nodded. In anyone's hands that kind of power was scary in and of itself. But what truly terrified him was the fact that those two creatures were stupid enough to actually do it, and not care about the consequences.

That's what War and Death were. Indiscriminate killers, without regard to the past, present, or future. They cared for nothing and no one. Respected nothing and no one. They could not be reasoned with.

And while Death was inevitable for everyone, War was not. It could be stopped and extinguished.

Both could be thwarted, avoided, and delayed.

That was what they had to do. Avoid and delay them and put Laguerre down as soon as possible.

Preferably before she got her hands on Nick.

Or Nick's son, whoever he was.

Determined, Jaden picked up their pace as he rushed to find Aeron.

True to his prediction and gut instinct, they found Aeron in the holding cells. And as expected, he wasn't alone.

Kaziel started for him, but Jaden caught him.

"You go in there and you'll get him killed."

"He's right, love." Rhibyn released her grip on Kaziel. "How do we distract them? Shall I have a go at it?"

Jaden shook his head. "They'd attack you if you did, and bring you down. No, for this . . . we'll need the big guns. But I don't have control so once I do this, get him, get out, and don't worry over me. Understood?"

*What about Zavid?*

Rhibyn scowled at Kaziel's question. "The hell-hound?"

*You know him?*

"Oh, yeah. They've been having a time with him," Rhibyn said bitterly. "Grim is a twisted beast. Livia even more so."

"He needs to return to the other side with Aeron and Kaziel."

"Easier said than done. That one is *officially* dead. You know the rules about removing the dead from Azmodea."

Jaden laughed bitterly. "Oh, sweetie, bringing the dead things back are what make me so coveted." Lowering his head, he summoned the Verlyn that lay dormant inside him. He tapped the primal Source powers that had once ruled him.

The powers he hated most.

They were what had allowed him to harm his own children. For whenever they ruled him, nothing else mattered. He had no heart or soul. No compassion.

Like Death, he couldn't be reasoned with or ran from. He was a creature of cold, callous rationale. The greater good was all that mattered.

In this form, he would sacrifice anything for the world.

Even his own children.

Cold comfort to know that his sons didn't really hate Jaden. It was the Verlyn who curled their lips and filled their hearts with contempt.

Because when all was said and done, *he* was the Verlyn. And all those despicable things the Verlyn did, were by *his* hand, too.

And when he wrenched the door from the hinges, the demons inside scurried like rats from a sinking ship.

Aeron, however, even though he was bleeding and bruised and barely able to hold up his head, didn't flinch at his approach. Rather the ancient god met his gaze as an equal.

"You don't scare or impress me. Take your theatrics and go. I've no use for you."

Jaden tsked. "Since you're what I've come for, I can't be doing that."

Aeron was stunned silent as the primordial, ancient being reached for him. As an older god himself, he'd heard many tales of the primary ones, but he'd never met one before.

He was not disappointed.

Seven feet tall and extremely well-muscled, Verlyn was said to be the firstborn of them all. The oldest, most powerful. Deadliest.

Dressed in a long, black coat with a high-standing collar that was trimmed in silver . . . silver that appeared to be stained by blood, the ancient god had shaved his head smooth to show off a wealth of dark, tawny skin. Symbols were tattooed down the center of his skull, culminating into a sharp point right between his eyes. His right eye was ringed with black and from the bottom of it was another set of symbols that went down his cheek to his chin.

The only color on his body was a splash of a bright green shirt he wore beneath the black coat. A vibrant green that matched the same color as his one single eye. While the other was a deep, dark brown.

A deeply unnerving and unexpected contrast.

With a terrifying ease, the god ripped off his manacles to free him.

Aeron started to fight, until he saw that Kaziel was with him. "Kaz?"

*Aye. We've come to take you home.*

"We?"

Rhibyn stepped out of the shadows. Aeron was even more stunned by his presence here. "I don't understand."

Verlyn laid a gentle hand on his shoulder. "My sons have bought your freedom. Remember what you owe them and treat them accordingly."

"Your sons?"

"Daraxerxes and Malphas."

Aeron choked on the last two names he'd ever expected to hear from the mouth of this powerful, primal god. Honestly, a part of him had thought Nick would have to be one of the sons. *That* would have made much more sense.

But *them*?

Why hadn't Caleb or Xev ever mentioned the fact their father was Verlyn?

Now *those* were some bragging rights.

Quickly, Verlyn led him from his cell.

In the dark hallway, he paused to look back at Rhibyn. "Where's this Zavid?"

"In the arena."

Verlyn cursed. "Of course he is." He clenched his teeth before he spoke again. "We'll have to move fast while Noir is incapacitated and Azura distracted by her errand. That at least works in our favor. But the minute they're not, you'll have to run for it. Zavid or no Zavid. Understood?"

They nodded.

With that, he led them toward the arena. It was where Noir sent the souls of those he cared least about to be entertainment for the others. All manner of violence was practiced here. Gladiatorial blood sports being the most common.

Aeron had no idea which poor soul might be the hellhound they sought. Not until he heard the chanting that came from the current fight where a dark-haired man wearing only a pair of ragged jeans was battling a demon. The man was ferocious and fought with the heart of a Fomorian.

He lifted the demon up, tossed him over his shoulder, and came down with a vicious pile driver so jarring, Aeron winced in sympathetic pain.

Even though they had yet to meet, he knew instinctively that this was the one Nick had saved.

Glancing at his companions, he jerked his chin toward that fierce combatant and spoke to them for confirmation. "Zavid?"

They nodded.

Oh, goodie. He was going to be a fun one to wrangle. "So how do we do this?"

"Well, we have to wait for . . ." Verlyn's voice trailed off as Zavid ripped the still-beating heart from the demon's chest. "Never mind."

Aeron passed an impressed look to his friends. "I like him already."

Vawn snorted irritably. "*You* would, like."

"Och now, with you. There was a time you would have, too." Aeron cocked his head back. "What are *you* doing here, anyway?"

"Long story, that. Not in a mood for it. Buy me a firkin of ale and we'll talk, now, in a minute."

"All right, then. Plan to hold you to that, and a full firkin, it is. Two actually. One for each hand."

Verlyn made a face at their rapid-fire conversation. "At what point do you people start speaking English?"

Vawn snorted. "Fancy that one, eh? What with the accent he has on him. Can't understand a single word he says half the time."

Aeron made a peculiar noise. "Just wait 'til you get around the Malachai's friends, Bubba and Mark. There's an accent for you, what'll make both ears bleed. And your noggin ache."

Suddenly, one of the demons turned toward them.

Too late, Aeron remembered he wasn't supposed to be out and about. Sadly, that particular demon hadn't forgotten it.

Before they could move, the demon cried out an alarm to his friends to attack them.

# CHAPTER 15

✳

Nick slowly entered Menyara's small duplex, just in case there was a trap waiting. Which there was, but luckily it was her normal one that she had set to keep out the unfriendlies they normally had to fight.

The walls lit up at his presence, activating the protection spells. Since he was known and not here to do harm, they slowly faded back to blend in with the paint.

Turning on the lights, he allowed his friends to enter behind him.

"No one's been here."

Kody bit her lip. "Why would they attack the shop? It seems like she'd be stronger there than even here."

Nick picked up an old photo of him with Menyara

from his third birthday party where he was sitting on her lap, wrapped in her arms. She'd kept it on her shelves as far back as he could remember. He had one identical to it in his own bedroom. "Maybe because they could get in there. This is personal space. Evil can't enter here unless invited. The store's neutral ground where the protection sigils aren't as strong. They could get in and up close before she'd be alerted to what they really were."

"Yeah, I guess that's true." Kody wrapped her arms around herself as they looked about for clues.

That action concerned him. Kody only did that when she was emotionally hurt and needing comfort. Nick set the picture down and drew her into his arms. "You okay, *cher*?"

She let out a shaky sigh. "Tired of burying loved ones. It's just stirring bad memories."

Nick flinched as her words awoke flashes in his own mind. He saw his future home and his mother . . . He staggered back from the image of her death and shook his head to clear it of an event that he couldn't bear to think about.

"Whoa, Nick! *You* okay?"

"Yeah, another vision. I'm starting to wish I'd never

touched that Eye. Just reminds me why drugs are a bad idea. I can't stand this. Who in their right mind would intentionally do this to themselves?"

She rubbed his back, then frowned. "You're burning up again." She placed her hand to his cheek. "You feel all right?"

"My hands are cold. Other than that, I'm fine."

Kody took his hand into hers. "That's not cold. It's arctic. . . . Caleb, feel this."

Frowning, he stepped over and did as she asked. His jaw dropped. "You're like a corpse."

Suddenly, he heard whispering in the aether around him. Subtle and light, it was barely audible. Only his Malachai powers could detect it.

The room and his friends faded. He was no longer in Menyara's home . . .

He wasn't sure where he was. It was somewhere he didn't know. Some place he couldn't identify.

Then, he saw Acheron . . .

No, not Ash. This man had short, curly blond hair and blue eyes, instead of Ash's swirling silver ones. But other than that, he was identical. Same towering, six-foot-eight height. Same athletic warrior's build. Dressed in black armor that was a cross between ancient

Greek and futuristic Kevlar, he stormed inside a palace Nick had never seen before to face a gorgeous blond woman. Her pale blond hair glistened in the darkness. It was so dark here. As if no light could reach this place.

Her gown was made of an ebony material so lightweight that it floated over her body like a cloud. She was the epitome of a regal queen and yet power and fury emanated from her. When she turned to face him, she held the same swirling silver eyes of Acheron, and features that were the feminine version of both his and Styxx's.

"What are you doing here?" Her gaze went from him to the army of Charonte he'd brought with him.

"Acheron sent me to evacuate you."

She laughed. "Where? I can't leave. He knows this."

"Ambrose is opening a gate for you. He and Acheron are going to face Cyprian's forces."

Her gaze softened as she swept his loyal body with her mercurial gaze. "Where's *your* family?"

"By their sides."

Tears filled her eyes. "I cannot believe we were so deceived. I will go so that they can battle without worrying for me. But before I do . . ." She pulled at the chain around her neck until it dislodged a vial from between her breasts.

Removing her necklace, she pressed it into Styxx's hand. "Give this to Ambrose. Should they fail today, should he fall in battle, it will be imperative that he drink it before he dies. Tell him this. If he doesn't drink of it, we will all be lost."

"I don't understand."

"I know. This is a matter of trust. Not understanding. All will be revealed in time. As with all things, it is never the enemy we see who destroys us. It is the one within we fail to notice, the one we trust, who deals us the fatal blow."

She pulled Styxx into her arms and held him. The agony in her eyes wrenched Nick's heart as she buried her fist in Styxx's curls. "My precious boys. How I wish I were there for this battle, to fight by your sides. I would drive them back to the corners of the universe and bathe in their entrails until I was blackened by their blood."

Styxx laughed nervously. "Now you're frightening me, *Matera*."

With a devilish grin, she kissed his cheek and

stepped back. "We've been through much, you and I. In all your lifetimes. Go, my mighty phoenix, and be the warrior I know you to be."

"Nick?"

Blinking, Nick was forced away from the future image of Apollymi and Styxx.

Was that real? Or was he hallucinating again?

It *felt* real.

He pressed his hands to his temples as he struggled to breathe. It was impossible. Nothing felt real. Nothing felt right.

His mind was snapping in two. Everything was wrong.

He reached for Kody to anchor him, but not even that worked as his breaths came in short, sharp gasps. His heart pounded in his ears. "I'm going crazy, Kody. I don't know what's true anymore. Are these possible futures? The real future? What really happened? How do I know the difference in what I see?"

Xev caught him against his chest. "Breathe, Nick," he whispered in his ear. "Slow . . . in and out."

He listened to Xev's soothing voice and followed his lead until he was calm again. Only then did Xev slacken his hold.

Still shaky and wrecked, Nick drew a ragged breath. "Well, look who got all maternal, suddenly."

Xev rolled his eyes. "It came with the new hair-style."

But that wasn't true. There had always been a deep vulnerability to Xev underneath that hate-filled kill-them—all-let-God-sort-them-out mentality he projected to others. It was what had caused Nick to reach out and help him when they'd first met. Why he'd risked much to bring Xev back with him.

He ruffled Nick's hair. "Get over there with your girlfriend before I spank you."

"Ooo promises, promises! You really shouldn't tease me like that, Grandpa. It's just so cruel." Nick batted his eyelashes at him while he rubbed at his posterior.

Caleb held his hands up in surrender. "You wound it up. It's on you now. I'm not tending *that*."

Xev gently pushed Nick toward Kody. "Tag, you're it."

Laughing, she shook her head. "You're all such big babies."

Nick sobered as he heard the whispering in the aether again. Louder this time.

Only now, it sounded like Mennie calling to him.

Pressing his fingers to his temple, he tried to concentrate. To pull the voice in closer so that he could focus on the words themselves.

As he did so, he began to see even more images. He felt a compulsion to . . .

Kody stepped back as Nick walked past her as if he were in a trance of some sort. "Should we be worried about that?"

Caleb and Xev watched him closely.

Xev stepped closer as Nick went to Menyara's altar cabinet. Without a word, he opened it and began some kind of peculiar preparations. Using a steel pestle, he slowly mixed salt and paints in one of Menyara's mortar bowls. "Not quite sure."

Caleb moved to stand beside Xev. "What's he doing?"

"Not quite sure," he repeated.

"Can he hear us?"

Xev glanced down at Kody. "There's only so many times I can say, *not quite sure.*"

Nick ignored them as if they didn't exist.

He went around Menyara's house gathering items as if he lived here, which kind of made sense. She had practically raised him and he'd spent a lot of his childhood in this home.

For that matter, he'd been born on her couch.

They gave him room to work—which ultimately resulted in a large summoning circle on the floor.

Only then did Xev begin to appear concerned. "He's not going to do something stupid like summon a friend we hate, right?"

"It's Nick. Of course he's going to do something stupid. When has he not? The only way this could go worse would be if we had Mark here, helping."

Kody would chastise Caleb for that, but he was right.

Still, she did feel an urge to defend her boyfriend. "It's not Nick's fault bad things happen around him. He always means well."

"Not helping, Kody," Nick said absently while he worked.

After a few minutes, he stood in the center of the circle, lighting incense, and began to chant in a language he shouldn't know.

Kody arched her brow. "Is that—"

"That primal language? Yeah." Caleb exchanged a shocked glance with Xev.

"Did one of you teach it to him?"

"No." Xev scowled. "But as Malachai, he should have knowledge of all languages. That's one of his powers."

A whirlwind began to swirl in the room. Slowly at first, but it quickly picked up speed.

Kody reached out to catch herself against the couch. "Is it supposed to be doing that?"

Xev shrugged.

Smoke rose from the painted circle. Menyara's protection sigils glowed and thrummed like breathing beasts that had run a marathon.

The lightbulbs over their heads and in the lamps shattered. Kody dodged as shards rained down on them.

She started for Nick, but Caleb stopped her. "You know better than to break the circle. There's no telling what harm you could do."

Just as she started to knee him and do it anyway, a bright flash blinded her. A beam of light burst through the ceiling, spreading down to engulf Nick who stood with outstretched arms as he continued to chant.

His eyes rolled back in his head before they turned a flaming red. The chanting became louder and louder. More like thunder than words.

She could feel it in her chest. A second heartbeat.

More white and gold light appeared in the circle around Nick. It danced and swayed. Stippling the air until it began to form something solid.

No, not something.

*Someone.*

At first, Kody thought it was a child in Nick's arms.

But as more details filled in, it became a tiny, delicate woman. One with glistening café au lait skin and a wealth of sisterlocks.

"Menyara?" she breathed.

Nick didn't stop chanting until she was whole. Then the light went out and the sigils on the wall dimmed. He carefully set her down so that she could stand on her own two feet. Using his telekinesis, he yanked a blanket from the couch and into the circle and used it to cover Menyara's wet, bare body.

Shaking and weak, Menyara leaned against him for support, both physical and emotional. "I wasn't sure you'd hear me, Baby Boo."

Nick held her. "I wasn't sure I was doing it right."

Laughing, she patted his chest. "My little Nicholas. Ever doubtful of himself. Whatever are we to do with you?"

"If you were smart? Throw the baby out with the bathwater. Toss the tub on top of him for good measure."

Caleb cleared his throat. "Is it safe to break the circle?"

"Yes." Menyara stepped away from Nick and tightened the blanket around her narrow shoulders.

Xev helped her toward the couch while Kody went to make her some hot tea. "What happened? Where were you?"

"I was attacked by mortents who caught me unawares in my store. They were on me before I could do anything. Pulled me into the Kassitu."

Nick cocked his head. "Kassitu?"

Her hand shaking, she wiped at her damp hair. "A prison of sorts where some of the worst demons to ever roam the earth have been banished."

"How could do they do that to *you*?" Kody asked as she brought her a cup of tea.

Menyara thanked her as she took it and cradled it in her hands. "I don't know. I've never heard of such a thing, and I didn't think I'd ever make it back. Every time I tried to call for help, I choked. I'm still not sure how Nicholas finally heard me."

"Don't give me too much credit. I barely heard you and I thought I was going crazy. Not to mention, my powers have been all over the place lately."

"What do you mean?"

"They're inconsistent. And most of the time, they fade out completely."

"He has a fever right now." Kody picked his arm up and held it out to her. "Touch his hand. It's ice cold."

The moment Menyara did, a deep frown drew her brows together.

Caleb nodded. "Yeah. Exactly. We've been told that Nick will have a son in the future. And we think he might have come back in time to kill us and alter time."

Menyara scowled at him. "Malachais can't time travel."

"They can with help."

She passed a look to Xev that said she didn't want his reminder.

Suddenly, Nick's phone went off. He jumped in startled alarm. Pulling it from his pocket, he saw it was his mom. Without hesitation, he quickly answered it, because any delay could result in his mom calling out the National Guard to recover him.

He really wished that were a joke. While she had yet to actually call the National Guard, she had been known to call all the local hospitals and police if he was out of touch for too long. Too long being defined as more than an hour.

And since he wasn't where he was supposed to be . . .

Time to prevent a national security panic.

"Hey, Ma."

"Why aren't you at home?"

"I'm at Menyara's."

That at least took the bite out of her temper. "Oh . . . are you okay? Did you get sicker? Do I need to take you to the ER?"

"Nah. It's okay, Mom. I still have my fever. And I was whining so much that I was afraid Kody would break up with her big baby boyfriend if I didn't find another person to annoy with it. Plus, neither of the guys are real long on sympathy. They just stare at me and tell me to suck it up, or throw things at me and tell me to stow it. So I came over here to whine and pout to someone who actually listens and tolerates me. Here, you want to talk to Aunt Mennie?" He handed her the phone, knowing his mom wouldn't calm down until he heard her voice and confirmed that he wasn't barfing up a kidney or something else.

"Hey, Cherise. Nah, your boy's fine. He's a little

pale and warm to the touch. But we're taking good care of him for you, sug. You don't worry your beautiful little heart for nothing. Enjoy your time with your new man."

"Um! No, Ma! Behave yourself with Bubba. Both of you!" Nick called out. "Remember, both feet on the floor at all times!" He looked at Kody. "What else does she always say to us?"

"Don't drag me into this."

"No ring. No fling," Caleb said in a dry tone.

"Leave the mystery in the relationship and it'll last longer," Xev added.

"Thank you! Did you heard that, Ma? God hates a hypocrite! There's another one of your sayings. . . . And the ever popular—just 'cause all your senseless friends are jumping into the Pontchartrain don't mean you need to follow them over the Levee of Stupidity!"

Menyara laughed. "I'll tell him, sug. Good night." She hung up and handed the phone back to him. "You're terrible, Nicholas!"

"I don't want to hear it. You half raised me. Besides, I'm only returning some of the grief she's given me over the years. It's actually kind of fun to be able to dish a little back."

She shook her head at him. "Help me up so I can get dressed. We've got some things we need to talk about."

"Do you need me to help?" Kody offered.

"No, *mon ange,* I'll be fine."

Weird, Nick had never noticed before how much Menyara and Kody favored each other. While he'd known for a while now that Menyara was her mother's aunt, he hadn't really seen the similarities in their features. But then Kody usually wore her hair down, with bangs over her forehead.

With them side by side and their hair pulled back from their faces, it was remarkable how similar their features were.

He didn't really see any of Styxx's features in his daughter. But his personality was there. By the bucketfuls, especially whenever they were fighting enemies. And while she might have her mother's exceptional archery skills, it was her father's sword skills that stood miles above everyone else's. Sword in hand, Kody was invincible.

"Kody? Nick's got that look again."

Nick barely heard Caleb as his mind replayed the night his father had died, and he'd first seen a vision of his own death at the hands of the Ambrose Malachai.

All this time, he'd thought it was just a guilty vision of him killing Kody's brother, and then killing her.

Now . . .

He again heard the sounds of horrendous fighting and saw himself in his demonic form. His gunmetal Malachai armor gleamed in the dull light of a fading sun while he fought against an army that was trying its best to destroy him. His soldiers pulled back to protect him. But he knew what they didn't.

They were about to be defeated.

Dumbfounded, he couldn't understand how this was happening. No one had ever equaled him in battle. Not even the Sephiroth. Jared had been a worthy enemy.

*He'd been an even better friend and ally.*

And then, through their demonic ranks, Nick saw his nemesis.

Their leader emerged like a dark angel of death, with his black wings fully extended. Drunk on his impending victory, he called out to rally his demon soldiers and push them forward.

Nick knew instinctively how to end this battle and war. If he killed their leader, they would scatter like frightened roaches. They would cower and run, and bother them no more. He would save them all.

His eyes flashed red, then silver before he launched himself at the fool who'd left the safe shelter of his army. Focused solely on him, Nick ignored everything else.

*I'm coming for you . . .*

He bore down on top of their leader with his sword raised. Leaving his horse, their leader launched himself at Nick.

Their weapons rang out as they clashed against each other. His enemy rained acid blood and fire down on Nick who used his own powers to drive his enemy back. To his credit, the demon stood strong and he fought against him longer than anyone else had ever lasted.

He might have even defeated him, but for one thing . . .

A sudden, familiar cry of pain.

Terrified, Nick turned from their fight to the smaller soldier several yards away. She was surrounded. About to go down. All-out panic filled him. Whatever it took, he would not lose her. Damn the rest. She would not be the cost of this.

Ever.

He kicked his enemy away and flew to her as fast as he could, scooping her up to carry her from the fray.

She ordered him to return to fight, but he wouldn't go. "There is nothing I will not do to protect my family," he said with a determination so raw, he felt it to the core of his rotted soul. "I made you my promise and I will keep it."

But he felt her blood coating his hands as he held her gently, trying his best not to harm her any worse. Her eyes softened through the slits in her helm as she clung to him.

"You were never good at listening to anyone, were you?"

He smiled down at her. "Contrary from my first breath to my last. But loyal to you with each and every one I draw."

A raw, furious battle cry sounded.

Nick looked over his shoulder to see his enemy headed for them, dodging through the combatants around him, slaying any who dared to charge his path.

Knowing this was about to get bad, he landed and did the last thing he ever wanted to—he handed his precious burden off to another of his men. "Get her to safety. Do not let her die!"

Her hand lingered on his as if she hated to let him

go as much as he regretted what was to come. As if she knew the future as clearly as he did.

But this had to be done.

With a deep breath, he forced himself to let go of the one thing he cherished most and turned back to fight, but it was too late.

His enemy was already on him. Before Nick could even raise his sword, the demon stabbed him straight through his worthless heart and drove him to the ground where he planted him with his sword pressed all the way through his body.

Choking on his own blood, Nick struggled as hard as he could to live—he had so much to live for . . . but there was nothing he could do except die.

And as his life faded from his body, he heard the scream that broke his heart. Why did she have to see this? Why had he allowed her to fight today?

With the courage that he'd loved since the day they first met, she ran to his side. "No!" she sobbed over and over again as she exposed his face. She lay her hand to his cheek and wept as if her entire world had been shattered.

"The vial," he breathed. "I can't reach it."

Sobbing, she pulled out the necklace Apollymi had sent for him and quickly helped him to drink. "Don't you dare leave me, Ambrose! Do you hear me? I won't lose you. I will go back and I will change this. Whatever the cost. I will find you and I will save you!"

He tried to touch her one last time. But the darkness he'd spent his whole life fighting claimed him first.

The moment he was dead, the woman holding him let loose the battle cry of a thousand Furies. She took his Malachai sword and ran at his enemy to finish what he'd started.

Their demon enemy raised his arm and caught her blow, then shot a blast at her that knocked her helmet free.

Dazed but undaunted, she jerked her head back to glare at him.

The sight jarred Nick this time. Before, it'd been Kody's face Nick had seen in his vision. But this face was different. Still beautiful, it was older and scarred.

He didn't know this woman, at all. Yet he recognized the hatred in her eyes that she bore for the demon before her. It was brutal and tangible.

And as Nick came out of his vision, he knew that

this time, the demon Malachai was his son who'd killed him that day.

The first time he'd seen that vision, he'd thought it was him transposing his face over Kody's brother's.

Now . . .

He blinked and turned to face her. "I'm so confused."

"Maybe this is what Grim meant when he threatened us."

"What do you mean?"

"Rule one . . . what's the best way to defeat your enemies?"

"Psychologically." Leave it to Caleb to know that. "You beat them down in their mind and it's easy to beat them down in their body."

She nodded at him. "Exactly. Maybe that's what this is."

"But Ambrose was the one who told me to get the Eye."

"The Eye of Ananke?"

He turned around as Menyara rejoined them. "Yes, ma'am."

She made a sound of supreme noise. "Child, you don't want any part of that. It'll make you crazy."

"Too late for that. It's already happened. And it won't stop spamming with crazy junk mail, either. How do I turn it off?"

"That's the problem. You're the Malachai. You can't."

"Lovely. That warning would have been much nicer *before* I touched it."

Menyara cupped his chin. "As if you would have heeded *any* warning. . . . One day, child, I hope you will learn to ask and look before you leap. You've always been too fast to act first. Look at what you're falling into, after you're already on your way down."

She was right and he hated that about himself.

Tapping him on the nose, she moved her hand to quickly smack his bottom before she stepped around him. "Now. What was this about another Malachai?"

Nick nodded. "But in my visions, I'm always older when he kills me. And so is he."

"Like he was hidden and brought in to kill you at a specific time and place?"

"Well . . . I hate the sound of *that*. But now that you've put it that way, that's exactly what it's like."

Kody scowled. "How could they get his child and he not know it?"

Menyara gave her a droll stare.

"Same way Jared had Cherise," Xev said slowly, "and has no idea she was ever conceived or born. It's easy to hide a baby from his father."

"It's what I begged Cherise to do with Nicholas and Adarian. But she refused. It's almost as if some part of her knew what had been done to her own father, and she didn't want to do that to another."

Nick rubbed his chin. "I'm thinking this *has* to be Grim. It would make sense, right? What better way to get ahold of a Malachai and control him than to raise your own?"

"In that case, I have an easy solution." Caleb pulled a butterfly knife from his pocket and twirled it open. "Xev, hold him down."

Nick made a most undignified sound as he teleported to land behind Kody for protection. "Hey! Look at me learning my powers finally. That was an impressive jump."

"Yeah, but not far enough." Caleb started for him again.

Kody blocked his path. "Okay, you've had enough fun. No more threatening the Malachai."

"Who said it's a threat? I think it's a viable option. No one will miss it." He looked to Xev. "You're with me on this one, right, brother?"

"It would save the headache later."

Nick went pale as terror consumed him. "Mennie, help!"

Oh dear heaven, even she appeared to be considering it.

"Menyara!" Nick whined.

"Ach, you're right. If it's meant to be, it would serve no purpose to maim him. However . . ." Menyara paused to pin him with a meaningful glare. "Until we figure this out, you need to make sure you keep your fishing pole in its closet. And not go visiting someone else's pond with it."

Nick screwed his face up at her. "I am *extremely* uncomfortable with this entire line of conversation. And have no fears, my fishing pole is quite happy where it is. It ain't going nowhere."

Sighing, Caleb closed his knife. "And I better not hear about any alien abductions or probes, either."

"You know," Nick snapped at them. "On second

thought . . . I liked it a lot better when the two of you didn't get along."

As soon as those words were out of his mouth, Menyara cocked her head. She turned slowly to face Xev. "What happened to your hair and eyebrows?"

Caleb moved to stand between them as if to protect his brother from the ancient goddess. "Our father did it. If you have an issue with it, I suggest you take it up with him."

"You're defending him now?"

"After everything I've done against him, he saved my life when he didn't have to."

Menyara opened her mouth to respond, but before she could, a furious knock sounded on the door.

Nick stiffened as he felt a surge of something profoundly deadly on that porch.

As Menyara reached to open the door, he started to tell her no.

He never got the chance.

A preternatural wind blew the door from the hinges and shattered it into a million splinters. Nick grabbed Kody to shield her with his body.

Ready to battle, he looked up and saw Aeron rushing into the room to join them.

Aeron met Menyara's gaze. "Drop shields to let me friends in."

"Friends?"

"Aye, we're coming in hot and there's the devil on our tails."

# CHAPTER 16

Nick manifested his sword as he glared at Aeron. "Dude, it's good to see you. But really . . . did you have to break the door apart? Makes it hard to slam splinters in their face."

"Wasn't me!" He gestured over his shoulder at the . . .

Nick didn't even have a word for *that*. No frame of reference whatsoever.

"Honey, what did you bring home with you? You know mountains don't fit at the dinner table. And it don't look like it eats gumbo, either." Then the sarcasm died as Nick saw the two wolves running at them.

One white, shooting flames from its nostrils as it ran.

The other was a huge piece of familiar ebony rage.

"Zavid?" he asked in disbelief.

Aeron clapped him on the back. "Aye, we found him just lollygagging about. Thought you might be missing your playmate."

The two wolves were being followed by a terrifying female demon. One with hair the color of Artemis's and eyes painted black to match her soulless eyes. When Nick stepped forward to blast her, Aeron caught his arm.

"Nae! One of ours, too."

"Pick up anyone else on your way home?"

Aeron laughed. "Nae, boyo. Just these two of me old mates and yours. Try not to kill them."

"Noted." Nick grimaced at the foul demons chasing them. "How many hell-monkeys did you invite over this time? No offense, we're going to have to go to Winn-Dixie and make some groceries. 'Cause the one thing hanging around Simi has taught me—demons all got tapeworms and hollow legs, and I don't think Menyara can cover it. They don't look like a sugared grapefruit will satisfy their cravings and I'm not about to give them sugar-coated Nick."

Caleb eyed the demons then Nick before he grinned at Xev. "Remember the story of Medea and Jason?"

"Yeah, what of it?"

"I'm thinking we start cutting up the Malachai and chucking pieces of him at them 'til they go away."

"I'm good with that. But you have to tell Cherise what you did to her boy. Because honestly? I'd rather face the hell-monkeys."

"You're right. Anyone else got a bad idea?"

"Yeah," Nick said with a laugh. "I got lots of bad ones, but I'm trying to hold out for a good one for once."

Kody gulped at the giant demon that was leading the hell-monkey pack. "I'm terrified past all rational thought." She manifested her bow.

The other girl was stopped at the door by Menyara's protection. She literally slammed into the invisible force field and cursed.

Menyara narrowed her gaze on Aeron. "What is she?"

"*He* is a *cyhyraeth* . . . a bean-sidhe."

She gave Aeron an irritated smirk. "I know what a *cyhyraeth* is, Aeron."

"Sorry, love. Most just stare at me blankly whenever I use the term. Didn't mean to judge you by their ignorance of me culture."

She dropped the shield to allow the *cyhyraeth* in.

Aeron inclined his head. "Everyone, meet Vawn. Now, me lovely, shall we light them up?"

A slow insidious smile spread across Vawn's face. "Aye, like it's *Nos Galan Gaeaf.*" And with that, he manifested a blue spectral ball of light while Aeron conjured his own short Welsh war bow.

"Is that a god-bolt?" Nick asked Vawn.

"Much better, like. It be a corpse-light. Care to see why we call it that?"

"Yeah, sure."

Vawn let it fly out the door, toward their enemies. The moment it neared them, Aeron dipped his arrow down for Kaziel to set on fire with his breath, then released it to ignite the corpse-light.

The instant those three things came together, they formed what had to be the equivalent of demon napalm. It let loose a wave of energy that backlashed and knocked everyone except Aeron, Kaziel, and Vawn off their feet. It shattered glass across the entire neighborhood, overturned cars, and set off every alarm within a two-mile radius.

It also wrapped around the demonic mountain and his friends like an inescapable, spectral webbed hand that plucked them up, slammed them down, and sucked them into some kind of vortex.

Along with a few other nearby objects the neighbors were bound to be pissed off about losing. But hey, that was what happened when you shared your zip code with an ancient goddess and lived too close to a hell-gate.

Sighing, Xev passed an I-told-you-so stare to Nick and Caleb. "Remember what I said about letting them get together? And that was without their new friend in the mix."

Nick crossed himself. "Keep them away from liquor, right?"

"Yeah. I'd even lock up the cough syrup. Just to be safe."

"Duly noted."

Proud and smug, the three Celts turned around to face them. With his hip cocked, Aeron held his bow against his thigh while Vawn crossed his arms over his chest and stood with his spine parallel to Aeron's. Still in his wolf form, Kaziel moved to sit between them, at their feet.

Nick shook his head at the frightening sight they made.

Caleb snorted. "And that is why on ancient battle-fields they were known as *arswyd gan drindod.*"

"What's that mean?" Nick asked.

"Terror by a trinity."

"Yeah, I can see that." Nick pushed himself up. "Don't get cocky, guys," he said to Aeron and crew. "Or else we'll make you explain this to the neighbors."

He went to help Menyara. "Speaking of, how do you explain these things to your neighborhood, any-way?"

"Hurricanes. Tornados. Gas explosions work some-times, too. When that fails, government conspiracy. You'd be amazed how quickly they seize onto that one."

"Not really. I'd much rather believe the government is out to get me than a pack of fire-breathing hell-monkeys." Nick approached Vawn respectfully. "So . . . talk to me about the corpse-light."

"What about it?"

"Do all Legolas banshees have them as weapons?"

Scowling, she tilted her head to speak to Aeron in Welsh. "What's a Legolas and is he meaning to be in-sulting?"

"Nae, he's attempting to be charming. Not so much with Legolas, but even that's more teasing than mean.

Though he be the Malachai, he's not a cruel beast. He's truly trying to come to an understanding of what you really are. And speaking of, as the Malachai, he understands your Welsh so it does you no good to switch to it in front of him, as he knows every word we be saying."

"Oh . . ." Vawn turned back to study Nick for a minute. "*That's* the Malachai, is it?"

Nick feigned a deep chest wound at the way Vawn said that. "Now who's insulting who?"

Vawn held her hands up. "No insult meant . . . exactly. You're just not what comes to me mind with that word. At all."

"Especially given the animals where we've been kept."

Nick went over to Zavid and held his hand out to him. "You've no idea how worried I've been since they told me what happened to you. I'm so sorry."

"Aeron told me." Gratitude glowed in his eyes. "Thank you." Zavid looked around at everyone in the room. "All of you. I didn't think I'd ever get away from Noir."

Caleb approached him and pulled the collar back from his black shirt to examine his neck. For what,

Nick had no idea. But it was obvious, he was hunting for something in particular on Zavid's skin. "How did he get ahold of you to begin with?"

"Livia. Bitch threw me to him. I was protecting her one minute and the next. . . ." His eyes flashed red. "If I ever get the chance to return the favor, I will open her throat and bathe in her blood."

Nick felt awful for him. He could only imagine how badly they'd mistreated him, especially given the horrors he'd seen Zavid suffer while held in Hel proper. "Why didn't your sister tell us where you were?"

"They destroyed her soul." Tears gathered in his eyes. "For that I will kill Grim one day. This is now a personal war for me. And I won't rest until I make sure he feels my full wrath."

Caleb clapped him on the back and stepped away.

Xev arched his brow at him.

His gaze sincere, Caleb inclined his head. "He's clean and telling the truth. Our father got him away without a mark. He's ours again, free of their powers."

Zavid gaped at them. "Verlyn's your father?"

"Yeah."

Vawn winced. "I hated to leave that one behind,

I did. Never did I think to feel sorry for one of his ilk. But we owe him everything. He put himself to the hazard for us and fell back to take the full brunt of punishment from *Y Tywyllwch*."

"Tho?" Kody asked.

"The Mavromino," Nick answered absently, though how he knew . . . well, he knew *how* he knew, it just still stunned him whenever his powers allowed him to comprehend languages he'd never studied before. "Is there any way to free him?"

They shook their heads in unison.

Caleb clapped him on the shoulder. "There are some problems not even the great Malachai can solve."

"Not helping."

Neither was the fact that Menyara repaired her door by holding her hand out, muttering in the primal language, and it reassembled as if nothing had happened to it.

*Oh to be able to command the elements like* that.

Nick pouted at her. "You could have done that *before* the monsters gave your favorite Boo a cardiac arrest, Aunt Mennie."

Cupping his chin in her hand, she snorted at him. "There is much here that isn't right."

"You think it could be tied to the deaths of the Squires?"

Menyara froze at Nick's question. "What deaths?"

"Ash and Kyrian were talking about it. There's been a bad outbreak in Squire deaths. They assumed it was from Daimon attacks."

"Or something worse." Menyara held her hand out. An old book came flying off her shelves to hover in the air before her. Using her powers, she flipped through it. "I think we're dealing with a Dîv."

Caleb let out a nervous laugh. "They're extinct."

"*Supposedly,*" Menyara mumbled.

Nick was sure he had the same look of tasting bile on his face that Xev, Kody, and Caleb wore. "Aunt Men, I think I can speak for the whole group here when I say we don't like that word. Not that I know what a Dîv is, but your tone says that whatever it is, it sucks to be human whenever one's around."

"Nice summation. And also very true." Caleb stepped closer to the book. "But it would make sense. A Dîv would drain your powers. Require human flesh to sustain itself . . ."

"And would have imprisoned me in the same realm their leaders were once banished to."

Nick's jaw went slack. "You were banished with them?"

She nodded slowly as Xev cursed.

They all looked at him.

"The body in the store that didn't decay? The one we fed to Simi? If that was a Dîv . . ."

Caleb turned pale. "We didn't destroy his soul. It would be intact wherever he had it hidden."

Xev nodded. "And with it intact, he could take possession of her."

Appearing as sick as Nick suddenly felt, Kody groaned at the sound of those words. "Are you telling me that we gave a Charonte to a Dîv?"

"We have to find Simi."

"Wait!" Nick grabbed Caleb's arm as he started for the door. "For those of us informationally challenged . . . hello? What exactly is a Dîv?"

"One of the scariest, most lethal classes of demon." Caleb passed a pained stare to Menyara. "They are a special nightmare. Like parasites, they're drawn to other powerful demons and gods. Once they find them, they can drain them and use their powers, similar to a siphon, except they don't have to make physical contact. They just have to be within a few hundred yards.

Then they move into the host and make him or her their bitch."

"You think it's what got Nashira and Dagon?"

"Maybe." Xev sighed. "I wouldn't put anything past one. They were a vital part of the Mavromino army, since it's hard to kill an army made up of the faces of dead loved ones." He passed a gimlet stare to Caleb.

"You're *never* going to let me live Zykesh down, are you?"

"No. You annihilated my entire army—right down to slaughtering all the city's chickens."

Caleb rolled his eyes until he saw the horrified gape on Kody's face. "My men were hungry after the battle."

"And used the bones of my men for skewers to roast those chickens."

"It seasoned the meat while it cooked—gave it a nice . . . okay, I can see your point. Your anger *might* have some merit."

Kody finally managed to close her mouth. "So what I'm hearing is that we owe a huge debt to Lilliana for pulling Caleb out of play for a time and taming him down a bit?"

"Yes," Xev said. "By removing Malphas from battle, it allowed us to gain the upper hand. He was one of their few generals who could and would strategize. And my brother knew exactly how to maximize damage. And hit you hardest where it did the most damage."

"Yeah, but Lil was right. I was a lot deadlier when I fought to protect her and her people, than I was while I fought because I was pissed at my father and wanted to get back at him."

"Indeed. Mal was the only commander we ever had who led his troops against the Dîv, and not only survived the battle—he won."

Nick arched a brow at him. "How'd you do it?"

"A Malachai sword will kill them and they're attracted to powerful enemies. We lined up our strongest and armed them with Malachai swords."

"How'd you get Malachai swords?"

"Trophies," Kody whispered. "Whenever a Sephiroth kills a Malachai, he or she takes the sword as a trophy of their skill. It's a badge of honor for them."

Caleb nodded. "Back then, there were Sephirii who had decorated their entire rooms with those swords."

Nick curled his lip at the thought of such a grisly thing. Not that it was *that* grisly. Just that he would have probably been one of those Malachai they were so proud of killing.

Aeron moved to squeeze Nick's shoulders. "If only we knew where to lay hands upon one of those swords, eh, mate?"

Nick snorted as he saw where this was heading. "So I'm the sitting duck . . . now there's a big surprise. Y'all might as well cover me with Mark's duck urine while you're at it, too."

Xev made an annoyed "heh" sound.

Ignoring them both, Caleb continued. "And we have to pull a Dîv out of a Charonte." He crossed himself.

"Dude, you're not Catholic."

"No, but much like Clovis, to win this round, I'm willing to convert." Caleb took a deep breath. "All right, crew. Let's go find Simi and try not to die."

"Let's do it." Nick clapped his hands together to encourage them. "Should I ask for our odds of survival?"

"No!" they all shouted at Nick in unison.

"Okay," he said slowly as his ulcer came back with friends. "To certain death, dismemberment, and undignified screams, let us march!"

# CHAPTER 17

N ick hesitated on the street, not too far from Menyara's store. "Are you sure this'll work?"

Caleb nodded as he took Nick's sword. "You didn't have your powers earlier. It's why the Dîv didn't try to possess you, then. Now, it'll sense them and leap. When it does . . ." He held the sword up pointedly.

Then collapsing it, he handed the hilt to Nick who slid the sword into his pocket.

As he did so, Nick froze. A peculiarly surreal sensation engulfed him. No, not engulfed.

Slapped. Like an enemy with an iron gauntlet that had just laid open his cheek to challenge him for a duel.

It felt like an out-of-body experience. As if something had jerked his soul from his body to hover over himself, and he was looking down at a stranger in one really tacky shirt. For the first time, he really saw himself as others did.

Taller than most, he was still a gangly kid whose body fit the same as a child trying to walk in their parents' shoes. Yeah, he faked it. Nick would never let anyone know just how insecure he truly was about every aspect of his personality and looks.

At the end of the day, he couldn't deny the feelings of inadequacy that forever stalked him like a hungry Daimon out to shred his soul. The never-ending terror that Nick wouldn't live up to being the man he wanted to be.

Worse, that he really was the monster demon he'd been bred to become. That the Malachai would emerge and tear down everything his mother had tried to teach him. Shred all the humanity inside him until he no longer cared who he hurt.

Nick's mind went back to Kyrian talking to him about *The Iliad* for class. "Life is always about choices, Nick. Sometimes we make them for selfish reasons. Sometimes we make them for others. Sometimes we run from them and sometimes they're forced on us against our will. Paris could have left Helen alone, regardless of what the goddesses had promised him. Hector could have given up his brother and saved his kingdom. Achilles didn't have to withdraw from battle out of spite. Patroclus didn't have to put on Achilles' armor to inspire their forces. Nor did Achilles have to kill Hector knowing that when he did so, it would mean his own death. Was it Helen's choice to go with Paris to Troy? She could have stayed in Sparta, and when Troy fell, she could have killed herself rather than return with the husband she'd originally fled. . . . Where is that line of free will and what is preordained by the gods? Do we choose our lives or are we merely pawns to some higher game we know nothing of?"

In that moment, the fog began to clear and Nick started understanding the significance of pith points and free will.

*I am the master of my own destiny and it is one screwed-up mess that I've made of it . . .*

And as he looked around at Caleb and Xev, a new respect for them rose up inside him. Like Kyrian, they'd been handed a raw deal by life. Both of them had made sacrifices for others and paid a bitter price.

Would it have been worse had they acted selfishly?

That was what Kyrian had done. He'd taken the self-ish route and his life had turned out no better.

If anything, his was worse. While Caleb and Xev had lost their hearts, it'd been through the actions of others who had taken what they loved. To the end, their wives had been loyal to them.

Kyrian's tragedy had been through the betrayal of the woman he'd given up everything for. She had carved his heart out and handed it to him.

Pith points.

Yet his friends had stood up through the rubble of their annihilated lives, dusted themselves off, and carried on with a resolute strength Nick couldn't fathom. Undaunted. Indefatigable.

Just like his mother.

And for them, he would fight the Malachai darkness inside him. Just like they had. Just like they continued to do every day of their lives.

*Every great legend begins with that one person who raises an angry fist to the sky and flips off the gods in defiance.*

Acheron was right.

And that was what Nick had been doing since the

moment he came into this world as a sick baby. Defying the odds. Defying expectation. Defying authority.

Defying his destiny.

And he had no plans to change his ways now. He knew no other way to be. "All right. Point me to the hell-monkeys. It's time to make them my bitches."

"Excuse me?" Kody gaped at him. "Your mother would be horrified."

"Probably. Most of what comes out of my mouth horrifies her." He gave her an adorable grin. "I have to admit, it surprises and embarrasses me, too, most days."

Laughing, she gave him a quick kiss. "And that's why the good Lord made you so adorably cute. Otherwise the impulse to drown you would override all others."

"Ah, *cher*, what have I told you about baiting the gator? You say such things and it just makes the devil in me want to say something even worse."

But as they reached Menyara's store, Nick sobered at what greeted them there.

Ah, crap . . .

Tabitha Devereaux stood on the sidewalk outside

the chained doors with her zoo crew. That was bad. Worse was the fact that her zoo crew included Madaug's older brother, Eric. Although Madaug was right. Sometimes it was hard to say if Eric was his brother or his sister.

Tonight was definitely one of those nights. With his hair dyed as black as Tabitha's, he had it braided up on one side and wore more makeup than Tabby. In fact, the sharp angles of his thick eyeliner looked like he must have gone to the same store Vawn had for instruction on how to wear *it*, and the black eyeshadow and matching lipstick.

"Why is Eric in a dress?"

Aeron rolled his eyes at Nick's question. "It's a kilt, man. Learn the difference."

Well, that explained the combat boots. But . . . "If it's a kilt, why's he wearing a . . . Kode, help me out here? Blouse? That's what that frilly thing's called, right?"

"Yes, Boo. It's a black silk blouse with lace French cuffs and a ruffled cravat. And as much as I can't believe I'm going to say this, it is Tabitha's shirt. I've seen her wear it before."

*Cravat.* Nick mouthed the word and made a face at Caleb, who laughed at him.

"Don't mock the boy, Nick. Least his clothes don't glow in the dark."

"Sorry, Cay. Without Madaug here to do it, I felt the inexplicable need for it. Besides, unlike M-dog, I'd never say it to Eric's face and hurt his feelings. I'm merely getting it out of my system before we approach and it slips out against my will."

Nick winked at them. "And, I have to say that I admire the man for the self-esteem that allows him to leave home looking like that. And I envy him the mirror he owns that told him it looked good, 'cause my mirror cackles at me every time I glance in its general direction."

As they approached Tabitha and her group, Nick glanced about for a sign of Simi, but didn't see anything.

"Hey, Tabby. What's up?"

She gestured at the closed store and the broken glass on the sidewalk. Luckily, the storm shutters were still in place so that she and her friends couldn't see into the store. "I was coming to get some new protection crystals for the group and . . ." She toed the glass. "I've never known the store to be closed like this. Any idea what happened?"

"Gas leak," Nick said, remembering Menyara's list of ready excuses.

"Oh . . ." Tabitha gasped. "That's awful. I hope no one was hurt."

"Nah, everyone got out."

*Except for the dead demons.*

Nick cleared his throat at Caleb's mental insertion.

Tabitha sighed heavily. "Well, crap . . . Guess we'll get our protection elsewhere. Everybody, head to my aunt's."

As they started away, Tabitha stepped over to Nick to whisper in his ear. "Future reference? You wrinkle your nose when you lie, Gautier. Might want to work on that. And I know this was a demon attack—they left their stink all over it. But I don't want any of my friends hurt, so I'm getting them out of here. *À bientôt!*" She glanced over to Kaziel. "Nice Cŵn Annwn, by the way."

Gaping, Nick watched her skip to catch up to her friends. "How does she do that? Or, more to the point, *know* that?"

Caleb and Xev shrugged.

Kody leaned against him. "She's an empath and a psychic. She knows all kinds of things."

He shook his head. How had he always ended up collecting the strange ones . . .

*You're the Malachai, moron. They're drawn to you.*

Oh, yeah. That was why they always found him. How could he forget?

Putting that out of his mind, he led the others into Menyara's shop to look for Simi. But she wasn't there.

An awful feeling went through Nick. What had they unknowingly turned loose on the city?

Yeah, that ulcer was spawning clones. "Who all thinks Simi is eating tourists?"

Caleb and Xev raised their hands.

Nick passed a curious stare to Kody. "You're not in on this?"

"Sorry. I'm trying to think like Simi. Where would she go from here?"

"If we had her scent, we could track her."

Nick liked Zavid's thought. But unfortunately, they didn't have anything that held her scent on it.

Suddenly, they heard something rustling in the back room. Assuming it was another demon that had stumbled into the store to do damage, they armed themselves and headed for the noise.

Nick licked his lips and braced himself to fight whatever would be on the other side of the break room door. He passed a quick glance to the others to make sure they were ready before he snatched open the door and made ready to cut the head off the intruder.

Simi stared at him with a cocked head and pursed her lips. "Why all you peoples look so strange? Even for you? Is this one of them irritable bowel syndrome thingies?"

Nick was truly confused now.

Simi *appeared* normal, although normal for Simi on any day was a bit of a stretch. "What are you doing here?"

"Well, less see. You done told me that the Simi could eats the demon. What you forgots to tell the Simi is that he a Dîv. Ever tried to eat a Dîv?" She gave each of them a condemning stare. "Didn't think so. Theys all gamey and . . ." She shuddered. "Not enough barbecue sauces in the world to make that taste pleasant. So the Simi done had to pop him in the head again. They all screamy like a bunch of them little half-sized people who smell funny and run around yards. And then,

when the Simi popped him in the head, he made a big
old gross mess and I was afraid that if akri-Mennie saw
it, she might not share her sparklies with the Simi. So
I wents and cleansed it and made it all smell nice again."
She grinned.

Kody hugged her. "We were so worried about you,
Simi. We didn't know he was a Dîv, either."

"Ah, then you all forgiven for almost getting the
Simi eaten. See the Simi likes to do the eating. She
don't like to be the eaten. Akri be all unhappy about
that, too, 'cause then he be alone and that would
just be all tragic. He needs his Simi to keep his heart
working."

Simi paused. "Oh, but the Dîv said something before I exploded him. He said that they's coming and
that this time, the Malachai can't stop them."

Nick went cold at those words. He met Kody's
frown and then Caleb's gape. Did that mean that Ambrose had originally stopped whoever was doing this?
Or that Ambrose had stopped them in one of his other
attempts?

Sick to his stomach and needing air that didn't reek
of dead demon guts, he headed for the door to the
back alley.

"Nick?"

He barely registered Kody's presence. His mind was too busy processing all the possible outcomes that invariably ended with him and everyone else dead in a bombed-out New Orleans.

No longer did he see the old French and Creole buildings around him. He saw the devastation they'd witnessed in the future. The fires. The bodies.

Simi's son and daughter.

*His* daughter.

The one he'd been forced to abandon while wounded.

No! It couldn't end like that.

"Nick?" Kody stepped in front of him and cupped his face in her hands. "Look at me and focus. I know where you are, but you can't stay there. Breathe."

His gaze blurry, he looked down at her. "Kyrian's daughter is named Marissa and she's blond."

"I know."

True panic set in as the full magnitude of everything hit him at once. "Oh God, Nyria . . . what have I done?"

"*You've* done nothing."

"But I'm Ambrose. . . . Or will be." He choked on a sob. "I am responsible for what happens to all of you."

Tears filled his eyes as he looked at Caleb and Xev. Zavid. Aeron and Vawn and Kaziel.

Unable to stand it, he pulled Kody into his arms and held her as he shook from the weight of his guilt and anguish for things he had yet to do. And for his fear of what he might have already done that would have set it all into motion.

The future was looming and he hated the weight of that guillotine over his head. Forget the sword of Damocles. This was *so* much worse.

"Maybe the Arelim were right," he whispered against her hair. "Maybe the only answer is to kill me before I rise."

"We've talked about this. You've already risen, Nick," Caleb reminded him.

"But something drained my powers. We could drain them again and then you could kill me. You said it yourself. It would stop it."

Xev shook his head. "Doesn't work that way. Another Malachai would rise. Most likely, your brother."

"Would that be so bad?"

Caleb choked. "Um, yeah. Lotta bit, as you would say."

"Why?"

Kody reached up to wipe at the tears on Nick's cheek. "Because right now, Boo, Madoc's emotions have been locked away for thousands of years. They're only just starting to return to him and he can't cope with it any better than you can. In fact, he's doing a lot worse."

"He's angry and bitter." Caleb sighed.

Kody nodded. "You will meet him before much longer . . . or at least you did. But until he is taught compassion—in the future, he has none whatsoever. For anyone or anything. The worst thing you could do would be to give him the power of a Malachai in his current state. To combine that with the blood of a god . . ."

"World would end a whole lot sooner," Xev finished for her. "And much more violently."

Kody rubbed at his arm. "It's why I haven't encouraged you to meet him. There's no need right now. You've met D'Alerian, the Dream-Hunter who tends Kyrian when he's injured?"

"Yeah."

"That's exactly what Madoc is like. They're brothers."

Nick winced at the memory of the Dream-Hunter who was impossible for humans to see. The only reason he had knowledge of him was because of his Malachai abilities. Whenever a normal human looked at one of their species, their gaze glanced away and registered nothing.

You could walk right into one and not know it.

Yet they were ethereally beautiful. Angelic. And as cold as the Arctic Circle because of a curse Zeus had placed on them aeons ago. All emotions, other than pain, which was a physical response, were banned from them. The only time they could experience any emotion whatsoever was inside human dreams. Because of that, some of them would become addicted to that experience like major drug addicts.

And as bad as that was for the Dream-Hunter, it was far worse on the human or preter they stalked. As with a drug, the Dream-Hunter would crave a deeper high and need to stimulate the dreamer to have more vivid, more horrific, and longer-lasting dreams to the point they'd drive their victims mad and ultimately kill them. Those addicts were deemed Skoti and their brethren who hadn't been turned into dream-demons were charged with policing them, or else they could all be rounded up again and punished by the gods.

Just as they'd been centuries ago.

"Why didn't you tell me my brother was a Dream-Hunter?"

"Because he's not just a Dream-Hunter, Nick. He's a *Kallitechnis*."

He scowled at her. "A what?"

"Madoc can move through anyone's dreams. He can even time travel through them. He is the leader of their council and has full access and control of their Hall of Mirrors. Now do you fully understand the dangers of allowing him to possess your powers? So long as you live, he can't do that. But if anything happens to you, he will be given them because the balance must be maintained. If a Sephiroth lives, so must a Malachai. Their life forces are joined together."

Caleb nodded. "His emotionless curse is what kept him from becoming a Malachai originally. Because he couldn't feel hatred or jealousy, he couldn't take Adarian's powers. But as Kody said, that curse is finally weakening. If you were to die, the powers-that-be would shatter his and he'd emerge full-blown, pissed-off, and ready to rain down his vengeance on us all."

Xev hung his arm around Nick's shoulders. "For the record, son, we don't want that to happen." He ruffled Nick's hair. "C'mon, let's take you home. It's been a long, hard day for us all. But yours has really sucked. . . . Get a good night's sleep and things will look better in the morning."

"All right."

Caleb let out an elongated breath. "Thinking I should have bought a bigger house."

Nick scoffed at his whining. "You've got eight bedrooms. What the heck, man?"

He swept his gaze around the others. "Thinking I need a bigger house."

Nick rolled his eyes.

Caleb paused next to Xev. "Where are you staying?"

As Xev hesitated, Nick didn't miss the shock and longing in his hazel gaze. "Is that an invitation?"

Caleb stiffened. "I'm not apologizing about my past behavior toward you. But I'm starting to understand and see things a little differently. So it's an invitation for dialogue."

Xev softened his features. "I appreciate it. Deeply. But for now, Mr. Fuzzy Boots will remain with He Who Can't Stay Out of Trouble. I don't want to leave either Nick or Cherise unguarded."

"Probably the best call."

Zavid moved to stand next to Xev. "Do you think your mom would object to a stray dog in her home?"

"Probably, but let's try, anyway. I can be pretty dang charming when I try. Just check the red eyes or she's going to be bathing you in holy water."

Nick grinned at Caleb. "You're down to only three guests. Better?"

"Only so long as none of them snores."

Xev let out an evil laugh. "They don't snore. But remember . . . lock up the alcohol."

"Och, now on with you!" Aeron groaned. "You're a mite cruel bastard. No need in all that, mate."

Laughing, Nick listened to them grumbling as they vanished to go to Caleb's.

Zavid changed into his wolf form and shrank it a bit to walk with them back to his house on Bourbon Street.

While they walked, he held Kody's hand until they reached the stoop of his condo building. "You coming up?"

"Better not make your mother angry. I'll surrender you to her custody and see you tomorrow at school."

"Yeah, I'm not looking forward to that."

"Ah, c'mon. Another day. Another survival."

Xev and Zavid wandered into the building to give them privacy while Nick kissed Kody goodnight. Honestly, he hated to let her go. There was always a part of him that was terrified that he wouldn't see her again.

And as he pulled away and nuzzled her cheek, he had the distinct impression that someone was watching him. All the hair on the back of his neck and arms stood up.

Scowling, he turned his head to find Nathan slowing down on the sidewalk as he neared the stoop. His arms were full of bags from the deli on the corner.

"Oh, hey, Nick, right?"

"Yeah . . ."

"You live here, too?"

Too? Nick wasn't sure about that as his stomach tightened in anger. "Maybe."

Nathan looked as confused as Nick felt. "Um, okay. Well, we just moved into the first floor. 1-C. My mom sent me out to grab sandwiches for everyone since we have yet to find all our kitchen stuff. Or buy any real groceries."

"Then you are neighbors," Kody volunteered. "Nick lives upstairs."

Before Nick could say anything, a little blond girl around the age of ten came running out of the building. "Nate! I'm starving! I'm going to wither up and die if I don't eat soon. Did you get food?"

"Oh my God! Yes! I wasn't gone but a minute. Hold your horses." He handed one of the bags to her.

Without a word to them, she grabbed it and ran back inside.

Nathan sighed heavily. "My little sister, Elise. She occasionally gets off the chain and blows free. So if you see her running amok, please let one of us know and we'll round her up. She doesn't mean any harm. She just has yet to realize not everyone in the world isn't her best friend. Anyway, I guess I'll see you two at school tomorrow. Goodnight."

Kody waited until Nathan had vanished. "You still think he's not normal?"

"Nah. That seemed pretty standard stuff. Guess I was overreacting to the way he looked at you."

"You? Overreact? Noooo . . ."

He rolled his eyes at her sarcasm. "All right. That

did not require the mocking tone." Grinning, he kissed her again. "Miss you already."

"You, too. Are you sure you're all right?"

"I will be."

"Call if you need me."

Nick gave her one last parting kiss before he reluctantly allowed her to teleport home.

He headed inside the building to find Xev and Zavid waiting for him in their animal forms. "All right, Mr. Fuzzy. You know the drill . . . no defiling my bedsheets." He took a moment to pet Zavid's head. "And it really is good to have you back. Now let's go see what my mom brought us to eat. I'll share anything except the Bananas Foster."

Everything went well until Nick opened the door and his mother saw his latest houseguest.

"What's that?"

"You know Mr. Fuzzy."

"Not talking about the cat, Nick. Who's his friend?"

"Oh . . . you meant Spot?"

She glared at him. "Nick . . ."

"Just for a day or two? Please, Ma? He's Caleb's. I told him you wouldn't mind. Besides, I wanted a little company while I recuperated, and I knew you'd object to me bringing Kody home and putting her in my bedroom, even if it was innocent."

"Now you're just being sassy."

"That I am, but I come by it honestly. Learned it straight from my mama."

She harrumphed as she snuggled deeper under her pink blanket while she watched TV. "You need me to fix you anything?"

"Nah, I'm good. You keep watching your program. I'm just going to head to my room." He paused next to her. "Did you pass a good time tonight with Bubba?"

A blush crept over her cheeks. "I did."

"That better not mean it was too good, *Maman*."

She laughed at him. "Stop!"

He stooped to kiss her cheek.

At least that was the plan until she waylaid him to check for a fever.

Nick forced himself to endure her fever check. "Told you I was better."

"Just wanted to make sure."

"Satisfied?"

She kissed his cheek. "I am. Now go on with you."

"Yes, ma'am."

But she didn't quite release him to his own recognizance. Rather, she caught his hand as he started away and kept him by her side a little longer. "Thank you, by the way."

"For what?"

"Michael told me what you said about us going out. You're a good boy, Nicky. Much better than I deserve."

Nick took a moment to savor the image of her on the couch, knowing she wouldn't always be there. "That's not true, but I love you, Mom."

"Love you, too, Boo."

Without another word, Nick left her and went to his room where Zavid and Xev were waiting in their human bodies. That wasn't the shocking part.

No, what floored him was that Zavid was fastened onto Xev's neck.

Gasping, Nick quickly entered the room and locked the door so that his mother didn't accidentally stumble onto this and stroke out. "What the devil?"

Zavid pulled away and shrank to the farthest corner of the room as if he expected Nick to beat him.

Xev wiped at the blood on his neck. "Remember when we told you that getting him out and restoring him wouldn't be that easy?"

"Yeah . . ."

"Now you know the price of returning him to this realm."

"And you're good with this?"

Xev fastened the collar of his shirt and rose with that regal grace that always reminded Nick of the way Acheron moved. Fluid and trained. "Would it matter?"

"I don't understand."

"Do you know what a Šarru-Dara really is, Nick?"

"Blood king."

Xev clenched his teeth before he spoke in a low, emotionless tone. "Blood *slave*. My blood isn't just used to seal in Noir and Azura. I was also damned to be used as a food source for a lot of different things."

Suddenly, Nick had an image he really didn't want of why Xev had hated being locked in his nether prison. "I'm sorry. How could you even talk to your father again?"

"He wasn't the only one who did this to me. And in the case of Zavid, for once, I don't mind. 'Course, I'd rather feed him with a cup. But your mother would most likely freak out if she saw *that*."

"Is this why you wanted to stay here?" he asked Zavid.

He wiped the blood from his lips. "Yes. If I don't feed, I'll return to them."

Xev sighed. "Because my blood is the lock, it can keep him on this side of the gate."

Nick winced as he felt bad for both of them. "Is there any way to make it permanent so that you don't have to keep doing this?"

"There's only one way I know."

"And that is?"

"The Cup of Hebe."

Nick frowned. "Is that like a cup of coffee? Where do we buy it? Neiman Marcus?"

Groaning in absolute misery, Xev pressed his fingertips to the bridge of his nose before he shook his head. "No, Nick. Hebe's the goddess of immortality. She's the cup-bearer for the Olympians. If he were to drink from one of her cups, it would restore him to what he was before Noir took his body over and pulled him out of this dimension."

Nick duplicated Xev's groan. "I'm going to assume we can't just walk up and ask to borrow one."

"No. She's going to want something for it."

And experience had taught him that it wouldn't be a Mardi Gras throw. Nor would it be pleasant or easy.

Great. Just great.

But right now, his fears weren't the important thing. He saw the expression on Zavid's face that said he was waiting for Nick to send him back and condemn him to living with Noir and his animals for eternity.

That was the last thing Nick would do to anyone.

"It's okay, guys," Nick said, offering them a reassuring smile he didn't quite feel, but one he hoped he was faking well. "We will get through this."

Nick had no idea how. Yet they would muddle through as they always did. Even though they still had enemies at the gate. Allies missing and unaccounted for.

And a future even more uncertain. With an unknown Malachai.

All they currently had in their corner was that his powers were holding. For the moment.

Of course, that could change in the next heartbeat.

Worse? Ambrose had been wrong. The Eye hadn't helped him even a little bit. If anything, it'd confused him more. And given him a migraine that still hadn't let up.

At this point, Nick was at a loss. They all were. Meanwhile, the Mavromino was gathering strength. Nick could feel it. The darkness would win if they didn't stop it.

And all the gates would come crashing down.

But come heck or high water, he would stand and he would fight. They all would. Because the only guarantee they had in this was that if they didn't fight, they would definitely lose, and losing wasn't in his stubborn Cajun genes.

*You're right, Grim. It's on. And I'm coming for you.*

# EPILOGUE

Kyrian listened to the police as he stood with Acheron and the parish coroner off to the side. "This is crap and you know it."

"Crap or not, those are the boys who attacked Nick the night you met him. How many times has he sworn, quite publicly, he'd get them back?" Acheron's voice was barely more than a whisper.

"Yeah, but you were there when he had the chance. He handed them over to the police."

"And now they've been found slaughtered. Nick's prints are all over the murder weapon . . ."

Kyrian cursed under his breath. "He didn't do this, Acheron. You know he didn't."

"Yeah, but they're calling in a warrant even as we speak. You better go warn him and Cherise, while I call Bill and let them get started on bailing him out. *If* they'll set bail for something this brutal." Acheron looked over at the mutilated bodies and winced. "Our little Squire's in serious trouble this time, Kyrian. And I have no idea how we'll get him out of *this*."

That was brutal, even for you."

Standing on the rooftop of the old building in the French Quarter, Cyprian didn't speak as Laguerre moved to stand by his side while he watched Kyrian and Acheron talking down below. "You wanted him shaken and destroyed."

"Have to say, you are definitely surpassing our expectations."

A slow smile curved his lips as he shifted his form to take on the appearance of Ambrose again. "Oh trust me, putting the Eye in his possession was just the first move. Before I'm done, he won't even trust himself."

Laguerre shuddered as she took in his disguise. "It weirds me out whenever you do that. You look just like him."

"I should, should I not, Mother? After all . . . I am his son."